"The author knows about the sea."—*St. Paul Pioneer Press*

Apparition Island

"With a mastery of details and a sailor's sense of land and sea, LeClair has given us another memorable story on an eerie island off the coast of Maine . . . a real gift for those who like their mysteries straight from the sea."

—Steve Thayer
New York Times Best Selling Author

"LeClair handles the island's rugged terrain and its rugged inhabitants equally well."

—*Publishers Weekly*

"Jenifer LeClair provides her fans with another thrilling investigation in a consistently excellent series."

—*Midwest Book Review*

"LeClair skillfully brings the setting into the mind's eye with wonderfully descriptive detail."

—*Foreword Magazine*

Cold Coast

"Brie is so likable and the plot so involving, it's not surprising this series has won several awards."

—Mary Ann Grossmann
St. Paul Pioneer Press

"This engaging police procedural vividly captures the Maine background. . . . The eccentric Mainers add depth to a fabulous step by step investigation."

—*Midwest Book Review*

"*Cold Coast* is superbly written. The characters are easy to follow and well-developed. . . . Brie is a strong female protagonist but in an endearing way, not the stereotypical hard-nosed female law enforcement officer. The descriptions of the harbor and the coast are exceptionally vivid . . . 5 Stars—excellent read!"

—*Reader Views*

"Tense . . . keeps the reader guessing until the final outcome . . . full of wonderful descriptions of life on a sailing vessel."

—*Armchair Reviews*

Danger Sector

"If you love sailing, grab this title and prepare to be immersed. . . . A strong sense of place and a fine little closed-room drama make this seafaring read a real pleasure."

—*Library Journal*

"Intelligent and well-written . . . The strong, smart protagonist is Minneapolis homicide detective Brie Beaumont."

—*St. Paul Pioneer Press*

"Recommend this agreeable mixture of adventure and crime."

—*Booklist*

"There is something compelling about the sea, particularly when it claims a murder victim. LeClair weaves a yarn that draws in the reader from the first page."

—*Midwest Book Review*

"LeClair combines police procedure, finely-honed investigative skills, psychological insights, and suspense . . . in this haunting story of unrequited love, deceit, and murder [that] involves all five senses. A creative imagination, a love for sailing, and gifted communication skills combine to make Jenifer LeClair a top-notch storyteller."

—Reader Views

Rigged for Murder

"A winning combination of psychological thriller, police procedural, and action adventure. It's a five-star launch for [LeClair's] aptly named sea-going series. . . . Tightly written and intricately constructed, LeClair's *Rigged for Murder* is first-class storytelling in a setting so authentic you can hear the ocean's roar and taste the salt from the sea."

—Mysterious Reviews

"An engaging New England whodunit."

—Midwest Book Review

"Brie [Beaumont] is smart and competent, and she uses her brain and not her gun. . . . Jenifer LeClair offers another appealing main character in *Rigged for Murder*, first in her Windjammer Series."

—St. Paul Pioneer Press

"A strong plot, non-stop action, and first-class character development combine to make this an exciting, page-turning adventure novel."

—Reader Views

"A debut mystery that is so well written you will hunger for more . . . well-developed characters and superbly good writing."

—Once Upon a Crime Mystery Bookstore

DEAD
ASTERN

ALSO BY JENIFER LECLAIR

Apparition Island
Cold Coast
Danger Sector
Rigged for Murder

DEAD
ASTERN

The Windjammer Mystery Series

JENIFER LECLAIR

Conquill Press
St. Paul, Minnesota

This book is a work of fiction. Names, characters, places and incidents either are products of the author's imagination or are used fictitiously. Any resemblance to actual events, or to actual persons living or dead, is entirely coincidental. For information about special discounts for bulk purchases contact conquillpress@comcast.net.

DEAD ASTERN

Copyright ©2017 by Jenifer LeClair

Conquill Press
387 Bluebird Alcove
St. Paul, MN 55125
www.conquillpress.com

Cover Design: Rebecca Treadway

Library of Congress Control Number: 2016954682

LeClair, Jenifer.
Dead Astern: a novel / by Jenifer LeClair – 1st edition

ISBN: 978-0-9908461-7-8

Printed in the United States of America

10 9 8 7 6 5 4 3 2 1

For my brother Jim Thibodeau, U.S. Coast Guard retired, and my brother Joe Thibodeau, writer and avid outdoorsman. Here's one set all at sea!

For your reference, the author has included a glossary of sailing terms in the back of the book.

"The North Atlantic is a hungry ocean, hungry for men and ships, and it knows how to satisfy its appetites."

—*The Grey Seas Under*
by Farley Mowat

The Isles of Shoals

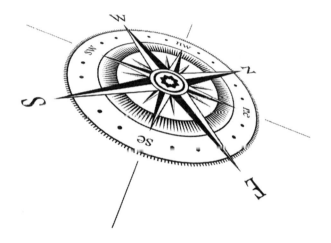

Chapter 1

Aboard schooner Maine Wind
10 kilometers off the coast of New Hampshire

An ill wind blew east by south over the Isles of Shoals, slowly circling the compass like a bird of prey. Schooner *Maine Wind* swung uneasily at anchor, and darkness came early. Second Mate Brie Beaumont patrolled the deck, lighting the hurricane lamps that nightly hung from the rigging when they were at anchor. The wind swung the lantern she hooked over one of the tarred ratlines and, as an afterthought, lifted her long hair so it billowed like a pale ghost in the lamplight. She felt a kind of unease, the sense of something brewing. Maybe just the weather.

At this season nautical twilight clocked in around 1900 hours, or 7:00 p.m. On a clear night, the light would linger, encouraged by its own reflection in the mirror of the sea, but this evening, a thick cloud deck, heavy as iron, pressed down on their anchorage, bleeding the last vestige of light from the day.

First Mate Scott Hogan headed below with an armful of orange Coast Guard-approved PFDs for the fore and aft compartments. Wearing a personal flotation device, or PFD, was mandatory when they were sailing at night or anchored out away from land.

Brie doubted there'd be any takers tonight. The seven men who had chartered the ship for this late season cruise had shown little interest in coming topside after dinner, what with the wind picking up and the chill of the sea in the night air. Six of the seven now lolled around in the galley, talking and imbibing spirits from a bottle of Laphroaig Scotch whiskey that one of the group, Peter Bendorff, had packed aboard. He'd made a point of explaining to her that this particular single malt was distilled on the remote island of Islay off the west coast of Scotland, a fact, he had said, that made it particularly appropriate for their adventure.

Now, as she approached the galley companionway, she could hear the men below decks getting up a game of Texas Hold'em. And here and there she caught snatches of conversation and laughter from Captain John DuLac and George Dupopolis, the ship's cook, as they waited for the coffee to finish brewing.

The sound of John's voice played on Brie's heartstrings like a sad refrain. This was the last cruise of the season, and her five-month adventure aboard *Maine Wind* was drawing to a close. There were lots of things in the wind besides her feelings for the captain—besides their feelings for each other. There was her job at the Minneapolis Police Department Homicide Unit, from which she was still officially on leave. There was her apartment back home and her personal ties, not the least of which was her mother, recently widowed for a second time. In short, there were the many trappings, the tangled branches of a life that up until this summer had remained rooted in one place for all of her thirty-six years.

The regular cruising season for *Maine Wind* had ended a few days ago, but John'd had a request for a charter from this group of seven men who'd offered to pay handsomely. Scott and George didn't quibble about a few extra days, and Brie had been able to push her flight home back a week. And though it delayed the inevitable—putting her affairs in order back in Minnesota—Brie's steadfast goal over the past five months had been to wring every drop of sea-time, every moment of shipboard, every hour of blue-water sailing with her crewmates from her precious sojourn here.

"Time to set the watch, Brie." Scott had just emerged from the amidships companionway that led down to some of the passengers' cabins. "I'll stay on till twenty-four hundred. Then you're on deck until oh-three hundred, when I'll come back on. Once we're finished with our chores on deck, you can head below for some sack time before your watch."

"These early sunsets make me want to hibernate."

"Plenty of time for that when you get back to Minnesota," Scott said. He went over to the storage box that sat amidships and took out two mops and buckets with long lines attached.

"Maybe, but then there's that five-month backlog of mail, and I told my mom I'd go up North with her when I get home."

"Up North? What's more north than Minnesota? You mean like Canada?"

"Lake Superior, actually. But 'Up North' is really Minnesota speak for freedom. It's as much a state of mind as a place. It can mean going to a lake cabin, backpacking in the north country, heading for the Boundary Waters with your canoe, or just driving with the compass needle fixed on the big 'N.' 'Up North' covers a lot of territory, both real and figurative."

Scott's hair and beard shone like penny copper in the lamplight. "So, while we Mainers have our 'Down East,' you guys have your 'Up North.'"

Brie smiled. "That's right." She took the mop Scott handed her. They lowered their buckets over the port-side gunwale to fill with saltwater, hauled them up, and started swabbing down the deck.

"So what's up at Lake Superior?"

"A wonderful cabin right on the rocky shore where my family has vacationed for decades. We'd go there every fall—hike up rushing rivers, sit in front of roaring fires, hunt for agates—Minnesota stuff."

"Sounds like your idea of a party, Brie. So what's an agate?"

"Well, geologically speaking, it's microcrystalline quartz with a few minerals thrown in that was deposited over thousands of years in gas bubbles formed by ancient lava flows and then broken free by the glaciers that scoured Minnesota during the Pleistocene."

"Well, when you put it like that, it sounds pretty impressive."

"It is impressive. You hold this beautiful piece of banded quartz in your hand that's been a billion years in the making. Where do you find quality like that anymore?"

Scott smiled. "You got me."

"What's more, the Lake Superior agate is the official gemstone of Minnesota. We call the pick of the crop 'lakers'—the ones that have been sloshing around in old Gitche Gumee there for about ten thousand years. Every now and then the big lake spits one out all smooth and round with these bands of creamy white and orange—a true rock hunter's confection."

"Never heard such enthusiasm over a rock."

"They're just rare enough to bring out the treasure hunter in one. Agate hunting's a Minnesota obsession."

"So, that's your plan as soon as you get home? Head for some more open water?"

"Now you see why I fit in here."

"Brie, long before you became part of the crew, I knew you and this ship were made for each other."

She looked around the deck, fighting a moment of panic at the thought of leaving her beloved *Maine Wind*.

Scott noticed her expression and changed the subject. "So you mentioned your mom. It's nice you're close like that."

"Mom moved to the Southwest a number of years ago, but she missed autumn in Minnesota, so she visits the family every year in October. I try to make time each fall to go up North with her to do some hiking. But this year—well, you know—if I make the move to Maine, it could be our last time together at the cabin."

"You'll always be from two worlds, Brie. You know that, right?"

"I guess."

"It's not a bad thing. Gives one perspective."

"I think we're all from two worlds, Scott. The one we grew up in, and the one we make for ourselves. Sometimes the geography's similar . . ." She shrugged, not finishing the thought.

Scott smiled. "My life sure is a seismic shift away from the one my folks had planned for me."

Brie knew Scott's parents had wanted him to go to medical school and become a doctor. That was eight years ago, and Scott was now 26. But over those eight years, he had earned degrees in math and music from the University of Maine, all the while working for John.

"They'll come around—see the wisdom in what you've chosen for yourself."

"Oh, they have. They really just want me to be happy. And truth be told, all the things they gave me, the really important things—I use them every day."

The two of them fell silent for a time, plying their salty work, giving the deck a thorough scrubbing with seawater—a ritual that kept the deck tacky for safe footing and tightened up the planks. Brie sloshed some water out of her bucket and pushed her string mop along the deck, working her way forward.

After a few strokes, she looked up. "So, Scott, just wondering. Have you had a sense of anything off about this cruise?"

"Like what, Brie? You mean something wrong?"

She shrugged. "I'm not sure. Just a strange feeling." To her, something felt off, like a nice sharp picture that slowly slips out of focus.

"I haven't noticed anything. Why?"

"I don't know. Can't put my finger on it. Could be nothing. This group has had an odd feel from the beginning."

"That's true enough."

She went back to her mopping, working her way methodically along the deck in the opposite direction from Scott and thinking about the cruise so far.

They were only two days out from port—maybe too soon to form any kind of judgment. But then again, two days in the closed environment of a ship on the ocean might be like two weeks in a normal setting. *You get a sense of people quickly when you're closely in their company,* Brie thought. And even though *Maine Wind* was big for a schooner, as a passenger vessel she was small.

The first day of the voyage had taken them out through Penobscot Bay to Isle Au Haut and Jericho Bays, then on to Monhegan Island, where a flourishing artists' community dwelt alongside sturdy, determined lobstermen who hauled their traps year-round. Today they had weighed anchor before dawn for the long sail—approximately 82 nautical miles—from Monhegan Island to the Isles of Shoals, where they now lay.

The Isles of Shoals perch along the watery boundary between Maine and New Hampshire. The group of seven islands lies ten kilometers off the New Hampshire coast, with three of the islands belonging to Maine and the other four to New Hampshire. One of the men aboard, a former history professor, had wanted to visit the spot of the infamous killings on Smuttynose Island that had been committed during the night of March 5, 1873.

On that ill-fated night, two women, Norwegian immigrants, had been brutally murdered, and a third woman had survived by hiding in a sea cave. And while a culprit, one Louis Wagner, had been convicted and hanged for the murders in 1875, controversy had continued to swirl around that verdict and the case for more than 140 years. Partly due to that controversy, Louis Wagner was one of the last people ever executed in the state of Maine. It was a haunting story, and the questions about what had really happened here all those years ago cast a kind of eerie pall over this place—a mystique—like an ominous fog that had never quite lifted.

From the Isles of Shoals, the plan was to sail down East, visiting coastal locales on their way back to the waters of Penobscot Bay. All in all, an ambitious itinerary, especially for this time of year, when violent weather systems can prowl the Gulf of Maine. So far, they'd been lucky, but Brie wondered how long that luck would hold.

She finished her portion of the deck, walked aft, and stowed her mop and bucket. As she closed the top of the storage box, a strong gust of wind swung the ship at anchor and keened through the rigging, slapping the halyards hard against the masts. She paused and studied the sky. Something in that wind tonight. Or was it the wind? She wasn't sure when or how, but despite the jollity currently issuing up from below decks, a vague sense of malaise had reared its head over the past forty-eight hours. Nothing untoward had happened, but a feeling had settled over her, crept into her detective bones. She turned and headed below to sleep until her watch rolled around.

Chapter 2

At the foot of the companionway ladder, Brie entered a different world—the warm and welcoming galley, where George's woodstove pumped out heat and smells of rich coffee and comfort food filled the cozy space. This was where passengers gathered to eat on cold or rainy days and where they came together in the evening, seeking camaraderie around books, games, and music. Often the captain would read to the shipmates from his collection of maritime stories, or Scott might play his guitar, coaxing from it folk music, salty sea ballads, or when the mood struck, plaintive blues or cool jazz. At sea, there was nothing like stories and music for bringing folks together and closing out the day.

The hurricane lamps cast soft light around the gold-hued wood of the galley's interior and the overhead. Forward in the bow, around the table, the six poker players had imbibed just enough spirits to raise the volume and the stakes in their game. One of their contingent, Paul Trasky, hadn't joined them for the game but had retired early instead. He'd been plagued by seasickness since they'd left port and had clung to his cabin, not wanting to eat much or socialize. Over the two days they'd been out, Brie had seen little of him. She'd hoped he'd come around once he got his sea legs, but sadly there are some passengers who never turn the corner but battle *mal de mer* from one end of a cruise to the other.

"Coffee's up, Brie." George turned and offered her a mug.

"I shouldn't, George—I want to sleep before my watch, but it's hard to resist that smell."

"How about a half o' cup?" He raised the pot enticingly. It was a big, black metal drip pot like one might use over a campfire.

Brie gave in and took the mug. When it came to George's cooking and coffee, her defenses were always down. George filled the mug halfway. It warmed her cold hands, and she held it up and inhaled the rich aroma before taking a sip.

"Everything done topside?" the captain asked.

"Shipshape." Brie met John's gaze and held it for a moment as she raised her cup again. "We weighing anchor before or after breakfast?"

"Let's see how the weather is in the morning. There's some rain passing through tonight, but if it clears and the seas are manageable, we'll haul anchor early and eat breakfast underway."

"Sounds good," Brie said.

"You up for a round of cribbage?" John asked, looking hopeful.

Brie checked her watch. It was just before eight o'clock. She knew she should hit the sack, but maybe a half hour wouldn't hurt.

"Okay, you're on. How about you, George? We can play three-handed."

"No, you two go ahead. I'll just sit with you and have some coffee."

"This calls for another half cup," Brie said, holding her mug out for a refill.

George poured more coffee, and they settled in at the other end of the community table from the poker players. Brie and John sat next to each other on the padded bench seat with the cribbage board on the table between them, and George pulled up a stool and sat down with his coffee.

A half-hour later the game went to Brie, as it usually did. Her dad had taught her to play cribbage at a young age, and he had taught her well. Even when they hadn't seen eye to eye during her teen years, somehow they'd always been able to reach a truce over the cribbage board. She kept those fond memories locked in her heart along with the other family treasures she stored there.

John put away the cribbage board and cards, and Brie brought the coffee cups over to the sink, washed them out, and headed for her berth on the port side of the ship behind the galley. It was a tiny personal space, consisting of her berth, a little bit of floor space in front of the berth, and a small mirror and battery-operated reading light, both of which hung from the bulkhead at the end of her berth. She pulled off her wool sweater and tossed it down at the foot of her berth, crawled into her sleeping bag, and reached up and flipped off the light.

She lay in the dark feeling the comforting rocking of the ship. But along with the darkness tonight came the disturbing thoughts that sometimes haunted her. Lately, she'd been think-ing of Phil again—reliving the intruder call in north Minneap-olis that they had responded to that ill-fated night—the night he had died. The night he had taken the bullet that would have ended her life, but instead ended his. Maybe it was because she was going home soon—back to where that horror had un-folded.

Over the past eighteen months, but especially since she'd come to Maine, the flashbacks from that terrible night had morphed into a less devastating form. It was rare that she was jolted from her sleep, disoriented and nauseated. But post-traumatic stress disorder (PTSD) is a beast. With a big enough whip, you can back it into a corner, maneuver it into a cage, but it's always there, ready to come raging forth, fangs bared.

Brie drifted in and out of an uneasy sleep for the next hour, slowly burrowing her way toward the deeper realms of consciousness. When the splash comes, she is down far enough that she incorporates the sound into a dream.

She is in the air, falling. Did she slip off the bowsprit or go over the side? She can't seem to remember, and then she hits the water with a tremendous splash—a disturbance far more spectacular than her slim body should cause. The extreme cold of the Atlantic makes her want to gasp—have to gasp—an involuntary reflex? She can't remember what it's called, but knows it is how people drown in cold water. The shock of that cold literally makes them gasp, and if they are submerged, that is usually the end. She fights now, mustering all her inner strength to not take that breath, but she is sinking deeper and deeper. She pulls with her arms and whip-kicks with her legs in a kind of a vertical breast stroke toward the surface, but she does not rise. Her lungs burn; her body burns despite the freezing water. Suddenly her skin begins to loosen. She swims free of it, and she rises as if pulled by some tremendous force.

Brie jolted up in her berth, gasping for air, flailing out of her sleeping bag. She was soaked in her own salty sweat, not the cold saltwater of her nightmare. She heard feet pound the deck above her, and the realization of what was happening hit her like the paralyzing cold of her dream.

Someone has gone overboard.

Chapter 3

B rie bolted out through the galley and up the ladder. John emerged from the aft companionway at the same moment, carrying a small flashlight. Outside of that beam and a lantern forward in the starboard rigging, the night was coal dark. Scott was on the port side of the ship, leaning over, lantern in hand, visually scouring the water below the ship, and a drizzly rain was coming down just hard enough to render visibility in the dark near zero. Seconds—probably no more than thirty or forty—had elapsed since the splash had registered on her consciousness, creating the dream that jolted her awake.

Brie crossed the few feet of deck. "What's happening, Scott?"

"Don't know yet. But something or someone went over the side."

Then John was there. "What's going on, Scott?" It came out more as a demand than a question, and even in the dim light, Brie could see the alarm in his eyes.

Scott repeated what he'd just said to Brie.

"Get below and check the passengers' cabins. Make sure all are present and accounted for."

Scott hesitated, lantern in hand.

"Do it now." There was a hard edge in John's voice that telegraphed his fears.

Scott headed aft, and Brie darted for the ladder leading down to the amidships compartment. With so few passengers aboard, each of the men had been given his own cabin, four of them in the forward compartment and three in the cabins aft.

Brie went first to Paul Trasky's cabin. He was the passenger who'd been plagued by seasickness. She realized she hadn't seen him since the afternoon, as he'd declined to come to dinner that evening. She knocked on the wood louvered door and waited, checking her watch in the dim light of the passageway. It was 2340, or 11:40 p.m. No response. She knocked harder this time and thought she heard a slight groan from inside the cabin.

"Mr. Trasky—Paul. Please open your door."

She heard stirring inside the cabin and tried to be patient, knowing Trasky hadn't been feeling well. But his voice was not enough; she needed to see his face. She knew the captain would require a face-to-face accounting of all passengers.

Finally, Trasky opened the door a few inches and peered out. His shaggy black hair stuck out from under a watch cap, and he wore baggy gray sweats for pajamas. He had put on his glasses but squinted and held up a hand to block the dim glare of the battery-operated light in the passageway. He looked pale in the diffused light and seemed to be shivering.

"What's wrong?" he mumbled, his voice gravelly.

"Sorry to disturb you, Paul. We're doing a cabin check."

"Why? What's the matter?"

Brie hedged the question. "Nothing right now. Go back to sleep. Do you need another blanket? You seem cold."

"I'm fine," Trasky mumbled.

The standard male response for anything from "I'm actually fine" to "I could be dying," Brie thought. She turned from his door as he closed it and saw that Leo Dombello was taking in the exchange from across the passageway.

Leo was a short man, maybe five-five or six, with a bald fringe of hair and protruding brown eyes. He was squat but muscly, and right now, his stance reminded Brie of a docile bulldog.

"Something's wrong, isn't it? I can tell, you know." He crossed his arms on his tee-shirt clad chest. His paddle-like feet stuck out from beneath blue flannel pajama bottoms.

Brie relented. "There was a disturbance on deck. We're just checking on the passengers."

He nodded but held his ground.

"Thank you, Leo. You can go back to bed."

He studied her for a moment and then retreated back into his cabin.

As she turned back toward Peter Bendorff's cabin—the one next to Paul Trasky's—she heard the door to the right of Leo's open and Joe Callum speak. She turned to see him bare-chested, wearing boxers only and a look of self-satisfaction like he'd just closed an important merger, albeit in boxer shorts.

"I hear you're doing room checks, so here I am." He fixed her with a look that felt just a little too familiar.

"Thank you, Joe. Noted."

He held her eyes for a moment, sending out an uncomfortably seductive vibe.

Brie brushed it off with one pragmatic swipe. "You may want to cover up tonight; the temp's headed for the fifties. Once the heat from the stove dissipates, it'll get cold fast." Brie turned and smiled to herself as she heard Callum's door close maybe just a little too hard. Brie had him pegged at mid to late thirties—too old to act like such a dope, that was for sure. But it was okay. She'd seen another side to Callum—an earnest, helpful side. So the cause was far from lost.

She stepped over to Peter Bendorff's door and knocked. His was the last cabin on the starboard side of the compartment. It was next to Paul Trasky's cabin, which was next to the storeroom at the foot of the ladder. She knocked again. "Peter, can you hear me? Could you open your door, please?"

No response. She knocked again, and now she heard Leo's door open and knew he was watching her. She tried the door and found it unlocked. Gingerly, she opened it while knocking. "Peter...?"

No response.

The light from the passageway did little to illuminate the cabin. She stepped to one side so the glow could filter in, and now she could see that the cabin was empty. She didn't enter the space—her cop instincts kept her anchored in the doorway as she let her eyes adjust to the darkness within. After a few seconds she could make out something at the head of the berth. A single sheet of white paper. She closed the door.

Leo Dombello was out of his cabin again, arms crossed on his barrel-like chest.

"Leo, could I ask you to step back into your cabin and stay there until further notice?"

"Why? What's going on? And where's Pete? I have a right to know."

"Leo..."

Dombello must have caught the note of authority in her voice, because he disappeared back into his cabin and closed the door.

Brie lingered a few moments in the passageway to be sure Leo was staying put and then headed back up the ladder to find the captain. John was walking the perimeter of the ship's gunwale, surveying the water below. He turned as Brie approached.

"Peter Bendorff is not in his cabin, and it looks like there's a sheet of paper at the head of the bed."

"Shit."

Brie knew he never would have let that fly with anyone but her.

"I didn't want to go in there till I talked to you. Cop instincts, you know."

"I wasn't keen on this cruise from the get-go. You know I wasn't. I should have turned it down." He looked toward the dark ocean. "What a mess this is going to be."

"Before I go back in Bendorff's cabin, I need to bootie and glove up, just in case." Brie had been deputized by the Maine State Police when she had worked a homicide case with them in August in Tucker Harbor—away Down East. Since then, she had kept a small box of crime scene supplies with her aboard ship, in the event that they assigned her to a case.

"Look, Brie, before I call the Coast Guard, I want you and Scott to start in the aft compartment and walk through each cabin just to be sure Bendorff isn't somewhere else aboard. I'll check the galley and then go below and check the forward cabins myself."

Brie started to say something, but John stopped her. "Don't worry. I won't enter Peter Bendorff's cabin."

"The passengers are going to want to know what's going on."

"I guess it's no secret. Tell them we're looking for Peter Bendorff. But advise them to stay in their cabins until further notice."

"Aye, Capt'n." Brie headed aft to find Scott. She understood John's thinking. It was a good idea to double-check the cabins. There was always the possibility Peter Bendorff could be in the cabin of one of his buddies. When she got below, she and Scott asked the three passengers in the aft cabins—Lyle Jarvis, Alexander Smith, and Rusty Boardman—to step out so they could do a visual check of the cabins. That didn't sit well with any of them, having already been disturbed by Scott, but they all came out into the passageway nonetheless. Brie told them they were looking for Peter Bendorff.

"What do you mean, looking for him? We're on a ship. How far could he go?" It was Lyle Jarvis, a jittery beanpole of a guy. Brie noticed his right eye begin to twitch. Over the past couple days, she'd gotten somewhat accustomed to his nervous tics and darting looks.

Alexander Smith stepped into Scott's path and locked eyes with him. "We have a right to know what's going on."

Brie couldn't help inwardly rolling her eyes. *Everyone has a right to know.*

"Look, you'll know what's going on when we know what's going on. Does that seem fair?" Scott returned Smith's steely-eyed stare.

The professor held his ground for a few more moments, but finally he nodded grudgingly and stepped aside.

The third passenger, Rusty Boardman, held his tongue but watched what Scott and Brie were about intently.

The two of them stepped into each of the cabins, turned on the overhead light and the bunk lights, and looked around. It took a matter of seconds for each inspection. The cabins aboard the windjammers are very small—one or two berths and a tiny bit of floor space. There's simply nowhere that an average-size human being could hide.

When they were done, Scott asked the passengers to return to their cabins until further notice. Brie left Scott there as the enforcer and headed up the companionway to find the captain.

She took a detour below, to her berth off the galley, to collect a pair of latex gloves, a zipper baggie, and a pair of shoe covers that police use when entering any potential crime scene. There was no actual crime scene—at best this was a crime against oneself. But the protocols were the same.

John was waiting for her at the foot of the ladder in the forward compartment. "Any luck?"

"Nope," Brie said. "And the natives are getting restless."

He smiled a weak smile.

"You checked the storeroom, right?" she asked.

"Yup. And the galley."

Brie nodded. "Well, let's see what we've got here." She stepped over to Peter Bendorff's cabin and paused to pull on the booties and gloves. "Wait here, John. I'll check this out."

She stepped into the cabin, flipped the switch to turn on the ceiling light, and moved to the head of the lower berth, where a single sheet of white printer paper lay like a forlorn ghost on the navy blue pillowcase. She lifted it by one corner and read what was there.

Dear Rebecca,

Please forgive me. I know this is the coward's way out but I can't help myself. I know this will make life immeasurably hard for you, but you will find your way through, I think. You always do. You always were the strong, resourceful one, so I know you will be fine. I hope someday you can forgive me. I did love you—guess I still do— but it's not enough to keep the hounds at bay any longer. Please forgive me, a selfish bastard.

Peter

Brie let out a sigh. The air in the cabin felt strangely close all of a sudden, as if the ghost of Peter Bendorff had already taken up residence there.

"Brie . . . ?" John spoke softly, but there was urgency in his voice.

She slipped the suicide note into the ziplock baggie she'd brought and sealed it up, turned off the light, and stepped out into the passageway. She nodded toward the ladder to signal John that she didn't want to talk down here. She removed the gloves and booties and followed him topside. The rain had stopped falling, but the wind, carrying a cold front on its back, had picked up. She pulled up the hood of her rain jacket as they stepped away from the companionway and out of earshot.

"The note confirms our worst fears, John. It appears that Peter Bendorff has used the ship and this cruise as a means to commit suicide. Whether he planned it before coming aboard, we don't know. All we have at this point is the fact that he's missing and this note." She patted her jacket where she had placed the note in an inside pocket.

"I need to call the Coast Guard."

Brie checked her watch, pushing the stem to light it up — 2352, or 11:52. A mere fifteen minutes since the splash had roused her from sleep. It seemed much longer.

"Will they come or wait till daybreak?"

"They'll come. There's always a chance he's still alive and in the water."

"What should I do, John?"

"You and Scott handle the passengers. I'll deal with the Coast Guard." He turned and walked aft.

Brie headed for the galley companionway to take the note below to her berth. As she hit the ladder, she heard the hail over the radio.

"Mayday — Mayday — Mayday."

When she had heard the splash, Brie had leapt from her berth, slid her feet into her deck shoes, grabbed her rain jacket, and headed topside. But the temperature was dropping, with more rain likely. So back in her cubbyhole, she slipped Bendorff's note into the box with the crime scene supplies for safekeeping and pulled a wool sweater over her long-sleeved tee shirt. She pulled on the bib overalls to her foul weather suit and swapped her deck shoes for sea boots. She donned her rain jacket again, stuffed her watch cap into the pocket, and headed topside to wait with John for the Coast Guard and discuss what his plan was for the other passengers.

Some of them would likely wake up when the Coasties arrived, so they needed a game plan. She also wanted to do some preliminary questioning of the men, either individually or as a group. She wasn't sure which just yet. But she knew one thing: it was going to be a long night.

Brie emerged from the companionway into the dim glow cast by the lanterns. The captain was back near the helm, staying close to the radio to intercept any incoming transmissions. At that moment Scott came up from the aft compartment, and John turned to speak to him. As she got closer she caught a few words that surprised her.

"I hold you responsible for this," John told Scott. "You left your post."

Brie hung back for a second, not wanting to intrude but surprised John would blame Scott for what had happened.

"Look, Captain," Scott said in a level tone, "I'd have to have eyes in the back of my head to keep track of every inch of the deck at every moment during a watch."

"You told me you went below for wood for the stove. That's not your job when you're on watch."

"Well, you'd better tell Brie, because it's common practice during watch. Or maybe there's a different set of rules for her."

They glared at each other, and Brie decided it was time to intercede.

"Did I hear my name mentioned?" she said as she closed the gap between her and the guys.

Scott turned, surprised to see her. "Sorry if you heard that, Brie. That was a low blow. I'm sorry." He stalked off toward the bow of the ship, leaving Brie studying John.

"It's not Scott's fault, you know," she said.

"He should have been more watchful," John said. "I think that's why they call it a watch."

"Look, John. There's something you need to understand, and this comes from Brie the cop, not Brie the sailor. If someone is determined to commit suicide, there's little that can be done to stop them. They will find and seize their opportunity. Look what happened on Apparition Island."

John looked away. "You're probably right. But this ship and the people aboard are my responsibility."

"I know that, John, and it's a heavy responsibility. Scott understands that, believe me."

"I'll talk to Scott later. Clear things up. But just for the record, no more going for wood for the stove during watch." He gave her his *this-is-the-captain-speaking* look.

"Aye, Captain. I'll change my evil ways."

"Don't make jokes, Brie. I mean what I'm saying."

"Right. I'll be more aware," she said, studying him earnestly. "So, any ETA on the Coast Guard?"

"Fifteen to twenty minutes on the response boat. They're coming from New Castle, New Hampshire, just east of Portsmouth. They're sending a chopper too. That's being deployed from the air station on Cape Cod. They'll drop flares and do an aerial search. The sky'll be lit up like the Fourth of July over New York Harbor."

"That should get the passengers good and riled up. They'll want to come topside, you know. So what are we going to do about that?"

"The noise of the chopper will likely wake them." He paused and looked at her. "Maybe not, though. They were hitting the sauce pretty hard tonight."

"My guess is none of them are asleep. They know something's up."

"Well, that may be, but I'm counting on you and Scott to keep them below deck while it's dark and the search is going on."

"At some point tonight I'm going to have to question them—see if any of them had a clue that Peter Bendorff was planning to use this cruise as a suicide mission."

"Not a mission, Brie, and thank God for that. I guess that must be the silver lining."

"You're right. At least he didn't take anyone else with him. Always something to be thankful for in this day and age." Brie reached out and put a hand on his arm. "You want to go below and get on some warmer gear?" John wore jeans and a sweatshirt, and even in the dim lantern light, she could see his clothes were wet. "I'll hang out here by the radio."

"May as well," he said. "The night is young."

Brie heard sarcasm there but also a hint of John's stalwart humor. "Atta boy," she said. "We'll get through this."

He disappeared down the ladder to his cabin and was back up in a few minutes dressed in his rain gear.

"I'll get you some coffee." She didn't wait for him to refuse it but turned and headed forward. George always left coffee in the galley overnight for those standing watch. Just as she reached the galley companionway, she heard a sound slicing through the night, way off in the distance, amping up with each passing second. She hesitated at the ladder, looking off across the dark sea toward the disturbance, listening to the deep-throated vibration that signaled the Coast Guard's approach. *Cavalry's coming,* she thought, *but I'm afraid they will be too late to save Peter Bendorff.*

Two Days Before

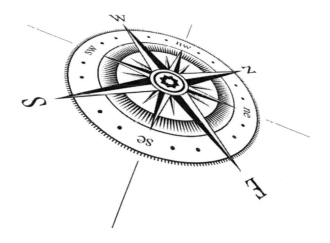

Chapter 4

Peter Bendorff pulled his Audi into the public lot north of Harbor Park in Camden, Maine. He stepped from the car and shook the road fatigue from his legs, then arched backwards, arms overhead, letting out a loud guttural sound approaching a roar that this particular stretch seemed to require. There was no one around, so why hold back? he thought. The drive from Portland had felt like a long one, and even though he enjoyed the way his R8 hugged the curves and hills of Coastal Route 1, today had tried his patience. He had a lot on his mind, and even though he'd blasted the music for most of the trip, troublesome thoughts had still managed to crowbar their way into his head, making the two-hour drive feel like a slow trip to hell.

Now, a tension headache crawled up the back of his skull like some slow-moving parasite. "Can't wait to crack open that bottle of scotch and get this show on the road," he said to himself. "Or maybe I should say, ship on the sea." He opened the trunk on the front of the Audi—it was called a frunk, which always amused him—and took out a large, black duffel bag, then reached back in for his Swiss Gear backpack. It was heavy, and he carefully maneuvered his arms through the straps and hoisted it onto his back, grimacing as the pain in his head slapped a vice grip on him. He shut the trunk and stood for a moment, hand on the front fender, surveying the car, then picked up the duffel and started toward the harbor to find the schooner named *Maine Wind* that they had chartered.

He made his way down through Harbor Park that lay just north of the public marina and landing. Some fall color still held forth in the park and around the harbor, but the peak of the New England leaf season was on the wane. At the west end of the park the Megunticook River thundered over a small waterfall before emptying into Camden Harbor. Bendorff paused, listening to the sound of the falls, and for a few moments his headache seemed to relent. He felt a pang of regret, remembering another waterfall, one from his honeymoon. That seemed like so long ago. He let out a sigh, but then he brushed the feeling aside—something he'd practiced for a lifetime. He squared his shoulders and continued down the hill and onto the long float that led to the *Maine Wind.*

As he approached the ship, he saw a boarding ladder attached to her starboard gunwale. He dropped his duffel on the float and shinnied up the ladder and climbed aboard. From the back of the ship a long-legged beauty moved toward him, and the swing of her blonde hair somehow perfectly fit the freedom of her gait. *Wow, what a knock-out,* and then all cohesive thought emptied down the fast-running drain of his libido. But he pulled himself into check. *Need to mind my Ps and Qs,* he thought. *Stick to business.*

The clear-eyed blonde stopped in front of him, and he noticed the eyes leaned more toward the blue of the sea than that of the sky.

"Brie Beaumont, second mate," she said, holding out her hand.

When she spoke he realized she was older than he'd first thought, and something about her—something in her demeanor —gave him pause, struck some note of apprehension in him. He shook it off and extended his hand. "Peter Bendorff," he said, but he couldn't help wondering what made her tick. *So helpful to know things about people. One never knows when it will come in handy.*

"Well, you're the first one," she said.

"Really?" Bendorff answered, swiping his hand over his bald head and looking around the deck. "I thought my buddies would be here by now." He felt mildly irritated. He never arrived anywhere first. He thought it made one look needy, or at least over-anxious. He liked the subtle control of making an entrance.

"Is that all you have?" the blonde asked, nodding toward his backpack.

"No, I left my duffel on the float when I climbed aboard. I'll go down and hand it up to you." He shinnied back down the ladder, handed up the duffel, and climbed back aboard.

"I'll show you below to your cabin," Brie said and started to pick up his bag.

"I can carry that," Bendorff said.

"Well, watch your step; the ladders are a bit steep. You're in the amidships compartment," she said, heading aft. When they got to the companionway she said, "We like folks to go down backwards for safety's sake, especially when we're at sea."

Bendorff climbed down the ladder, keeping one hand on the rail, and waited at the bottom, enjoying the view as the foxy second mate came down after him.

"You're in Cabin Two," she said, nodding toward the corner cabin on the starboard side of the passageway. She opened the door for him, and he stepped inside and looked around. "With so few of you on this trip, we were able to give each of you your own cabin. The head's right there." She pointed to the door to their immediate right. "Please make sure nothing goes into the head except the toilet paper provided."

"Got it," Bendorff replied.

"Well, I'll leave you to unpack. The cook will be putting out some snacks at around eight o'clock, but you're on your own for dinner tonight."

"That's what the letter the captain sent out said. I'm sure I'll have to run back into the village for something, once I un-pack and see what I forgot. When the others get here, we'll make a dinner plan."

"Great. I'll leave you to it then." She turned and headed for the ladder.

Bendorff looked around the cabin and took everything in at a glance—it was that small. There was a double bunk fitted right in along the hull of the ship, and in the corner by the door, a small washstand with a stainless steel bowl and a wooden cask of water with a small spigot at the bottom. *Well, they promised adventure*, Bendorff thought. *I guess it starts with washing up in the morning.* He studied himself in the small mir-ror, trying to focus on his totally bald head. He was still getting used to the look, but one thing was for sure: it drew attention away from the weak chin he'd inherited from his father. *Dear old Dad*, he thought, *chin to match his character.* He'd spent dec-ades convincing himself that he was different from the old man, but in the final analysis, life had proven him wrong. On the darkness spectrum, Dad was maybe the color of the New England granite, while Peter rated himself, rightfully or not, black as a basalt flow.

He lifted his duffel onto the bunk and started unpacking. The upper bunk would not be in use, so he stacked his clothes and toiletries up there for easy access and then went about the job of making his bed with the sheets and blankets provided.

Chapter 5

Brie emerged from the companionway just in time to see Scott helping a short, rather stout man over the rail. Once aboard, he gestured down to the float where he had left his bags—what looked like enough for a slow boat to China. Brie smiled to herself, glad Scott had fielded this one. By the time she got to the rail, Scott had climbed down to the float and was handing the first large suitcase up to the man. Brie jumped in to help. There was another suitcase nearly as large as the first, a briefcase, a camera bag, a medium-sized duffel that was open at the top and looked like it contained an assortment of footwear, and finally a square box that felt like it contained books and who knew what else. All the time they were wrestling the bags aboard, the man was gesticulating wildly, his hands talking a mile a minute, as he told them about his drive from Portland and how he'd nearly hit a moose on Route 1 near Waldoboro.

Scott climbed back aboard. "Brie, this is Leo Dombello. Leo, Brie Beaumont, a member of the crew."

Leo did a gallant little bow and, as if just noticing her for the first time, became suddenly shy.

"Nice to make your acquaintance, Leo. We'll help you get your gear below so you can get unpacked."

"I'll get Leo settled below if you want to help George." Scott nodded toward shore, and Brie turned to see George Dupopolis, the ship's cook, just making his way onto the float with a wheelbarrow full of provisions. "Once I'm done with Leo here, I'll come help you two with the supplies and the wood."

"Roger that," Brie said. She leaned over the rail and waved to George, who navigated the bobbing float with surprising ease while balancing an all-too-ambitious load of goods in the barrow. Brie waited at the rail as George made his way up to the ship and parked the wheelbarrow at the foot of the boarding ladder. He had four crates of wood at the bottom of the precarious pyramid, and on top of them more crates containing vegetables, including two filled with a variety of lettuces, and several others that held potatoes, carrots, onions, beans, broccoli—you name it, George had it. All those veggies were good for health, but truth be told, they had another more immediate and crucial purpose, which was keeping everyone regular aboard a ship with only two heads.

Brie leaned over the rail, and George started handing up crates to her. She stacked them on the deck as they came aboard. When the barrow was empty, George mounted the ladder, and he and Brie wrestled the crates of wood down to the galley. They piled some of it under the stove and left a couple crates alongside.

"We'll put the rest of the wood in the lazarette when it comes aboard. This should be enough for tomorrow."

The veggies went down the amidships companionway, where they were stored under the floorboards of the passageway in a metal tray that hung above one of the bilges. This space was colorfully known as the vegetable bilge, and just aft of it lay the dairy and egg bilge. The ice chests up on deck were reserved for those items that needed to be kept frozen—primarily the meat for the trip. There was no such thing as refrigeration on a windjammer, so storage of food had to be carefully thought out, and the Atlantic Ocean that surrounded the hull of the ship below the waterline made a fine natural refrigerator.

As they were loading the food into the bilges, Leo Dombello stuck his head out of Cabin 3 on the port side of the compartment. "So that's where I go if I need a snack," he joked.

"Believe me, the way George cooks, you won't be needing any snacks," Brie said. She introduced Leo to George, and Leo shook his hand enthusiastically. She noted that both men bore the look of Mediterranean ancestry—George's from Greece and Leo's from Italy. But, whereas George still had a thick head of curly black hair, the decades had been less kind to Leo, whose bald pate was nut brown and smooth as an acorn, except for a fringe of dark hair running around the back of his head from ear to ear.

Brie and George climbed the ladder. "Want me to come up to the parking lot and help you with the next load?" she asked. She knew John's pickup truck would be full to the gills with provisions for the trip.

"I can handle it, Brie. You wait here in case any passengers show up."

"We've already got two aboard." She leaned in close to George. "And Leo down there brought enough stuff to sail to China."

George smiled at that as he went over the gunwale and down to the float. He reversed the wheelbarrow and headed for shore, and Brie went to the stern and sat down on the deck to wait for the next load or the next passenger, whichever came first. She could hear Scott below in the yawl boat tinkering with the engine. She propped her arms behind her and lifted her face to the sun. It had lost most of its summer intensity, but the heat felt good on her skin, and she basked in its glow, knowing her days of sunning on this deck were numbered.

That thought brought a moment of sadness, but before it could take hold, she heard voices and the hollow sound of footsteps approaching on the float. She waited a few moments, not wanting to abandon her spot in the sun, and now she was picking up snippets of their conversation. She should have stood up so they knew she was there, but something held her in her spot. Call it curiosity or call it the detective gene, which was really a nice way of saying she had a snoopy side, but there was no help for it when one had spent her career following clues, interrogating suspects, and employing any means necessary to ferret out the truth.

She knew one thing for certain: since *Maine Wind* was the only ship reached by means of this float, these must be some of their passengers. She quickly identified three distinct voices as the men approached.

"Nice looking ship. I had no idea it would be so big," said voice one.

"Sailing's not my thing. I'm not loving the idea of this," a second voice said. It was slightly higher of pitch, and Brie detected a note of nervous strain there.

"Relax, Jarvis. Peter's in charge and the die is cast, so you may as well try to enjoy yourself," voice number one said.

"I hate the ocean—it scares me. Don't see why everyone's always wanting to get out on it. Water's fine for drinking, but beyond that, it makes me nervous," Jarvis remarked.

"Pete's been good to us. We owe him this," a third voice said.

"Still, it's crazy, don't you think?" Jarvis again.

Brie waited for a response, but none came. It was as if someone had brought a silencing finger to his lips and the conversation had abruptly stopped. Or maybe the other two had just had enough of number two's prattle.

Brie scooted to port and up alongside the cabin trunk before standing. She didn't want them to know they'd been overheard. She crossed the deck and called down to them from the rail.

"You guys here to board the *Maine Wind*?"

"You got it, gorgeous."

Brie recognized voice number one from their approach. She was equal parts flattered and bugged by the "gorgeous" bit but decided to let it pass—one time.

"Well, hand up your gear and I'll show you to your quarters. I'm Brie Beaumont, one of the crew."

"Joe Callum," the guy formerly known as voice number one said. He gave her a wink. "These are my buddies, Lyle Jarvis and Rusty Boardman."

Brie nodded to them, at the same time assessing the three men on the float with the discerning eye of one trained in the study of human nature. Callum had buzzed brown hair and a two-day scruff. He was lean and lanky and wore confidence as easily as a pair of favorite jeans. Jarvis was beanpole thin and clearly uncomfortable in his own skin. His restless eyes roamed over the ship but never once made contact with her. Rusty Boardman, on the other hand, studied her with laser-like intensity. There was an austerity about him—the stamp of a military background, Brie thought. Maybe Special Forces. She was momentarily put in mind of Nate Freeman, the ex-Navy SEAL she'd met while working a case with the Maine State Police in Tucker Harbor in August. Boardman's face, neck, and hands were tanned copper, and the long white cord of a scar ran down the left side of his neck like captive lightning. He wore an Aussie hat and cowboy boots—something you don't see a lot of on the Maine coast. Plenty of boots in Maine, but they're sea boots—rubber, knee high, with siped bottoms for navigating slippery decks on lobsterboats and other craft.

Brie took the large backpack Boardman handed up and lifted it over the gunwale with an ease that earned a look of admiration from him. Just then Scott climbed over the stern and headed her way. When he got to the rail, she introduced him to the three men on the float, and then they muscled the rest of the bags aboard as they were handed up. Finally, the three guys climbed aboard, and Scott's eyes immediately traveled down to Rusty Boardman's cowboy boots.

"Sorry, mate, but you can't wear those on deck," Scott said, in a way that left no room for argument.

"No problem," Boardman said. He squatted down, unzipped his pack, and in a matter of seconds produced a pair of deck shoes from among personal effects packed with military precision.

Callum looked around the ship in a proprietary sort of way. "Where's the captain?" he asked.

"Ashore on personal business," Scott said. "He'll be aboard this evening."

Callum nodded. "It's clear he runs a tight ship."

"The captain takes great pride in his vessel."

"Yeah, but any ship can sink," Lyle Jarvis mumbled under his breath.

Scott gave him a look, and Brie thought, *Uh oh.* She knew Scott was fiercely loyal to Captain DuLac and maybe second only to her in his admiration of John's skill as a master mariner and helmsman.

Scott studied Jarvis for a moment before speaking. "There's really no reason to be nervous about the voyage. You're in very competent hands."

Well played, Brie thought, sending Scott a look of approval.

"Two of you are in the aft compartment. If you'll follow me, I'll show you to your quarters below so you can get unpacked. Mr. Callum—Joe—you're in the amidships compartment. Brie will show you to your cabin."

With that, Scott picked up two of the bags and headed for the aft companionway. Rusty Boardman jumped right in to help, leaving nothing for the overly nervous Lyle Jarvis to do except follow along like a prisoner being assigned a cell. Brie had never seen anyone more joyless or apprehensive about a cruise.

"Right this way, Joe," Brie said. She started to pick up one of Callums's duffel bags, but he beat her to it.

"I'll get those," he said. She led the way forward and offered to take one bag so he could navigate the ladder, but

Callum hoisted the duffels up in front of himself and went down the ladder frontwards with surprising agility. Brie warned him that when they were at sea he'd be best to go down the ladder backwards for safety. She expected some macho retort, considering the "gorgeous" bit when he'd boarded, but surprisingly he gave her a serious nod of consent.

As they descended into the passageway below, Peter Bendorff came out of his cabin to greet Joe Callum. "Joe, old man, it's about time. For a while there, I thought I was being stood up."

Callum dropped one of the duffels and they thumped each other on the back with what Brie liked to call the one-armed guy hug. She could see right away that these two were the best of friends, and despite Bendorff referring to Callum as "old man," he had a good fifteen years on old Joe. She interrupted their party to give Callum his cabin assignment—Cabin 4—to deliver the instructions on use of the head, and to tell him there were extra blankets and pillows aboard should he want one. She was just about to head up the companionway when Leo Dombello stuck his head out of his cabin and greeted Callum. From his owl-like look, it was clear to Brie that Leo had been sound asleep in his berth. Brie put Leo's age at mid-sixties, making him the senior member of the group so far. He obviously liked his afternoon nap. She left the three of them standing in the middle of the passageway and headed up the ladder.

Chapter 6

B rie met Scott amidships. "Well, just two more to go," he said.

"Make that one." Brie nodded toward a man working his way out the float. Every few yards he stopped to look around as if each pause held some new, exciting vantage point. He seemed lost in his own world and actually walked right past the ladder and might have continued off the end of the float had Scott not hailed him.

"Yo, mate. Heads up there!"

The man stopped abruptly and came back to the ladder. "Thanks," he said. "I nearly walked off the end. The harbor here is beautiful." He tossed his large round duffel up to Scott and shinnied up the ladder in an old pair of Birkenstocks that looked like they'd walked all the way from Germany.

"Alexander Smith reporting for duty," the man said, giving them a sardonic little salute. "Where're the rest of the brigands?"

"Stowed away below decks," Brie quipped.

"Am I the last one, then?" Smith asked.

"Not quite." Scott checked the manifest in his hand. "We're still waiting on a Paul Trasky."

"Ah, yes. Trasky," Alex said, surveying the standing rigging.

Brie, in the meantime, was studying him with some interest. Totally different from the others who'd come aboard, he put her in mind of an academic—maybe a college professor. But if that were the case, he'd be roaming a campus somewhere at this time of year. He had the kind of demeanor one might expect from an academic, though—a look of perpetual alertness, coupled with a touch of cynicism. His brown hair was just long enough to be slightly unkempt, and he slouched, which seemed to say simultaneously, *I'm cool but I don't care what anyone thinks.* Brie placed him at late fifties and thought he leaned toward arrogance, but also something else—maybe insecurity.

"Your name is somehow familiar," Scott said. "Your face a little, too."

Smith was still studying the rigging. "Did you know that the *George W. Wells,* the world's first six-masted schooner, was built right here in Camden, Maine?"

"So, you're a maritime history buff," Brie said, "or maybe a history teacher?"

"Was," he said. "Was a history professor."

Brie was about to ask what he did now when Scott interrupted.

"Wait, are you the Alexander Smith who wrote the recent biography of John Paul Jones that received so much acclaim?"

Alex's eyes moved off the rigging and came to rest on Scott. "That's right," he said, but he looked uncomfortable, like he wanted to bolt. He stooped down and picked up his duffel.

"Look, I don't want to be rude, but I'm on vacation this week, getting away from my work, you know. So I'd appreciate if you didn't tell the others."

"You mean your friends here on the cruise?"

"No, of course not. I meant everyone else." He waved his hand in a circular motion.

Scott smiled. "Well, we're only a crew of four, but mum's the word. Step right this way. You're in the aft compartment with Rusty Boardman and Lyle Jarvis."

Alex shuffled along after Scott, who had headed aft. Brie heard Scott toss one more comment over his shoulder. "*Jumping Ship.* That's a great title for your book. But I'll say no more."

Brie turned toward the harbor just as a gust of wind sent a blazing little cyclone of orange maple leaves into the water. She decided Smith did indeed have a bit of arrogance about him. *After all, who but another maritime history buff like Scott is going to recognize his name?* she wondered. *It's not like we have Stephen King aboard.*

Scott arrived back on deck just as George came trundling out the float with his next load. The three of them hauled large bags of ice aboard and the meat and other provisions that needed to stay cold. With George's careful supervision they filled the big icebox on deck, placing meat closer to the top that he planned to cook first. Then the three of them headed back toward shore to empty the rest of the provisions out of the truck. More crates of wood went in the wheelbarrow, and Scott carried the last two that didn't fit while Brie juggled three crates of produce down to the float and out to the *Maine Wind*.

So the afternoon ticked away, and the passengers went back and forth between the village and the ship. Camden village wraps itself around the harbor, enticing visitors into its array of seaside shops and restaurants. Known as the "Jewel of the Maine Coast," the village is famous for its beautiful mansions that march up the hill north of the village. Many of these residences belonged to wealthy sea captains in their day, and some now housed lavish bed and breakfast inns. West of the village, the Camden Hills rise up sentinel-like and can be seen for miles out at sea—a familiar landmark for windjammers heading to their berths in the harbor.

While *Maine Wind* had come and gone from this spot all season, Brie had spent little time in the village. Their layovers between cruises were short, and the ship required the active attention of the crew to bring everything into Bristol-fashion for each new group of shipmates. She promised herself she would prowl the village at the end of this cruise and find gifts to bring home for her mom and her friend Ariel.

Chapter 7

By the time their last passenger arrived at the ship, the sun had dipped behind those painted hills, and the rest of the group had already gone ashore to eat dinner. Brie had asked if they didn't want to wait for the last member of their party, but Peter Bendorff, the one who had been the first to arrive at the ship, told her their friend Paul Trasky was perennially late and that, when he arrived, she should send him ashore to Waterfront, where they planned to eat.

Brie was the first to notice the forlorn-looking character glancing to left and right where the shore met the float. He had in tow a small carry-on size piece of luggage. He stepped reluctantly onto the float like he might be boarding a sinking dinghy and made his way gingerly toward the ship, as if terrified by the darkening water on either side of the float. By the time he hove to at the starboard side of the ship, his face looked slightly damp from the ordeal. *Boy,* Brie thought, *this is a bunch of landlubbers the likes of which I've yet to encounter in my five months aboard.* The man had black-framed glasses, shaggy dark hair that stuck out from under a Red Sox ball cap, and a full beard—the only part of him that looked like it belonged at sea.

"You must be Paul Trasky," Brie called down to him. "We've been waiting on you. Hand up your bag and climb aboard."

Trasky did as ordered with his bag and then tried the rope boarding ladder with both hands, like he didn't trust it. When he finally stepped off the float onto the rung of the ladder and felt the movement of the ship, he froze.

"It's okay," Brie encouraged. "Just climb up one rung at a time." Scott had joined her now, and as soon as the fellow's shoulders cleared the gunwale, they got a good grip on him.

"Just one more rung," Scott said. "Now swing your leg over the gunwale."

Brie had stepped back, because at a point it was a one-man job, and Scott had Trasky securely in hand.

"Thanks," he mumbled, not looking at them. "Don't like heights."

Brie glanced over the side. It was eight or nine feet down to the float. She imagined what it was going to be like getting him to board that ladder from the thwart of a rocking yawl boat. Since the ship was always anchored away from shore, navigating the boarding ladder down to and up from the yawl boat was a feat each passenger had to muster the courage for, or they weren't going ashore for the whole cruise. She was so used to shinnying up and down that ladder under all conditions, it was easy to forget how daunting the task could be for some.

"Your buddies went ashore to eat dinner," Scott said to Trasky. "They said you should join them. They're up at Waterfront in the village."

Trasky glanced over the side, and Brie was pretty sure he'd gone green around the gills, had there only been enough light to see it.

"That's okay," he mumbled in a soft gravelly voice that sounded rusty from disuse. "I think I'd like to go to my cabin and unpack. It's been a long day. I can live without dinner."

"No problem," Brie said. "I'll show you below. You're in the forward compartment. Our cook, George Dupopolis, will be putting out some snacks later on if you get hungry." She picked up his suitcase and went forward and down the companionway ladder, telling him to turn around and come down backwards. Trasky handled this ladder better, it being brass rather than rope, and she showed him into Cabin 1, just forward of Peter Bendorff's on the starboard side of the ship. She gave him the spiel about the head and then left him to his affairs and headed for the galley. The ship was provisioned, and she wanted to check in with George and see if he needed any help.

"Hey, Brie," he said as she came down the ladder. "Captain aboard yet?"

"Not yet, but it's getting dark. He should be boarding any time now." George already had a couple of lanterns burning in the galley, which gave things a cozy feel, and over to starboard, she could hear the wood crackling and snapping in the woodstove, building up enough heat to brew the coffee.

"Need any help with the snacks?" She saw he had fruit laid out and cheese and crackers ready to be arranged.

"You bet. Why don't you get all of that attractively arranged, and I'll get on making the coffee."

"Roger that," Brie said. She opened one box of crackers and started arranging them in a ring on the large platter.

"Everybody aboard?" George asked.

"Just welcomed the last one. He doesn't look any too happy to be afloat either." She started to unwrap the cheese.

"Early sign of *mal de mer*?"

"Maybe. We'll find out tomorrow, I guess, once we get underway. John always advises them to take a Bonine or Dramamine the night before we sail, but as you know, not everyone listens."

"Well, this'll be like a vacation, cooking for so few this trip. You and Scott can have extra portions."

"That's the best pay right there, George."

He waved off her compliment, and Brie smiled to herself. *The great ones are often humble.* To her way of thinking, nobody topped George. She would never have dreamed she could enjoy food so much before coming aboard *Maine Wind* in May. It suddenly struck her that besides being the last cruise of the season, this was the last week she would be eating George's wonderful fare, and she was feeling a bit downtrodden about it.

"What am I going to do without your cooking, George?" The words rushed out involuntarily, because to Brie, George's meals weren't just food. Over the past five months they had provided comfort for her weary mind and sustenance for her troubled soul.

George turned from the stove, where he'd just put the water on to heat. "I'll tell you what. You promise to come back from Minnesota ASAP, and I'll promise to cook for you and John—oh, heck, Scott can come too—as often as you guys like. No coercion—I'm just sayin'."

Brie smiled. "No coercion, eh?"

George shook his curly dark head, and she could see his smile. "None whatsoever," he said.

Brie washed the fruit—green and red grapes, and straw-berries—and had just finished arranging it on the second plate when she heard the captain come aboard and greet Scott. A few moments later he stuck his head down the galley compan-ionway.

"Hey, you two," he said. "Are we ready to go to sea?"

"Once more unto the breach," George joked.

"I think George has battle fatigue." John gave Brie a wink. "Too many hungry shipmates over too many months."

"And here he is offering to cook for all of us if I'll just beat it back from Minnesota in a hurry. Might you be behind that, Captain John?" She gave him a quizzical look.

"No, but good idea, George. I think if we all keep at it, we'll wear down her defenses."

"I'm right here, you know, guys."

"And that's where we want you to stay," George quipped.

"Scott said all the passengers have checked in," John said.

"They've all gone ashore for dinner except Paul Trasky. He's in his cabin."

"Good. If you and Scott would join me in my cabin in a few minutes, I'd like to go over the itinerary and the weather reports."

Brie nodded. "I'll meet you down there in a couple minutes."

John headed back up on deck, and Brie asked George if he needed help with anything else.

"Nope. We're all good here," he said. "After you're done meeting with the captain, and the passengers get back aboard, we'll bring all this up on deck. You know how the first night aboard is. Everyone likes to hang out and visit till the wee hours. This'll give them something to snack on until they turn in."

"Sounds good, George."

"Oh, and tell Mr. Trasky, if he's hungry, to come on down any time and eat some of this."

"Will do," Brie said. She headed topside and then down the ladder to the amidships compartment, where she knocked on Trasky's door. She could hear him moving things around inside the cabin.

"Yes?" Trasky said from behind the louvered door.

"If you get hungry, George, our cook, has food out down in the galley. Feel free to go down there any time," Brie said through the door.

"Thank you," came the reply.

She headed back up on deck and walked aft. Scott had lit the lanterns while she'd been down helping George. The last flames of sunset were giving way to a starry night, and a warm Indian summer breeze carried mingled aromas from village restaurants out over the harbor. *Good sailing tomorrow,* she thought, taking a deep breath. Even over the scents wafting from the village, she could smell the sea, and as always, it called to her.

She descended the ladder to the aft compartment and knocked on the captain's cabin door.

"Come," he said.

She opened the door and stepped in. Scott was already there.

"Ah, Brie, good. Let's get started," John said. "I've had a few requests from our group, so we'll do our best to cover those bases. I plan to haul anchor and get underway by oh-five-hundred."

"What's on their list?" Brie asked.

"Well, they'd like to sail down East toward Acadia National Park. I thought we'd head out toward Isle Au Haut and Jericho Bay. There are great vantages of Mount Desert Island from there, and it should be perfect sailing weather tomorrow."

"How about going ashore at Stonington?" Scott asked. "We'll be right there."

"You know, I think I'd rather keep them aboard tomorrow —let them get their sea legs in case we hit higher seas down the line."

"The marine forecast for tomorrow is for winds fifteen to twenty-five knots and seas three to six feet," Brie said. "That holds right on through the next day, when things could get a little soupy toward nightfall."

"Alexander Smith, one of the guys back in this compartment, mentioned they were hoping to see Monhegan Island and possibly the Isles of Shoals," Scott said. "The guy's a historian and former professor. Probably wants to visit the site of the infamous murders."

"Yup, they've got those two spots on their list," John said. He reached under his chart table, pulled out a chart, and unrolled it on top of the table. "I'd like to head for Monhegan

Island by early afternoon tomorrow and anchor in the harbor there tomorrow night. If we make good time, the passengers can go ashore and walk around; otherwise, we'll get them ashore the following day, before we set our heading for the Isles of Shoals."

"Sounds like a plan," Scott said. "Brie, you've got the first watch tonight. I'll come on watch at twenty-four hundred."

They heard footsteps on deck, and voices carried down the companionway.

"Sounds like our shipmates are back aboard. Anything else, Captain?" Scott asked.

"Nope, we're good here. Should be a fine cruise if the weather holds."

Chapter 8

The three of them left John's cabin and headed up the ladder. Everyone had congregated amidships, where George had put out some red wine and the fruit and cheese plates. As they headed forward, Brie noticed that even though they'd just eaten, two or three of the passengers were huddled around the food. Paul Trasky, the last one to come aboard, was not with the group.

She and Scott headed down to the galley to help George bring up the coffee and mugs. "Coffee ready?" she asked.

"Just about. I had a short visit with Paul Trasky before the others came back aboard. He said he wanted to turn in and asked if he could have a snack. I told him to help himself and also advised him to take some Bonine before bed to ward off seasickness tomorrow. So I think we've seen the last of him for tonight."

George transferred the coffee into the pump pots they used on deck, and the three of them carried the coffee service topside. George produced a pan of warm brownies he'd baked in the woodstove, and those went topside too.

Brie informed the captain that Paul Trasky had turned in for the night, and with that, the captain called the group to order by dinging his spoon against his coffee mug.

"I'd like to welcome all of you aboard. I'm Captain John DuLac, and this is my crew, Scott Hogan, mate, Brie Beaumont, second mate, and this is our wonderful ship's cook, George Dupopolis, who keeps us fed every day with his amazing fare."

George raised his hand in acknowledgement but then looked at his shoes, never knowing what to do with too much praise.

John gave the shipmates the projected itinerary they had just discussed at the meeting in his cabin. He advised them that plans can change quickly, though, if the weather should take a turn—something it was known to do in the North Atlantic. He also told them that they planned to haul anchor at five a.m. and that breakfast would be served on deck at eight o'clock.

"So, enjoy yourselves up here, and if you are prone to seasickness, there are over-the-counter remedies down in the galley in a basket on the table. If this is your first time at sea, I would advise you to take some Bonine as a precaution. There are also bracelets for seasickness in the basket down there. We have lots of returning shipmates every year who swear by those. Brie will be on watch until midnight, when Scott will come on. Should you need anything, she can help you." He raised his coffee mug. "Here's to fair winds and following seas for our voyage."

Everyone raised their glasses, and with that, the captain said goodnight, and he, Scott, and George headed for their berths. Brie took up her watch on deck. The night was unseasonably warm, with the temperature right at seventy and just the hint of an offshore breeze.

As she went about her tasks on deck, she observed the six men. She was hard-wired for such duty. Her work as a detective had made her a student of human nature to the extent that it was virtually impossible for her to ignore the dynamics of any particular group of people.

Alexander Smith, the author and former history prof, stood slightly apart from the others, observing them with a mildly condescending expression, as if they were some laboratory study of humanity gone wrong. Rusty Boardman, of the captive lightning bolt, also stood apart. He had his Nikon camera on a tripod and was taking time-lapse shots across the harbor toward the village. Brie had him pegged as a loner who used his camera as a buffer from the others.

Lyle Jarvis moved back and forth like a retrograde satellite in a minor arc behind the rest of the men, who were clustered around the food on the cabin top. Stationary was not a word in his physical vocabulary, and Brie had already come to think of him as "Jumpy Jarvis."

Peter Bendorff and Leo Dombello were sharing center stage. Bendorff, in his big voice, regaled the others with tales of shark fishing off Montauk, while Leo Dombello, possibly inspired by the wine, told of working in his grandmother's vineyard in Tuscany as a boy. He intricately illustrated his stories with his hands in what Brie thought of as the Italian manner, although she knew this was stereotyping.

Finally, Joe Callum stood to Bendorff's right, laughing at all the appropriate times and sending smoldering glances in Brie's direction, which she pretended not to notice. She was working on a strategy for dealing with him, since it was becoming apparent she'd need one on this cruise.

After a time the men broke up and prowled around the ship, visiting each other's cabins to compare notes and see who had more space. As it turned out, no one did; small cabins are the way of it aboard the windjammers. When Peter Bendorff and Joe Callum expressed their amazement to her, she reminded them that they were here for the experience above decks, not below.

"As the trip unfolds, I think you'll come to appreciate the coziness of your cabins. Nights at sea this time of year can be cold. A small cabin and warm wool blankets can be most inviting after a long day on deck."

"You make it sound nice," Callum said, stepping uncomfortably close to her side.

"Think of it as part of the charm of a sailing ship," Brie said, taking a step back. "And best of all, everything is close at hand. If we get into rough seas, you'll appreciate that."

Peter Bendorff smiled like *she* might be part of the charm of the sailing ship as well.

Since they were there, Brie corralled Bendorff and Callum to help carry the dishes down to the galley. The food was all gone except for a few brownies that went on the table under a piece of plastic wrap. Brie filled the sink with hot soapy water that had been heated on the woodstove and washed plates and coffee mugs. The wine had been served in disposable paper cups. Callum and Bendorff offered to dry the dishes, to which Brie said, "See, you two are already getting the hang of shipboard etiquette." The clean mugs went on a tray that was stored behind one of the rails that held dishes in place when *Maine Wind* was under sail.

By the time Peter Bendorff and Joe Callum headed for their cabins in the amidships compartment, all the others had retired. Brie dodged into her berth behind the galley and pulled on a hooded sweatshirt, knowing the night would get cooler by the end of her watch. She commandeered the one mug of coffee left in the pot and headed up the ladder, but she paused partway up, hearing someone above her talking. It sounded like Rusty Boardman, but the gentleness in his voice surprised her.

"Listen, Lise, I'll be home soon and everything will be different. We'll make it a new start."

Brie didn't want to eavesdrop on his private conversation, so she continued up the ladder with her coffee. As she emerged, Rusty Boardman looked up, startled. He'd been sitting on the deck, leaning against the port gunwale, one knee pulled up with his arm draped over it in a casual pose. He struggled to his feet.

"Hello, Rusty," Brie said casually, not wanting to add to his apparent discomfort. "I thought you'd turned in."

"Just making a quick call," he muttered.

"No problem. Stay up as late as you want."

She continued aft with her coffee but heard him say into his phone, "Nobody. Just one of the crew."

She smiled as the lines from a childhood poem came to mind. *I'm nobody! Who are you? Are you nobody, too? How dreary to be somebody! How public like a frog. To tell one's name the live-long day to an admiring bog.* That got her thinking about Alexander Smith, their resident author, who probably considered himself "somebody."

Rusty Boardman wasted no time ending his phone call. He came aft, head lowered, hands in his pockets. "Night," he muttered as he ducked down the ladder to his cabin.

"Night," Brie said. She tried to picture him having girl problems, and it made him more human somehow.

Although she never minded the solitary nature of the watch, tonight she was not alone as plenty of people ambled along the wharf that fronted the harbor. This was the last hurrah for the village's restaurants, shops, and bars as the peak of New England's leaf season began to wane. Soon, cold Canadian air masses would begin making up and dropping down from Hudson Bay and Quebec, and then the snows would come in earnest.

Chapter 9

Joe Callum stepped quietly out of his cabin and checked his watch by the dim light in the passageway. Eleven-thirty. The others were long asleep, and he could hear Leo snoring in the cabin next to his. He walked across the passageway and rapped lightly on Peter Bendorff's door.

"Peter," he said in a voice just above a whisper. "Peter, we need to talk."

After a moment he heard rustling from within, and in a few more moments Bendorff opened the door and motioned him inside. "What's this about, Joe? I was sound asleep."

There was just enough room for them to stand facing each other in the small space in front of the berth.

"We need to talk, Peter," Callum said, *sotto voce.* "We need to get something straight before we leave in the morning."

"Okay, shoot," Bendorff said. He kept his voice low, as well, but there was a hint of irritation in it.

"Look Pete, I owe you a lot, I guess. But I've paid my dues."

"That's for me to decide," Bendorff said. "Not you."

"Look, when we get back from this trip, everything's going to be different, and I'm telling you right now, I'm done keeping tabs on Lyle Jarvis. I know he's your nephew, and I know what I promised in the beginning. But I'm done with it." Even in the dim light filtering in from the passageway, Callum thought he saw Bendorff's face darken.

"I'll say when you're done with something. You work for me, and keeping tabs on Lyle is part of that work. That goes for now, and that goes for when you get back. I made a promise to my sister, and I am, by God, going to keep it."

"Your success in this current endeavor depends on all of us cooperating and supporting you. If you want things to go smoothly, then you'll do what I ask."

"Are you threatening me?" The menacing storm that darkened Bendorff's face seeped into his voice.

"I'd prefer to think of this as a negotiation. You see, I know where all the bones are buried. I scouted a lot of your talent at the company, remember? So I know that Rusty Boardman is eminently qualified to keep tabs on your nephew."

"You think you have some kind of power, Callum? I could send you to jail any day I saw fit."

Even though the space between them was minimal, Joe Callum stepped eye to eye with Bendorff. "And I, you," he gritted through his teeth.

"Ironic, isn't it?" Bendorff let out a cynical laugh. "That's the beauty of it, don't you think?"

"I think you'd better watch yourself, Peter."

Surprisingly, Bendorff's expression softened. He put an arm around Joe's shoulder and turned him toward the door. "Listen, son, I'm depending on you. That won't change."

"I'm not your son," Callum muttered, and yet, deep down, those words played on him; solace for a hungry heart. They meant everything. He stepped out into the passageway and heard Bendorff shut the door behind him. He stood there for a moment in a black fog of ambivalence. Finally, he crossed the passageway and quietly reentered his cabin. He crawled under his blankets and lay there thinking dark thoughts.

Eventually, though, the effort of all that anger was too much to sustain. He didn't like being angry. He liked being approved of—being liked. It was his tragic flaw. Maybe now was the time to change all that.

Chapter 10

Alexander Smith woke in the middle of the night feeling disoriented and thirsty. He sat up and banged his head on the berth above him. "Damn," he said, flopping back down. He rolled to one side and fidgeted his way to the edge of the berth, swung his legs out and sat carefully up. The cabin was dark. Before turning in, he'd hung two towels over the louvers on the door to block out the dim light from the passageway. He stood and stepped across to his wash basin. He fumbled for the small plastic glass, took it from its holder, and filled it with water. He drank, filled the glass again, and drank some more. Then he felt his way back to the berth and, reversing his awkward disembarking maneuver, reboarded the berth.

He lay there for a few minutes, feeling the gentle movement of the ship at anchor. It felt comforting, and he thought about the irony of that. There was nothing comforting about any part of this trip for him. Peter had insisted he come, and he'd finally given in and agreed to become part of the plan. No point resisting. He'd tried abortively to end his friendship with Bendorff a year ago. Tried and failed.

He'd met Bendorff while moonlighting as a history teacher at the local community college in Portland, back in the day when he was always strapped for money. Damn drinking—it had led to all his problems, and still he couldn't kick the precarious habit. He'd been teaching a course in the history of theater, and Peter Bendorff had been a student one semester. Bendorff was in his forties at the time and taking courses related to theater as well as acting classes, hoping to become good enough to break into community theater. They were close in age, so at first it had seemed natural that they would become acquainted.

Peter had been the befriender, and he'd been the be-friendee. Soon, friendly chats after class led to Peter inviting him out for a beer, and that had been the beginning of it. And it hadn't been all bad. Pete had been a true friend in many ways. Cheered him up when he was down, gotten him to start exercising, stood by him through the divorce. But something in it never felt comfortable, and of course, eventually, he learned why. He still remembered their conversation—that veiled confrontation the night he had tried to sever their friendship, over a year ago.

"Best to remain friends, don't you think?" Bendorff had said. "One never knows when one may need a powerful friend, or a good attorney, for that matter. I've got two outstanding ones at my company."

"I just need to make some changes in my life," Alex had said. "Move in some different directions."

Then the gloves had come off.

"You never know when someone might learn what you've done, Alex," Bendorff had said, putting his hand on his shoulder in a false gesture of solidarity. "It could come out, you know."

"How?" Alex had said. "You're the only one who knows."

Bendorff had studied the fingernails on his left hand but had not given him an answer.

And so their ostensible friendship had continued. Alex had never been good at ending things or breaking bad habits. Things had passed the point of no return the night he'd had too much to drink and told Peter his secret.

He lay in his berth for quite a while, castigating himself about his poor decisions in life, and when he heard the anchor start to come up, he thought about bursting from his cabin and running for the float, while there was still time to escape. But some time in his past, after good judgment had been sacrificed, any real chance for escape had also been forfeited. It was the price he had paid for one devastatingly bad decision.

Chapter 11

At 0500 they hauled their anchor. Darkness still gripped the harbor as Scott climbed over the ship's stern and down to the yawl boat. He turned over the large diesel engine, sending a deep-throated rumble of disturbance across the silent water. He butted the yawl up to the stern of the *Maine Wind*, and with the captain at the helm, began slowly pushing the ship out of the harbor, where they would raise sail. Brie was busy taking down the halyards from where they hung on the ratlines and getting them laid out on deck to port and starboard for raising sail. Sunrise was still an hour and forty-five minutes away, but the captain was eager to get underway so they'd be near Isle Au Haut Bay by breakfast time.

The plan was to sail through Merchant Row, which was peppered with beautiful islands, and up into Jericho Bay. By afternoon the captain planned to head around the eastern side of Isle Au Haut and sail the Great Circle out around Matinicus and Criehaven and on to Monhegan Island, where they would anchor for the night. If the wind stayed up, as was forecast, they would make Monhegan in five to six hours.

Outside Camden Harbor, John brought the ship upwind for raising sail. Scott put a towline on the yawl boat and came back aboard. They would haul the yawl later, once the passengers were on deck to help man the lines.

John and Brie stood by on the throat halyard for raising the mainsail, and Scott and George manned the peak halyard, and they hauled away alternately until the big sail was up and the halyards were made off. The foresail was smaller and lighter, and once it was set, George returned to the galley, where he was getting the stove up to temperature for baking biscuits. He had told Brie he planned to serve up a big basket of them with the coffee by 0700. George always put some savory treat out with the coffee, first thing in the morning, for those who came on deck early. This early fare might be pie or coffee-cake left over from the day before or toast, hot from the wood-stove, with butter and honey or jam. Something that went down perfectly with that first cup of coffee to warm body and soul early in the morning.

The October wind blew chill as they picked up headway, and Brie pulled the hood of her sweatshirt up over her *Maine Wind* ball cap. They were on a heading east-northeast with the wind on their beam—a fast point of sail. She and Scott went forward to raise the headsails—jib and staysail—and when the sails were set and trimmed, she reported back to John. He put her at the helm so he could go below, pull charts, and make a log entry. She noted the compass bearing as she stepped be-hind the wheel.

"We'll change course just beyond North Haven and head southeast toward Isle Au Haut Bay," he said, heading for the ladder.

"Aye, Captain."

The wind was blowing 18 knots—a fresh breeze. Brie felt it on the right side of her face, and if she turned her head that direction, she caught the briny smell of the sea. The sails were full and drawing well, and that ever-present roar of the wind in the canvas was ramping up.

The eastern sky began to glow gold now as their heading took them straight into the breaking dawn. *Gold, the color of il-lumination and wisdom,* her friend Ariel would have reminded Brie. Ariel felt that colors denoted certain spiritual traits or the lack thereof. Brie smiled, wishing she could absorb enough of that golden illumination to feel confident in the upcoming decisions she had to make. In a few minutes the sun crept above the horizon—a magnificent saffron presence, born of the sea. In these early approaches to winter, it was truly the coin of the realm, more sought after than all of Midas' gold.

John came up from below with three charts stuffed under his arm. He slipped two of them into the cuddy that held the nav equipment, unrolled the third chart, and fed it under the bungees to hold it open atop the cuddy. He stepped over next to Brie at the helm, and they watched the sun make its entrance up the eastern sky.

"Last cruise of the season," he said a little wistfully.

Brie studied his brown eyes, trying to read his level of anxiety about the situation, but this morning she saw only happiness there—the happiness of being able to share one more adventure together aboard *Maine Wind*.

Shortly after the sun rose, so did the first shipmate. It was 0650 when Paul Trasky's head poked out of the amidships companionway, soon to be followed by the rest of him as he climbed on deck. Brie wasn't surprised. He'd turned in quite early last night.

"I think I'll go check in with George, see if he needs any help," she said. She handed the helm over to John, but as she started to walk away, he caught her by the hand. She turned and their eyes embraced for a moment. "We'll make this a good last cruise," she said.

"And by last, I hope you don't mean last," John said jokingly.

Brie opened her mouth to say something, but John interceded. "It's okay, Brie. I know the future is a bit uncertain right now. You go ahead and check in with George."

She glanced forward. Trasky was occupied with the sunrise. She leaned in and kissed John lightly on the lips. "I promise you we will chart this course together."

"Whatever you choose, it can't be because of me," John said.

"What would be so wrong with that?" Brie asked.

"Because you'd come to regret it," he said.

"There's no way to know that, John. But here's one thing we do know. You're part of the equation now. Yes, there are unknowns—variables—but it's a different equation than it was six months ago. And, like it or not, you're a factor now."

"I never said I didn't like it." His brown eyes warmed. "It's hard not to like a girl who can draw a good analogy."

Brie couldn't help smiling at that.

"You go and help George. We'll have plenty of time to talk during the cruise."

She headed forward, but before going below, she stepped over to the starboard rail. "Good morning, Paul," she said to Trasky. He looked pale as biscuit dough, and his drab gray hoodie and heavy black-framed glasses did nothing to enhance his color. He had on the same baseball cap he'd arrived in, and Brie wondered if he'd slept in it, considering the disorganized scruff of hair sticking out.

"The ride's a little smoother astern—not so much rise and fall as up here in the bow. Why don't you head back and talk to the captain? He'll show you where we're headed this morning on the chart, and we'll have some coffee and food on deck shortly."

"I don't think I can eat," he said, looking bilious at the mere mention of it.

"It's important to get some bulk in your stomach the first day out. George, our cook, will probably have oatmeal or pancakes this morning—something to put a base in your stomach."

Trasky nodded. "Well, I'll try to follow your advice and get something down. The back of the ship, you say?"

"Yes—less motion."

He nodded and walked aft, serpentining along the deck the way all the passengers do on the first day out, or until they acquire their sea legs. Brie paused to watch him and then headed below.

Speaking of biscuit dough, there was George with a sheet full of cinnamon-sugar-topped biscuits just heading into the woodstove. The coffee was brewing atop the stove, and Brie got busy hauling down the coffee mugs from behind the dish rails.

Scott came below just then. "I smell cinnamon," he said with a smile.

"You can start taking things topside," George said. "It won't be long now."

Scott went up the ladder with a tray full of coffee mugs, and Brie followed with a second tray that held napkins, cream and sugar, butter and jam. She noticed that Rusty Boardman and Lyle Jarvis had come up from their cabins in the aft compartment and joined Paul Trasky and the captain astern. She and Scott got things laid out on top of the galley house. She could see Boardman and Jarvis looking their direction. Even from a distance, the vibe told her they were more than willing to risk eating at sea; in fact, they were chomping at the bit to do so.

Brie and Scott went back down to the galley, and by the time they returned topside with the coffee and a large basket of hot cinnamon biscuits, Joe Callum and Alexander Smith had joined the others on deck. Everyone crowded in around the coffee and biscuits for a miniature feeding frenzy.

"Remember, if we run out of biscuits, a full breakfast will be served in about an hour," Scott said.

It was looking like running out of biscuits was a certainty, and Jarvis piped up. "Maybe we should leave some for Peter and Leo."

"I didn't hear either of them stirring when I came up," Callum said. "They'll probably sleep in till breakfast time." Shortly after this statement, the biscuit basket was empty, and the men took their coffee and dispersed around the deck.

A few minutes later, Paul Trasky stopped Brie amidships. "I think I'll skip breakfast and just see how the biscuits sit, if that's okay," he said.

"No worries," Brie said. "We don't force feed anyone onboard."

"I might go below and grab some more shuteye," Trasky said in his gravelly voice, whose range was hard to hear over the roar of wind in the canvas. "I didn't sleep very well last night."

"You'll sleep better as the week progresses," Brie said. "Being at sea, in the wind and sun all day, can be surprisingly tiring." She started to walk away but then turned. "Remember, when you're below decks, stay horizontal. Standing up down there for very long will make you seasick. The motion of the ship is felt much more below the waterline, so if you're below, it's best to be lying in your berth."

Trasky nodded. "I'll remember that. Thanks." He headed for the amidships companionway, and Brie continued aft.

Chapter 12

At 0720, just beyond North Haven, they changed course and came to a new compass heading—east southeast—for Isle Au Haut Bay and Merchant Row. So far, the breeze had held steady at 18 knots, but Brie knew it would pick up as the morning wore on. Just after 0800, Brie and Scott rolled out the mats on the cabin top, and crew and shipmates formed a bucket brigade line from the foot of the galley ladder to the amidships house on the starboard deck—the windward deck. Up came a kettle of oatmeal—the captain always asked that oatmeal be served the first day out—and there was a big platter of pancakes laced with wild Maine blueberries and served with butter and Maine maple syrup. A roasting pan filled with thick-sliced bacon came up next, along with a basket containing oranges, apples, and bananas. Finally, the beverages came up the companionway—coffee, orange juice, and water—and when the last receptacle was in place, everyone formed a line on the opposite side of the deck.

Brie noticed that Peter Bendorff and Leo Dombello had arisen in time for breakfast. The captain addressed the group, as he did every morning before breakfast, and gave them the proposed itinerary.

"We're just entering the northern end of Isle Au Haut Bay. Lying straight off the bow, in the distance, you can see beautiful Isle Au Haut. The southern half of the island is part of Acadia National Park. As we make our way through Merchant Row and up into Jericho Bay, you'll see some stunning vistas of Mount Desert Island, home of our wonderful national park.

This afternoon we will leave these waters and sail for Monhegan Island, where we'll anchor for the night. We'll be on the lookout for whales throughout the day as we get farther from the coast. We expect to make Monhegan in time for you to go ashore, if you wish, and visit the island.

"The following day, Sunday, will be a long day of sailing to the southwest toward the Isles of Shoals, and we'll be on the lookout for whales that day as well. Now, let's all enjoy George's fare, and after breakfast, anyone interested can track our position on the chart back here near the helm."

After all the passengers had gone through the breakfast line, Brie took her oatmeal and coffee forward to the bow, where she stood looking out to sea. The salt tang in the air was a better wake-me-up than any cup of coffee could be. It was a cool morning, and remnants of fog hemmed the rocky islands of Isle Au Haut Bay, a hauntingly beautiful place. Here and there the deep-throated rumble of an engine broke the stillness as a lobsterboat prowled among the buoys off one of the spruce-capped islands. Brie drank in the scene, committing each sensory component of the watery paradise to memory, imprinting each upon her heart: a watercolor for the mind to be viewed at will, long after this voyage, this season, had ended.

After a while, Scott came forward, and Brie went below to help George clean up from breakfast. Scott stayed in the bow on watch. Whenever they were underway, there was always a crew member on watch in the bow.

*   *   *

Lyle Jarvis looked up from his plate of pancakes and darted his eyes around the ship. From where he sat on the storage locker amidships, he could take in the parts of the ship, as well as those aboard, without actually focusing on the water that was everywhere around them. Right now the food on his plate commanded his attention, and he mopped up some of the syrup with a hefty forkful of blueberry pancakes. The cakes were good —really good. Something to take comfort in. He glanced behind him at the food line to see if he might finagle a second helping. He noticed the cook had brought up a second round of pancakes, stacked high in a roasting pan.

Leo Dombello, who was seated across from him on a bench that faced the back of the ship, got up and waddled in the direction of the pancakes. That was all the prompting Jarvis needed, and he rose and followed Leo. Some of the other guys saw them heading for seconds and followed suit. When Lyle got to the pancakes, there were a couple dozen left. He figured he could nab four more of them without looking too greedy, so he did. He pilfered three more strips of bacon and drowned the whole thing in maple syrup.

It took all his concentration to hold the plate and pour from the pitcher on the tilting deck. He'd found if he kept his feet spread wide, it steadied him. He did his little dance to one side and another along the deck till he regained his seat on the locker. Why was it so hard to walk in a straight line? One of the crew—the girl—had said something about sea legs. He had no idea what that was supposed to mean, but since it had the word "sea" in it, he wasn't interested either. He hated the thought of water, and knowing he was out on it, surrounded by it, and stuck here for the better part of a week made him almost homicidally angry.

Dear Uncle Pete, who tracked his every move like a bloodhound, had made his life a living hell. It was bad enough that he had to work for his uncle, but that was only the beginning of the suffocating rein Peter Bendorff kept over his life. First off, there was the apartment—the one his uncle had chosen for him so he could live close by. "We can carpool to work," Pete had said shortly after he'd moved into the apartment. More suffocation. But the final blow was finding the surveillance cameras in his apartment. He'd removed them, of course, after a bloodthirsty battle with his uncle, but Peter was cagey, and he had no confidence that those cameras hadn't been replaced by others even more subtly hidden. And why not? Bendorff had plenty of tech-savvy employees who could have pulled it off.

He knew his mom, Uncle Pete's sister, was behind all the misery. She would have said that it was all about keeping him safe—that he had proven he couldn't be trusted. All bullshit. Sure, he'd screwed up when he was eighteen. Who didn't? But now he was thirty—a man. How dare the two of them keep invading and controlling his life. After many heated arguments, he'd agreed to this trip for one reason and one reason only. He thought, somehow, he might finally be free of Uncle Pete's clutches.

He got up and headed over to the rail, where the crew kept a bucket of seawater for scrubbing off dishes before they went down to the galley. He dropped his silverware into the bucket and, squatting down, used the brush attached to the handle to swab off his plate and cup and then stacked them in the adjacent dish rack that sat on the deck. As he finished, he happened to glance through one of the scuppers at the sea streaming by and was certain he saw a trace of red. He stood up, horrified, and in an uncharacteristic move, looked over the rail into the sea. The motion of the ship through the water sent a wave off the bow, but swirled into that wake, he saw deep, claret red—blood red—a backwash of death. It trailed away from the ship, taunting him. He clutched the thick lifeline, transfixed by the sight of that blood red trail. It couldn't be. Why was it there?

"Are you all right, Lyle?"

The voice jarred him from his nightmare reverie. He turned to see the second mate, Brie, staring into his eyes, clearly concerned. He glanced down at his hands and saw that the knuckles had turned a livid white from gripping the lifeline. He backed away from the rail, staggering a bit, and she actually reached out to steady him. He recoiled from her touch. "I'm fine," he blurted out. He turned from her and, weaving along the sloping deck, headed for the back of the ship.

By the time he got to the ladder that led to his cabin below, his hands were shaking so badly he could hardly take hold of the brass rails for the ladder. *You'll be fine,* he mentally told himself. He'd been a fool to look over the side. The sight of that moving water had brought things back—things he kept tightly locked away. And he'd been a fool to come aboard this ship. He swore to himself it wouldn't be for nothing. *Peter's agenda be damned,* he thought. Maybe he'd have his own agenda—a hidden agenda. Maybe that was all that mattered from here on out.

Chapter 13

And so the next two days unfolded. Saturday was a glorious day of perfect weather and sailing, and yet something was missing from this voyage; everyone on the crew noticed it. Absent was the sense of joyful abandon that had accompanied every cruise throughout the summer, that had lit up the eyes of every passenger as they stepped aboard, left behind set schedules, and gave themselves over to the surprises, the unpredictability of life at sea. Call it a feeling of expectation—the welcoming of adventure—because at sea, plans only work to the extent that the gods of wind and water allow.

Early in the afternoon, John was at the helm and Brie was running a plot on the chart. She turned when done, and John motioned with his head for her to step closer. She tucked the pencil under the bungee cord on top of the chart and came over.

"Do you think it would kill them to have a little fun?"

Brie laughed. "You'd think we'd hogtied them and dragged 'em aboard."

"It does feel a little like a press gang, doesn't it? It's like some of them had no idea what to expect."

"And then there's the rest who came aboard predisposed to dread."

That got a laugh from John. "Well, we'll see how it shakes out. Even the unhappiest passenger has been known to come around. We'll let the sea work its magic."

"That might work. I've got a lot more faith in the sea than in humanity," Brie said, waxing dark.

"Too nice of a day for that kind of talk," John said.

"You're right. Can't let this bunch of Eeyores rub off on us."

After that they grew silent, standing together at the helm, hearing the wind in the canvas, feeling the soul-stirring power of *Maine Wind* galloping along under full sail.

Thanks to a fine breeze that moved into the west and stayed there all afternoon, as if the captain had paid it to do so, they made good headway toward Monhegan Island. When they were still far off the island, they spotted a pair of Northern Gannets—large white seabirds with black wing tips and wingspans to forty inches—soaring overhead. Farther along they spotted Great Shearwaters and Sooty Shearwaters, Northern Fulmars, and several Great Black-backed gulls, with wingspans nearly as impressive as the Northern Gannet's.

Over the sailing season, Brie had worked at learning her seabirds and could now recognize many of them in flight. But today was her lucky day, because as they sailed around the northern side of Monhegan, a Magnificent Frigatebird, of huge wingspan and distinguished by its forked tail, soared out over *Maine Wind*. Brie had hoped to see one of these marvelous creatures all summer, and she took it as a sign this cruise might be looking up.

They sailed down the western side of the island and dropped anchor in the small harbor that lay between Monhegan and its stone's-throw-away neighbor, Manana Island. Brie had learned that the name Monhegan derived from "Monchiggon," Algonquian for "out to sea." And so it was, with the island lying about twelve nautical miles off the mainland. The shipmates were itching to go ashore and explore the island, except for Paul Trasky, who sent word through Leo that he didn't feel well enough to join them. Brie wondered if Trasky was just too afraid of the boarding ladder, remembering the fiasco the night he had boarded.

"I told him it would be good to get off the ship—get his feet on land," Leo said, using his hands to illustrate *ship, feet,* and *land.* "But he refused."

"It's okay," Scott said. "We never like to pressure folks. The point of these cruises is to let them do whatever their hearts desire."

"Anyway," the captain added, "it may be better for him to stay onboard so his ears continue to acclimate to the sea."

"Ears?" Leo said, holding his hands out in a praise-the-Lord posture. "I thought it was legs that had to adjust. I keep hearing about sea legs."

"Well, it's actually the ears that are adjusting to being in a continually moving environment," the captain said. Brie and John ushered the six guys, one by one, over the gunwale and down the boarding ladder to the yawl boat. Scott told them he would run them ashore and come back for them at 1800, or 6:00 p.m., so they could return to the ship in time for dinner.

"We'll see if a little shore duty lightens their mood," the captain said as the yawl boat pulled away.

"Like we said before, they're a pretty tightly wound bunch. I'd sure like to know why."

The captain stared at the retreating yawl boat. "Sometimes one person gets an idea to plan something like this for a bunch of friends or family members, but, much as *we* love the ship and the sea, not everyone does. This guy Bendorff is the ring-leader—he made all the arrangements. Sounds like some of these guys work for him. Maybe they felt they had to come. You know, keep the boss happy. Over the years I've had plenty of passengers who weren't thrilled with the experience once they got aboard. Not everyone adapts to the sea. Look at Trasky."

"Ever had anyone this seasick before?" Brie asked.

"More than once. I had a guy a couple seasons ago so seasick he made me put in on the second day of a six-day

69

cruise and let him off. Didn't care about a refund—just wanted out."

But to everyone's surprise, the shore trip worked some kind of magic, because the men returned in a more amiable mood. A couple of them went below to take a nap, but the others popped open some beers they'd brought aboard on Friday and struck up a card game on deck. Paul Trasky even came topside for a while and ate some of the pork roast and potatoes George served for dinner.

On Sunday the anchor chain rumbled up through the darkness, breaking the still silence of the harbor. Monhegan is a lobstering outpost, and a serious one at that, and normally the small harbor would have been buzzing with activity at this hour, but it was Sunday and the village still slumbered.

To reach the Isles of Shoals, approximately 81 nautical miles away, by nightfall meant a serious day of sailing. Even with good prevailing winds, John told Brie that they could be ten hours underway. So, long before breakfast, they were already making headway to the southwest and monitoring the NOAA marine forecasts and Coast Guard advisories for possible changes in wind and seas.

Just before breakfast Rusty Boardman came topside with his camera. He stayed on deck all morning and just after 1130 hours was rewarded by sightings of humpback whales. Alexander Smith, the history prof and author-turned-adrenaline-junky, also braved the elements, standing at the rail, feet spread wide on the pitching deck, gripping the ratlines to steady himself—John Paul Jones reincarnated.

John hoped to be safely anchored among the Isles of Shoals by late afternoon. Squalls were predicted by evening, so it came as no surprise when around 1330 hours the wind marched into the east, muscled up to 25 knots, and the seas started making up.

Unruly seas occasionally invited themselves aboard, took a run down the deck, and sloshed out through the scuppers. Just after 1400, the wind huffed up to Force 7, and the captain ordered the crew and all able hands to mount the cabin tops and reef down the main and foresail. At 1430 they corrected course to the west and came to compass heading 2-5-0. By 1500 hours, or 3:00 p.m., large following seas were piling up astern, bringing on what mariners descriptively refer to as the corkscrew plunge, whereby a ship, in this case *Maine Wind*, slides down the back of a wave and wallows momentarily in the trough before clawing her way up the face of the next sea. A wild ride, to be sure.

Below decks, Paul Trasky clung to his berth like a barnacle to a rock, finding it the only safe place to anchor himself. Leo Dombello, Joe Callum, and Peter Bendorff, his shipmates in the amidships compartment, had also opted to stay below as conditions roughened up. As for Lyle Jarvis, he had disappeared below to his cabin in the aft compartment immediately after breakfast and not been heard from since.

For now, the weather seemed to hold all the trump cards as *Maine Wind* battled toward her anchorage and wind and sea bullied around them. If only Brie could have known that the wicked elements currently holding sway would prove to be the least of their concerns that day—that a much greater drama was about to unfold, the scope of which would outstrip even the blackest of gales.

The Coast Guard Search

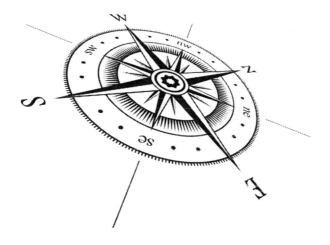

Chapter 14

The 45-foot Coast Guard RB-M—Response Boat-Medium—rumbled into the Isles of Shoals at 0017, or seventeen minutes past midnight. With the heavy cloud deck, it was a moonless night, and the crew turned on their search lights to locate the *Maine Wind* and motored slowly up to her starboard side. They heaved their lines fore and aft, and Brie and Scott caught the lines and made them fast. John disconnected the lifeline and lowered the boarding ladder. The chief petty officer put the boat's engine in neutral and stepped from the pilothouse, and with all the agility of one totally acclimated to the sea, jumped from his port gunwale to the boarding ladder and climbed aboard the *Maine Wind* to speak to the captain.

At that moment Brie saw Rusty Boardman emerge from the aft companionway.

"I'll get this," she told Scott. "We need to keep them below in their cabins for now."

"I'll check the other compartment," Scott said. But as he walked forward, the captain called him over to talk to the Coast Guard officer.

Brie walked over to Boardman. "We need everyone to stay below, Rusty," she said.

"I'd like to know what's happening." He didn't say it with hostility, but there was authority in his voice which spoke of former command.

"And you will," Brie said. "We'll be calling everyone together shortly. But until then, we'd like you and the others to stay below."

"I'm ex-military. It's not hard to spot a crisis. I'd like to help if possible." The lightning bolt on the side of his neck gave off an eerie reflection in the lantern light.

"Thank you," Brie said. "I'll pass that on to the captain."

Boardman nodded. He looked toward the captain and the Coast Guard officer, and Brie could sense his desire to join them, as if being part of command decisions was in his blood. But he respected her wishes and went back to his cabin below.

Brie descended the ladder a few rungs—far enough to see the passageway and the other cabins. No one was stirring from what she could hear, so she headed forward to talk to the captain. When she joined the three men at the starboard rail, they were discussing the currents and tidal flow. The tide was ebbing, and because they were almost on a full moon, they would be dealing with "spring currents"—tidal current velocities that are much stronger.

"We have divers aboard," Petty Officer Barston said, "and will deploy them, but the chances of spotting the body at night are greatly diminished. A Jayhawk helicopter is being sent from Coast Guard Air Station Cape Cod. They'll drop flares and do sweeps of the area outside the islands where the tidal flow may have carried the victim. They have a Coast Guard rescue swimmer on board just in case. We will treat this as a search and rescue initially, even though the note you found indicates a suicide."

"We appreciate that," John said.

"Well, it's standard procedure at this point in the search," Barston replied. With that he turned and descended the boarding ladder and reboarded the response boat. Brie and Scott heaved the lines, and the Coast Guard vessel motored to a position about fifteen yards off their bow, where they prepared to deploy their diver.

Brie turned to John. "I'd like to congregate all the passengers in the galley and ask them a few questions. See if anyone had an inkling that Peter Bendorff was planning to kill himself."

"That's fine, Brie. I'd like to know that as well. So let's wake them up and find out."

"I'll go roust the three from the aft compartment and tell them to head forward to the galley," Scott said.

"I'll notify the three below in amidships," Brie said.

"I'll station myself back at the helm to intercept any radio calls," John said. "But I'd like to know what you find out later." He turned to Scott. "You join Brie for the meeting in the galley, but afterward I'd like you topside as an extra hand."

"Aye, Captain," Scott said and turned and headed aft to get the passengers.

Brie went down the amidships companionway and knocked first on Paul Trasky's door.

"Yes, what is it?" A sleepy-sounding voice came through the louvers, and Brie wondered if it was an act.

"Mr. Trasky—Paul. We're asking all the passengers to come forward to the galley for a meeting, immediately."

"All right," Trasky said. "Is something wrong?"

"We'll talk about the details once everyone is assembled," Brie said. She stepped across the passageway and was about to knock on Leo's door when it opened. He stood there looking defensive, arms crossed on his barrel chest.

"I heard what you said to Paul." His brows knit together, and he fixed her with an accusatory look. "So something is wrong."

"We'll talk to everyone in the galley, Leo. Please come forward right away." She stepped over to Joe Callum's cabin just forward of Leo's and knocked.

Callum opened the door, and she delivered the message. He appeared to be wide awake and didn't ask any questions, just nodded and said, "I'll head right up there." The others had been wearing the sleep attire she'd seen them in when they first went looking for Bendorff, but Callum was dressed in jeans and a hooded sweatshirt, like he might have been planning to come topside and see what was going on.

Brie nodded. "I'll see you forward in the galley in a few minutes," she said, and with that she headed topside. She descended the galley companionway and dodged into her berth to take off her raingear and get her small notebook and pen in case there was anything she wanted to jot down. By the time she headed back out to the galley, the shipmates were already congregating. Some wore what looked like sleepwear, while others, like Rusty Boardman and Joe Callum, were dressed. Scott came down the ladder last and took up his position just behind her.

Brie asked everyone to take a seat around the table, and when they had all slid onto the benches, she began.

"It seems that Peter Bendorff has gone missing from the ship, and we have reason to believe he has committed suicide."

There was a stunned silence as if no one wanted to be the first to speak, possibly believing if the words went unspoken, the act could somehow be called back through some conjuring of magic. The glowing oil lamp, hung from the side of the foremast that bisected the table, swung almost imperceptibly with the motion of the ship, like a ghost wanting to be heard. Outside, the deep vibration of the approaching Coast Guard Jayhawk throbbed through the black night, like a death knell tolling the sad reality of the situation.

Leo Dombello, who sat at the end of the table just to the right of Brie, finally took out a handkerchief and wiped his eyes. She scanned the faces of the others. Next to Leo, Alexander Smith stared straight ahead, and even in the yellow glow from the lamp, Brie thought his face looked ashen. She paused momentarily when she got to Lyle Jarvis, and though he sat at the farthest end of the table where little light shone, she could have sworn she saw a slight smirk on his face. The moment Jarvis realized she was studying him, he lowered his head.

Across from him in the opposite corner skulked Paul Trasky in his ball cap and sloppy gray sweatshirt. He was hidden so deeply in shadow where the hull of the ship narrowed into the bow that she couldn't see his face clearly. Next to Trasky, Rusty Boardman met her gaze with his sphinxlike expression, never blinking but returning her look with eyes devoid of any hint of emotion. As a cop she'd seen everything, but there was something chilling in that gaze, former military or not. Joe Callum was the last of the group, sitting directly to her left. His youthful, athletic face seemed to have aged, and except for Leo, he appeared to be the only one in the group genuinely stricken by the news.

In an unfolding crisis, time ticks in slow motion, so this entire scene following the announcement of the suicide unfolded in what Brie knew was little more than seconds. She was frankly surprised at the lack of reaction from most of them, but wrote it off to the fact that they'd already done a sweep of the ship looking for Bendorff, so some of them most likely had already divined that something was wrong.

"Did he leave a note?" It was Leo who broke the silence.

Brie regarded him for a moment. "Yes, he did," she said.

"Can we see it?" Joe Callum asked. And then as if to qualify, "I mean, it's a shock. This was supposed to be a holiday. I guess I'd like to know why."

It was the moment for Brie to reveal her police connections, since she knew the note would not be shared with them, but turned over to the Maine State Police.

"I'm sorry, but that won't be happening. In any case where a person dies alone, there has to be a death investigation. Since no one actually witnessed Mr. Bendorff go overboard, he died alone. If the Coast Guard recovers his body, it may explain certain things. If not, the case will become more complex." She then explained as briefly as possible her background as a homicide detective with the Minneapolis Police Department and her current connection to the Maine State Police, all the while watching their faces to see how this revelation was received. It was met initially with stony silence.

Then Alexander Smith spoke up. "Well, I'm glad there's someone aboard capable of sorting out this mess and getting to the bottom of what's going on."

Spoken like a former professor, Brie thought. Teachers are a lot like cops in their propensity for maintaining order—marshaling the troops, so to speak. Being intellectuals, they also like answers—ones that employ logic—which puts them, if not in the realm of the homicide detective, at least in a neighboring kingdom.

"I gather you were all friends or work colleagues of Peter Bendorff," Brie said. "Did any of you suspect he was in this state of mind? That he might be planning to use this cruise to end his life?"

"This was supposed to be a celebration of a year of record profits for the company," Joe Callum said. "It doesn't make any sense at all."

"Suicides often don't," Brie said. "Humans are good at hiding their emotions and sometimes the true complexion of their lives. Often their families don't even know the depth of despair or depression they suffer from. And sadly, all of that goes double for men."

"Still, I feel responsible," Leo said, gesturing with his handkerchief. "Even if I'm just responsible for not noticing something was wrong." He wiped his eyes again.

Even overlooking his Mediterranean lineage, which may have made him more emotional than the others, he and Callum were the only ones who seemed genuinely grieved by the situation, and Brie couldn't help wondering why the others didn't appear more moved by their friend's death. She could write off Boardman's inscrutable demeanor to his military background, but the others' lack of response was an enigma to her, even considering their maleness. The thought crossed her mind that maybe some of them just didn't care that much about what had happened to Bendorff, which was sad.

"So what happens now?" The gravelly voice of Paul Trasky came out of the shadowed corner where he lurked.

"I assume we're going back to Camden—that the cruise is at an end," Joe Callum said.

"We won't be sailing anywhere until the Coast Guard gives us the go-ahead," Scott said from behind Brie.

She had almost forgotten he was there and now stepped back and stood next to him.

"The search will most likely continue through the night. Our next move will be determined by what the Coast Guard finds. Their diver is already in the water looking for Bendorff's body," Scott said.

"I wouldn't think it would be that hard to find," Alex said.

"On the contrary," Brie said, "the tide is ebbing, and because we are on a full moon, the tidal currents are unusually strong. That means the body could have been carried well outside the islands here."

"Unless he used something to weight himself down." Rusty Boardman said it in a coldly analytical way, as if it were part of some battle strategy.

Leo looked horrified at the thought. "For God's sake, Boardman, show some sensitivity."

"I'm just stating the obvious." Boardman fixed his stony gaze on Leo. "If a person is going to drown himself, he might use something to weight himself down. Isn't that right?" he asked, turning his eyes to Brie.

"Yes, it's quite possible," she said. "I know you guys have been visiting each other's cabins. Did anyone happen to notice anything Peter Bendorff might have used for this purpose? Did you see anything that seemed out of place in his cabin?"

No one responded. But she was thinking about the back-pack Bendorff had been carrying the day he'd boarded the ship. Specifically, she was remembering that she had started to reach for it when she was about to show him below to his cabin. She recalled he had quickly picked up the pack, saying he could handle it. But for some reason she'd had the impression it was heavy.

The sound of the approaching Jayhawk had increased to the point where it was becoming harder to speak, and Brie knew its arrival must be imminent. She stepped closer to the table. "That's all for now. The captain would like all of you to stay below in your cabins while the search is being conducted, and he will have an update for everyone in the morning. So please head back to your cabins and try to get some sleep."

The men looked at each other for a couple moments, then slid out from behind the table and filed toward the ladder. Scott had already gone topside to keep an eye on them and make sure they headed for their respective compartments. Paul Trasky was the last one up the ladder, and Brie followed him. She watched as he, Callum, and Leo headed down to the amidships compartment. Scott had followed the other three men aft to be sure they all returned to their cabins as directed.

Within a few moments the Coast Guard Jayhawk was overhead, and any communication on deck became virtually impossible. The chopper crew immediately began deploying flares and searching the waters within and around the Isles of Shoals. The air smelled of sulfur, and with the flashes of light and smoke from the flares, the waters quickly took on the eerie feel of a war zone. The response boat made slow sweeps back and forth among the islands, scouring the inky waters with their search lights. Two divers had been deployed from the Coast Guard boat, and Brie knew they would be searching the bottom near the ship and then working their way out in the direction of the tidal flow, trying to locate Peter Bendorff's body.

The rain had ceased, but the night was thickly overcast, with no hint of the nearly full moon that shone somewhere above an iron-like cloud deck that had locked itself down over the sea and the seven islands. The captain stayed near the helm, where he could intercept any radio communication, and Brie and Scott patrolled the rest of the deck, and even though plenty of space separated the three of them, she could still sense the tension aboard.

The islands themselves were totally deserted. Even though they were a popular anchorage for sailors, these isles were not home to much of anything besides seabirds. There was one hotel on Star Island, but it had closed for the season. The remoteness of these waters—this place—juxtaposed with the noise and frenetic activity of the Coast Guard's search lent an oddly surreal tone to the unfolding drama, Brie thought.

The search went on through the night, but the sea is a vast and mysterious place and does not always easily give up its dead. A body will float when it is ready, but it can take a few days to a week for this to occur. That's a lot of time in the tides and currents of the ocean, and ultimately, discovery requires that someone is there to find the victim in that sweeping and trackless environment.

At three a.m. the captain told Brie and Scott to head below and get some sleep in case they were given the all clear to sail come daylight. Brie headed below, eager for the peace and warmth of her berth. She turned on the small light at the head of the berth. As she took off her raingear and hung it on the hook at the far end of the berth, she was thinking about the expressions on each of the men's faces when they were told about the disappearance of Peter Bendorff. Now she methodically recalled each expression in a kind of mental line-up. She took out her small notebook, and as each face passed before her mind's eye, she jotted down a single word. Then she stripped down to her long-sleeved tee shirt and leggings and crawled into her berth. She lay there thinking about Bendorff, about what could have driven him to an act so desperate. She remembered her disturbing dream—falling overboard, being pulled down and down. But then, thankfully, sleep, not the sea, was claiming her, pulling her down, down—peaceful, dreamless sleep.

Chapter 15

Morning dawned with no trace of Peter Bendorff. The Coast Guard gave the okay for the *Maine Wind* to return to port, with Petty Officer Barston telling Captain DuLac that they would continue searching for Bendorff throughout the day and would keep the captain informed of their progress. Barston also informed the captain that the operation was no longer search and rescue, but search and recover.

At 0300 DuLac had sent his sleep-deprived crew below for some sack time with just this eventuality in mind. George had been allowed to sleep through the night, but he was up and at his post in the galley by 5:30, getting the woodstove lighted. No matter what happened aboard, the cook had to keep to his routine. There were passengers and crew to be fed, and that simple reality took precedence over whatever other drama might be unfolding. So, rain or shine, gale winds or calm, George was in his galley doing his duty.

For whatever reason, John took comfort in that fact on this particular morning. With his world turned upside down, at least he could depend on a hot cup of coffee and a hot meal. What's more, his passengers had signed up for a cruise, a vacation, and despite last night's tragedy, or maybe because of it, he needed to provide the best he could for them on their return to port.

The unimaginable had happened, and even though the hellish night was done, the reality of the situation weighed on him, heavy as a tropical low. He had lost a passenger overboard, and even though the situation had nothing to do with negligence on his part, he still felt one hundred percent responsible. This was his ship, and something unthinkable had come to pass. Suddenly his brooding feelings about Brie's leaving had been supplanted by a terrible sense of guilt. *How could this act have been averted?*

At 0630, shortly before sunrise, he went below and woke Scott.

"There's a problem with the head back here. Jarvis discovered it after you and Brie turned in. I told him to put a note on the head telling the others to use the one in the amidships compartment."

"I'll check it out right away," Scott said, climbing out of his berth.

"Come topside as soon as you can," John said. "We need to get underway and back to port."

"Aye, Captain."

Last night, after they had confirmed that Peter Bendorff was no longer aboard, he had communicated with the Coast Guard and given them the contact information he had for Bendorff so that the Maine State Police could notify Bendorff's family of what had unfolded. Brie had told him that the police would make contact with the family and give notification of the death.

He heard movement in Rusty Boardman's cabin, but the other two cabins were silent. *Not for long*, he thought. Once we start cranking up the anchor, the rest will wake up. He stepped into his cabin to pull some charts for the voyage home, and when he came topside, he saw Brie just emerging from the galley companionway.

*   *   *

As Brie emerged from the forward companionway, a raw wind bit her face. She pulled up the hood of her foul weather jacket and stuck her hands in the pockets. The ship had swung at anchor to face into a north wind that carried with it a reminder that this was indeed the last cruise of the season. She guessed the wind was blowing around 15 knots—strong for this early in the morning. If they were allowed to weigh anchor, they'd be going up into it on the voyage home, which meant rough seas. But somehow that seemed preferable to being stuck here, helplessly awaiting news of Peter Bendorff—news that almost certainly would not be positive. In the distance she heard the drone of the Coast Guard response boat as it continued its search of the waters outside the island. She did not hear the Jayhawk and assumed it had returned to the station for refueling.

Astern she saw John appear on deck with several charts under his arm. She headed toward him, knowing he must feel exhausted and disheartened by the bizarre turn of events. John ran a tight ship, which in no way meant that he was controlling. It was simply the job of a good captain to do so. As she got nearer, she saw the dark circles under his eyes. His hair was matted from the rain overnight. He looked ten years older than when they'd left port a few days ago. The weight of responsibility.

"Morning, Brie," he said as she approached. "Did you get some sleep?"

The words sounded formal, and the light that normally warmed his eyes when he spoke to her had been extinguished by concern and lack of sleep.

"I did, but you need to do the same," she said. He stood catty-corner from the wheel, unrolling a chart on top of the cuddy that held the radio and nav equipment. "You've been up all night." She studied his face in profile as he tucked the chart under the bungee cords that held it in place and clothespinned it to the cords.

"Maybe once we're underway, I'll grab some sleep," he said, studying the chart, not looking at her.

"John." She laid a hand on his. "You're not at fault here."

He drew his hand away, leaned over, and tuned the radio receiver to one of the WX channels for the NOAA weather broadcast. In a few moments the forecast for the coastal waters came across the airwaves. Winds 15 – 20 knots, increasing in the afternoon to 25 knots, and seas running three to six feet.

John tuned the radio back to Channel 16. "The Coast Guard has cleared us to head for port," he said, "Considering the suicide note we discovered and the fact that no trace of Bendorff's body has been found, the Coast Guard has downgraded the operation to search and recover."

For the first time he turned his eyes on her, and she saw a bit of the old gentleness and humor creep into them. "This is certainly the most interesting season I've ever had."

"It hasn't been all bad," she said, holding his eyes with hers for a moment.

"I didn't say bad; I said interesting."

"Which is usually a euphemism for bad," Brie said. Her eyes shifted from him to the desolate island that lay off their port bow: Smuttynose, where the murders had taken place in the 1800s. The winds of time had blown over that spot for 150 years and changed it not at all. There was a permanence about things in New England—in Maine. It had a feel very different from where she hailed in the Midwest, a feel that she found comforting—one that over the past few months she had come to equate with safety, or at least stability.

She turned back to John. "Do you think there's a reason for things happening as they do?" It sounded out of the blue, even to her. She watched him study her, possibly trying to discern where that question had come from.

"I don't know if I've had enough sleep to wax philosophical," he said. "So would that include everything from us—" he waved a hand between them—"to this current catastrophe?"

"I think it would have to include everything. I think it's an 'all in' way of thinking."

"Do you buy into that?"

"I didn't use to. In fact, I found the thought of things happening for a reason to be ridiculous. Too many years as a cop, I suppose, witnessing terrible things. Those things can make one question whatever one might call faith."

"And now?" John asked.

"Don't know," Brie said. "It's just a thought or a question that has visited me frequently this summer."

"So there must be a reason for *that* happening." He smiled sardonically.

At that moment, Scott emerged from the aft companionway with a freshly scrubbed face, his red beard still glistening with moisture. "Head's working again," he said.

"Good. We've been waiting on you."

Brie detected a note of stiffness in John's voice when he addressed Scott and wondered if he still held him responsible for what had unfolded last night. It wasn't like John to act this way—not see the bigger picture. But neither was it like him to draw away when she touched him, as he just had.

"We've got the go-ahead from the Coast Guard to sail," he said.

"Have they found anything?" Scott asked.

"Nothing. Not a trace. The operation will continue but as search and recover. We've been cleared to return to port."

Official sunrise this morning was 0720—just five minutes away. Brie studied the eastern sky for any glimmer of color, but on such an overcast day, sunrise meant little more than the sky morphing from very dark to a lesser shade of gray. Just then, she noticed movement forward and saw Joe Callum and Leo Dombello emerge from the amidships companionway.

"Do we wait until after breakfast?" Scott asked.

"No, I'd like to haul anchor right away. Go help George get the coffee up on deck for the passengers and then tell him we need him topside to help raise sail."

At that moment Rusty Boardman and Alex Smith came up the ladder from below.

"Ah, good, gentlemen. We can use your help with the sails. We're heading back to port."

"Is there any news of Peter?" Alex asked.

"I'm sorry, but no," the captain said. "We've been cleared by the Coast Guard to sail for home. The seas will be a little rough, but conditions are passable. So we go."

"But . . ." Alex started to say.

"I'm sorry, Mr. Smith," John said, cutting him off, "but little can be accomplished by staying here. The Coast Guard has things in hand and will complete the search."

Alex stared at the captain, obviously taken aback by his abruptness. He looked like he wanted to argue, but after studying John's face for a moment, he shrugged, turned away, and walked along the deck toward the bow, where Leo and Callum stood. Boardman trailed behind him, hands stuffed in the pockets of the leather bomber jacket he wore against the cold of the morning.

Brie and Scott headed for the galley to help George get the early morning coffee on deck for the shipmates. When they descended the ladder, he was just pulling a large baking sheet of scones from the woodstove, and the smell of warm blueberries filled the galley. A little bit of sunshine on a downtrodden day.

He saw them smiling. "I thought folks could use a little extra something with the coffee this morning. I've got another tray in the oven, so everyone can have as many as they want."

"That's great, George," Brie said. She remembered him coming on deck last night, bleary-eyed, asking what in the world was going on, after he'd been awakened by the Coast Guard Jayhawk making its passes over the islands as it dropped flares.

"We'll help you get everything on deck for coffee, and then the captain wants to weigh anchor," Scott said. "We've got the go-ahead from the Coast Guard to sail for home, and the seas are passable this morning."

George nodded. "The coffee's ready to go. I'll just get these into the basket and follow you up." One by one, he placed eighteen steaming scones into a basket lined with a gingham cloth big enough to easily cover them.

Scott pulled the tray full of mugs out from behind the dish rail on the starboard side of the galley and handed them to Brie. He followed her up the ladder, carrying a tray with cream and sugar and pump pots full of coffee and water for tea.

The captain came forward and spoke to Scott and Brie. "We'll all have some coffee and whatever George has in that wonderful-smelling basket, and I'll make the morning announcements now instead of before breakfast, as we'll be underway."

The three of them stepped aside and let the shipmates get their coffee and scones, and then they took their turns filling their mugs and helping themselves. In a few minutes, George brought up a second sheet of scones and refilled the basket before heading back down to the galley. Brie envied him that warm space this morning, but before long, the hot coffee started to take the chill off her bones.

Lyle Jarvis had joined them on deck just after the coffee came up. Paul Trasky was still below. So far, to her recollection, he'd only once come on deck for early coffee. Brie walked over and commandeered a second scone just as the captain tapped his spoon on his mug to get everyone's attention.

He started by bringing the passengers up to date on the Coast Guard's search. "I know this is both an unexpected and very terrible turn of events," he said. "But all we can do is leave the search in the hands of the Coast Guard. They're the experts in situations like this. There's nothing we can do but wait for them to complete their work." He looked around at the group. "We have sent contact information for Mr. Bendorff's next of kin through the Coast Guard to the Maine State Police. They will make notification to the family of what has unfolded." John paused in what felt like a respectful silence. No one spoke, and for a moment the ship lay shrouded in an uneasy stillness.

Finally he continued. "We will be weighing anchor shortly and sailing back to port. The seas may be rough outside the islands, and we can expect some boarding seas as the day wears on and the winds pick up. So please stay well clear of the bow of the ship. If seas get rough, those on deck need to stay aft. If the seas get too high or the weather deteriorates, we will put in somewhere along the coast."

The captain looked around to see if there were any questions. "Please go ahead and finish your coffee, and in a few minutes we'll ask for your help to raise sail." He turned to Scott and Brie. "Prepare to raise sail."

Brie went down the starboard side of the deck and Scott the port side. They took the heavy coiled halyards down from where they hung on the ratlines and began unwinding and stretching them out along the deck, where the crew and shipmates would line up to raise sail. Situated as they were among the islands, the raising of sails and weighing of the anchor had to be carefully synchronized. Scott and Brie got the men lined up for raising the mainsail.

John and Brie took the lead position on the throat halyard, with Scott and George at the head of the line on the peak halyard.

"Haul away," John shouted, and the vast mainsail slowly crawled up the mast as crew and shipmates pulled hand over hand, alternately hauling on the peak and throat halyards that raised the heavy gaff—the spar at the top of the sail—and the massive mainsail itself. Then Brie took Joe Callum forward to crank up the anchor; the captain went to the helm while George, Scott, Rusty and Alex raised the foresail and the headsails.

Brie always thought of getting underway as a kind of precise choreography in which everyone aboard took a role in a carefully staged ballet, the goal being to get underway without any mishaps.

When the anchor was up and they'd secured it to the starboard bow, the captain spun the wheel, and the *Maine Wind* began to fall off the wind to starboard and slowly make headway. Brie heard the familiar shoosh of water against the hull as the ship heeled to starboard, settling into the sea. Gosport Harbor in the Isles of Shoals is a very small harbor ringed on the north, east, and south by Appledore, Smuttynose, Cedar, and Star Islands. They sailed out the same way they had entered the day before, keeping Lunging Island to starboard and Halfway Rocks to port and passing east of White Island.

Once clear of the islands, the captain set a course down East on a heading east by northeast. The wind was clocking at eighteen knots. They picked up speed, and with a fresh breeze on their port bow, they were soon galloping along at seven and a half knots. The bite of the north wind had cleared the deck except for Rusty Boardman and Alexander Smith. Both men stood at the stern of the ship, capturing shots of the receding islands with their cameras. Dead astern lay the infamous Isles of Shoals, and somewhere beneath those cold Atlantic waters, the body of Peter Bendorff.

Once they were underway, Brie and Scott brought the coffee service back down to the galley, and Scott immediately headed back topside to take up watch in the bow. George stood at the woodstove on the starboard side of the galley, feet spread wide for balance. The galley smelled of pan-roasted onions, peppers, and spicy sausage, and notes of blueberry still lingered from the scones. Brie peeked over his shoulder at the two-handed magic act he was performing, stirring a large skillet filled with scrambled eggs with his right hand and flipping potatoes with his left.

"Brie," he said, "can you put the scones that are left on that baking sheet?" He nodded toward the end of the table. "I'll put them back in the oven to warm a bit, and we can serve the rest of them with breakfast."

"We setting up topside?" Brie asked, heading over to the table.

"I don't know. What do you think?"

"Wind's got a bite to it. How about down here?"

"Fine by me," George said. "With such a small group, it's easy to stage things here in the galley."

Brie got busy laying out ten place settings, enough for the passengers and crew, around the table. At George's request, she combined several containers of berries into a fruit bowl and sliced in several bananas.

When George gave her the go-ahead, she went topside and rang the ship's bell for breakfast, and then went aft and told the captain they'd be eating in the galley and asked if he'd like her to bring him a plate.

"Scott's taking over at the helm. I'll come below for some breakfast, and then I'm going to my cabin to sleep."

Brie nodded and went back to the galley to help George get the food on. Within a few minutes the shipmates started filing down the ladder and taking their places around the table. At George's request, she got down some serving platters from behind the dish rails, and George filled them with eggs and hash browns and handed them to Brie to place on the table. She set the basket of reheated scones on the table as well, along with the bowl of fruit and two carafes of coffee.

Brie and George were just dishing up their plates at the stove when John came down. George handed him a plate and heaped it up with eggs and hash. "Eat hearty, Captain, you've had a long night," he said.

"I'm almost too tired to eat," John said, "but I can never sleep on an empty stomach."

John turned down the coffee, but George poured out mugs full for Brie and himself from the big drip pot on the stove, and then the three of them sat at the end of the table with George across from John and Brie. Everyone ate silently for a few minutes, and Brie was savoring the wonders of George's Italian hash when Alex announced in a professorial way, "Did you know that Maine has fewer thunderstorms than anywhere in the northeast?"

"Especially at this time of year," John quipped, studying him with interest.

It was pretty random, Brie had to admit, but maybe it was his awkward attempt to fill the silence. However, it didn't work. Everyone went back to their meals, and Brie couldn't help thinking, *silent as the grave.*

It may have been that thought that triggered something in her, because a strange feeling suddenly crept into her gut. It felt like a hand closing tight. She paused with her fork halfway to her mouth and looked around the table. She silently set her fork down and excused herself. She stood up from her place and headed for the ladder, not bothering to put on her jacket. John must have picked up the vibe, because he slid off the bench and followed her.

As she stepped up on deck, a stinging north wind saturated with sea spray, cold and salty, hit the right side of her face. She saw Scott back at the helm as she leaned to windward, compensating for the pitch of the deck, and headed for the amidships companionway, moving toward what she hoped was nothing more than a thought fueled by lack of sleep and an overactive imagination. Acquiring the ladder, she gripped the brass rails and went down frontwards. At the foot of the ladder she headed for the first cabin on the starboard side. The fist around her gut had tightened even more, and her cop sense told her that was a bad sign. She heard John somewhere behind her saying, "Brie, what's going on?"

She stopped in front of Paul Trasky's cabin door and knocked three times. She waited for a moment. She didn't know why his absence from breakfast had suddenly troubled her—he'd been missing meals the whole voyage. She knocked again. "Paul? Are you awake?" Nothing.

"Mr. Trasky," she said louder, knocking a third time. John stepped up next to her and knocked, calling his name. He tried the cabin door. It was unlocked.

"Stay here, John," Brie said as she stepped into the darkened cabin, reached up to the ceiling and slid the cover off the deck light—a prism inserted into the deck to provide light down below. Gray, overcast daylight filtered into the cabin, and she immediately saw the grim reality of the situation. Paul Trasky lay still in his berth, a plastic bag over his head, a length of rope coiled around his neck. Even in the diminished light, Brie could see the face was blue with death, and though the bag obscured his face, something seemed wrong about it. The floor of the cabin was littered with a black substance, and she carefully stepped over to the berth and reached for his wrist to feel for a pulse. As she did, her eyes moved to his head, and she drew in a sharp breath. The mottled blue face that stared back at her from its death rictus was not the face of Paul Traksy, but the bald-headed visage of Peter Bendorff.

She stood perfectly still for a moment, trying to make this compute. Then she looked down at the floor and understood. The cabin floor was covered with what looked like tufts of animal fur attached to pieces of pelt. She squatted down, picked up a piece and felt it. The feel of human hair was unmistakable. She knew she was looking at Paul Trasky's hair, or rather, what remained of the wig that had turned Peter Bendorff into Paul Trasky. And while the beard was still in place, there was no mistaking who lay here.

"Brie . . ." John said from the doorway. She was so focused on the scene at hand she'd totally forgotten he was standing there. His tone of voice told her that he had guessed the worst.

"Stay there, John. Don't come in." She stood up and ever so carefully extricated herself from the scene of the crime, stepped back into the passageway, and closed the door to the cabin.

"My God, Brie. What's going on?"

"It's only partly what you're thinking. He is dead and obviously murdered, but the victim is not Paul Trasky. That is the body of Peter Bendorff in there."

If Brie had slapped him across the face, John couldn't have looked more startled.

"Say that again," he said, studying her, trying to understand.

"It appears that Peter Bendorff and Paul Trasky were one and the same person. The black stuff on the floor in there—that's what's left of the wig Trasky was obviously wearing. And let me say that this was a good and careful disguise carried out by a man who seemed to know what he was doing. I'll bet the autopsy will reveal he's wearing contacts that would have changed the color of his eyes. And he easily could have padded himself up to look like a slightly overweight Trasky."

"So, the suicide was a ruse," John said under his breath.

"Clearly, since he's lying in this cabin right now. My guess is that Peter Bendorff faked his own suicide with the intent of disappearing as Paul Trasky."

"And obviously someone aboard didn't like his plan," John said.

"Which leads to the conclusion that some or all of them knew about it. That would explain the odd behavior over the past couple of days."

"So some or all of them lied to us," John said, and Brie noted the edge of disgust in his voice.

"At least indirectly, yes. Which should make getting to the truth that much harder. Starting an investigation with a group of people who have lied feels a little like trying to build a house on quicksand."

"I have to radio the Coast Guard and tell them what's unfolded so they can call off the search." He started to leave and then turned back to her. "Can I ask what made you get up from the table and come down here?"

"Just an odd feeling—the kind I never ignore." But as she thought about it, she had to wonder what had triggered that odd knowing or suspecting, seemingly out of the blue. Had she picked up some kind of telling vibe from the killer? Some subtle telepathic signal about what he'd done? Because the fact was that one person at the table knew Trasky/Bendorff was dead. *Wow*, she thought cynically, *Ariel would be really proud of me, thinking about vibes and telepathic communication.* Ariel was her friend back home with the far-out ideas. So far out that Brie affectionately called her "Airy." Still, there had been several times this summer when Ariel's ideas had seemed strangely rational.

She turned back to John. "Can this door be locked from the outside?"

"Yes, I have a skeleton key in my cabin that locks all the doors. I'll go get it."

"We need to put into shore. The Evidence Response Team will have to come aboard and clear the scene, and the body will have to be removed."

"The closest harbor I'd be comfortable putting into is Boothbay. At current cruising speed, that's six to seven hours from our position now."

"That will have to do," Brie said. "Before you go, we need to keep the passengers in the galley until I can address them. And I'd like you to be present when that happens." She was thinking about the bold nature of this act, particularly considering that she had shared her police background with the passengers when Bendorff went missing.

"I'll tell George to keep them in the galley until you get back down there. I'll go for the key and be right back." He paused for a second. "Do you think it's better to address them as a group or inform them one by one?"

"The killer will feign surprise. The rest will be genuinely surprised. It will be hard to tell the difference. I think it's probably best to put it out there and then send them to their cabins until I call them for questioning. It will give them time to reflect on the fact that I know they lied. The fact that they all know each other may be good or bad. They'll either band together or turn on each other. I'm banking on the latter."

Chapter 16

John went for the key, and Brie was left with the silence below decks and the consoling sounds of the ship—the creaking of all the wood surfaces as *Maine Wind* flexed under the pressures of wind and sea. But as she waited outside Trasky's cabin, she was already thinking about who'd had opportunity and who was physically capable of committing this murder. She ran through the passengers in her mind, and the only one who seemed questionable for the act was Leo Dombello, because of his age—mid-sixties—and his short stature. Also, he was the only one who had seemed genuinely grieved when Bendorff went overboard. But now she reminded herself that could all have been a ruse. So maybe that made Leo the best actor of all. What's more, he was powerfully built, so, short or not, he might have managed it. She left him on her mental list for now.

The one thing she did know was that this murder had depended on the element of surprise. It was clear that Trasky/Bendorff had not locked his cabin door last night, or the killer would not have had access to him. It told her that Bendorff had complete confidence in the plan he'd cooked up and that he trusted his chums to help him carry it off.

She knew of any number of cases of people disappearing this way at sea with the intention of starting a new life elsewhere. Sometimes they were criminals, sometimes not. But they had all banked on one thing—that the sea has a way of swallowing bodies, so it's often hard to prove whether or not a person has actually gone overboard. If a ruse is suspected, then the investigation must focus on digging into the person's life for clues as to where he planned to go. No such problem here—Bendorff had never gotten to the second half of his plan.

John came down the companionway with the key and locked the door to Trasky's cabin. At Brie's request, he also locked the door to Bendorff's cabin. "Everyone is still eating happily in the galley," he said. "I told George to keep them there for a meeting. Scott has adjusted course for Boothbay Harbor and is calling the Coast Guard to inform them of the situation. I've instructed him to tell them that we'll put in at Boothbay, where the Maine State Police will take over."

"I'll get a call in to Dent Fenton and Joe Wolf, the medical examiner, right after we deal with the passengers. Dent will notify the crime lab team to be ready to meet us in Boothbay."

"We're making good time, and the seas are manageable. If conditions hold, we should make Boothbay around oh-sixteen-hundred, give or take."

"Good. That gives me time to do preliminary interviews with all the suspects. At least we don't have to ferret them out and track them down. They're all right here, aboard ship."

"Will that make it easier?" John asked.

"Only in that we know who the suspects are. Now we begin the process of discovering who among them actually had a motive to kill Bendorff. That requires finding out how each of these guys was connected to the victim. We start with the assumption that some or all of them were propagating a lie. So that speaks to their characters."

"And it doesn't say anything good," John said. "Is it possible all of them were in on this plan—the faked suicide?"

"Totally possible. It's difficult to carry out such a ruse. Bendorff may have gathered a select group for the express purpose of helping him pull it off. Just think about coming aboard as two different people. That had to be carefully orchestrated. They all went to dinner, and obviously Bendorff put on his Trasky disguise and came back to the ship as Paul Trasky."

"And when they all came back from dinner, we were below having a meeting," John said.

"And even if we hadn't been, I'm sure they had a plan. What's more, I'm sure they all had carefully concocted stories about what drove him to commit suicide."

"But one of them went totally off script and killed the guy."

"Yup. And who knows? If the rest feel threatened, in danger, they may begin to turn on each other. That could help the investigation."

"Is it a crime to fake a suicide, Brie?"

"Not in and of itself. And by the way, there's a name for the act. It's called pseudocide. But if the pseudocide connects to a criminal action in the past or is used as a device to commit a crime in the future, then yes. And then there's the matter of involving a government agency—the Coast Guard, which is a branch of Homeland Security—in a bogus search, and the sizable funds used to carry out such a search and rescue operation. Anyone who collaborated with Bendorff may be charged with misuse of federal funds."

"Is there any danger to the others, Brie? Or to us?"

"There's no way to know for sure, but I don't think we have a spree killer aboard. I think someone wanted to make sure Bendorff was gone for good."

"When do you think he was killed?"

"My guess is sometime between when Scott and I turned in at three a.m. and when either George or Scott and I arose between five-thirty and six-thirty. My money's on the wee hours, though. The body's not in rigor yet, but that can begin anywhere between two and six hours after death. And the cabins are cool down here, so that will keep rigor at bay longer."

Just then Brie remembered something. "John, you said earlier there was a problem with the head in the aft compartment in the middle of the night. When did that occur?"

"Well, it was after you and Scott turned in. Sometime around three thirty, I think."

"And who reported it?" Brie asked.

"It was Lyle Jarvis. He came up from below. Said he needed to use the head, but it was stopped up. I told him to go forward and use the one in the amidships compartment and to put a note on the door of the aft head telling the others to go forward and use the one up there."

"Did he go forward to use the head amidships then?"

"Yes."

"And how long was he up there?"

"Maybe five, ten minutes. I can't say for sure, because right around that time I took a radio call from the response boat, reporting that they were moving their search outside the ring of islands."

"But you saw him come back?"

"I guess I did, but I didn't take any notice of him."

"And the others back aft—Boardman and Smith—did they also go forward to use the head during those two or three hours after Scott and I turned in?"

"Both of them did, I'd say within an hour of when Jarvis went forward. I suppose that means they all had an opportunity to commit the murder."

"That's right," Brie said. "Convenient of the head to malfunction."

"Do you think one of the three men back there stopped it up on purpose? So he'd have a reason to go forward?"

"It's possible," she said. Although, if she thought about it, similar situations had occurred on almost every trip throughout the season. It wasn't unusual for the heads to develop problems with that many folks sharing them.

She checked her watch. Fifteen minutes had elapsed since they'd left the galley. "We need to go back down there and inform them of what's going on."

"Do you want me to tell them?"

"You're the captain, so I think that would be best. It will give me a chance to study their initial reactions. But they already know about my police connections, so once you've made the announcement, I'll take over."

"Bold move to commit a murder with a cop aboard."

"Bold or desperate," Brie said. "I'll be considering both those possibilities as I begin to profile these guys." She looked around the passageway for a few seconds. "I'd like to use your cabin to question them, John. It will afford more privacy. But you were going to catch some sleep."

"With what we've just discovered, I don't think I'll be sleeping. You use the cabin."

"I can ask Dent Fenton to leave one of his men aboard when we get to Boothbay so you can get some sleep."

"That might be a plan. But right now, with the current situation, I need to be present."

"Understood," Brie said.

He paused a moment and then said, "I'd like you to wear your firearm for the rest of the voyage."

"That goes without saying, John." She nodded toward the ladder. John took the lead, and they climbed up to the deck. "Let's call George up and inform him of what's going on."

So, at the top of the galley companionway, John called down for George to come up on deck. Even though the roar of wind in the canvas would have covered their words, the three of them stepped away from the companionway, and John informed George of what they were dealing with.

George's dark eyes grew intense as he listened. He spread his feet wide, as if the information required extra stability, and crossed his arms on his chest. "Do you have any idea who might be responsible?" he asked, looking at Brie.

"None whatsoever," Brie said.

"What can I do on my end?"

"Just be aware of what's going on, George, and be observant of the passengers—what they say, their general demeanor. You can be a second set of eyes and ears for me as you go about your work."

George nodded seriously.

"I'll be questioning the passengers one by one in John's cabin. I'm going to ask the three men from the aft compartment to go forward to the galley while that's happening. I doubt that they'll say much in front of you, but keep your ears open just in case."

"I'll be a spy in their midst." But then he looked at Brie as if he shouldn't be making a joke at such a time.

She smiled. "I'm counting on that, George. And by the way, be observant of them when we break the news. You too, John."

Just then a gust of wind savaged the surface of the sea, hurling spindrift over the port bow. They turned their backs to the spray and headed for the galley companionway. Brie went down first so she could catch their expressions—see if anyone looked curious or particularly watchful of their entrance, although she suspected the killer would be keeping a low profile, biding his time until the body was discovered.

Alex and Leo sat near the end of the V-shaped table, carrying on an animated conversation across from one another. Joe Callum and Rusty Boardman, who sat next to Alex on the portside bench, were also talking to each other. Lyle Jarvis skulked in his corner up in the bow at the far end of the table, cattycorner from Boardman.

John and Brie stood at the end of the table. Slowly conversation ceased and everyone looked up at them.

For one pregnant moment all that was heard was the creaking of the ship's timber and the disembodied moan of wind in the rigging. All that was felt was the rise and fall of the bow as it plowed through the seas. Yellow light flickered in the lantern—a miniature ghost under glass, hung from the trunk of the foremast, casting phantasms into the shadowy corners of the galley.

"There's been a death aboard," John said simply, looking around the table.

Brie cast her glance over them as well: a police officer's glance, like a net thrown wide—one that hopes to catch some nuance, some clue from the eyes of those held within it.

"Not just a death," John continued. He paused for the briefest of moments. "Paul Trasky has been murdered." There was a silent gasp from Alexander Smith and Joe Callum. Rusty Boardman's steely exterior remained fixed, as Brie had guessed it would. But the announcement activated a nervous twitch on the left side of Lyle Jarvis' face, and she saw him raise a hand to rub it away. Leo seemed to puff up like a blowfish, so full of real or feigned emotion that Brie thought he might burst.

John pressed on. "Here's the biggest shock, though I doubt it will surprise all of you," he said, casting an accusatory look around the table and pausing to let it sit heavy on them. "The dead man is Peter Bendorff. Apparently, Paul Trasky never existed, except, of course, as the star in a play that I believe some or all of you took roles in. However, I don't think this was any part of the script, except for one of you, of course," he said, looking slowly around the table.

"I'm going to let Brie take over at this point. As you already know, she is connected with the Maine State Police. We've changed course for Boothbay Harbor, where we will put in later in the day. I expect all of you to keep to your cabins or be here in the galley until we make port. No one on deck. Is that understood?"

The men nodded, and Brie noticed a couple of them looked intimidated by the captain's demeanor.

"Brie . . ." he said, turning to her, handing over the reins. But he stood his ground next to her.

"I'll be questioning you one by one," Brie said looking around the table. "I'll be using the captain's cabin, so once we get started, I'd like the three of you who have the aft cabins to come forward to the galley and stay here until you are told you can return to your cabins." She looked from Smith to Boardman to Jarvis. "Is that clear?"

They nodded, and she continued. "Who amongst you was closest to Peter Bendorff?" She didn't know what to expect, and though she had her reasons for asking, she knew the response could mean any of a number of things. For instance, a savvy killer might see it as a loaded question—he might know that most murders are committed by someone close to the victim and so not raise his hand. On the other hand, a not-so-savvy killer might raise his hand, thinking closeness to the victim would give him some kind of immunity.

At any rate, three of the five—Leo Dombello, Alexander Smith, and Joe Callum—raised their hands. Brie nodded but didn't comment. She did note that there seemed to be a trace of genuine sadness in Callum's eyes.

"I'd like to start with you, Mr. Callum," she said. "Will you please come aft to the captain's cabin in fifteen minutes?" She looked from Callum to Leo. "You two in the amidships compartment have the option to return to your cabins. If you choose to do so, please keep to your own cabin, and please lock your cabin doors."

That brought a look of alarm, and the men glanced around the table at one another.

"You other three will remain here in the galley until further notice. You may go to your cabins to get something to read or do, but come directly back here. The captain will accompany you."

She studied their five blank faces, wishing she could read their thoughts, knowing that a killer dwelt amongst them, surreal as that seemed in this setting. As she looked from one to the other, thoughts were indeed circulating around that table.

Someone actually killed him? What the hell?

What do I tell her? She'll think it was me. What a botched-up mess.

I'm glad he's dead. I'm free of his stranglehold.

He's gone. Really gone.

It was surprisingly easy, killing him.

John drew Brie aside. "After I see the passengers to their cabins, I'll be at the helm. Scott will be on bow watch, and George will be on galley watch down here." He said the last part *sotto voce*. "That will leave you free to do the questioning."

Brie nodded. "Since you're going aft, could you take one of the stools from the galley here and put it in your cabin? I'll need something for the men to sit on during the questioning. Also, I'll need my gun from your lockbox." After the case she had worked in September on Apparition Island, Brie had started keeping her gun in the captain's cabin in a small lock box he used to store important documents, such as passengers' passports during voyages to Canadian ports.

"No problem." He slid one of the stools out from under the table, picked it up, and then turned to the men. "Let's go, mates."

The men from the aft compartment followed him up the ladder, followed by Leo Dombello and Joe Callum. Brie brought up the rear. John continued aft with the three men, and she followed Leo and Joe Callum down the amidships ladder far enough to see each of them enter his cabin. Then she headed back down to her berth behind the galley to get her cell phone. She needed to call Lieutenant Dent Fenton at the Maine State Police.

Chapter 17

When Brie came on deck with her phone, John had already relieved Scott at the helm. The thick overcast still held the sky in irons, and the sea was making up to a good roll. The north wind had clocked up to twenty knots, and *Maine Wind* was driving up into it. Scott stood watch in the bow, dodging the cold spray each time they took a plunge.

Brie made her way aft along the windward deck, the roar of the wind in the canvas an ever-present reminder of the stupendous forces at play here. She hoped her phone would get reception down in John's cabin below decks, so she wouldn't have to compete with the thunder of the canvas. There's no mechanical noise aboard a sailing schooner, just nature's own fracas, but when it starts to blow, the deck is a surprisingly noisy place.

When she got to the helm, she leaned in. "I'm going to see if I get reception below in your cabin. I need to reach Dent Fenton."

John nodded his acknowledgement, and Brie headed down the companionway, stepped into his cabin and closed the door. *So quiet compared to topside*, she thought. She took out several items she'd collected from her berth and laid them on the chart table—small flip notebook, pen, digital pocket recorder, and her cell phone.

She had met Lieutenant Fenton—then Detective Fenton—in July, after becoming involved in a case that unfolded during their visit at Sentinel Island. Later in the summer she had been deputized by the Maine State Police and had helped with a complicated and dangerous case in Tucker Harbor, Maine. Her connection to the Maine State Police had been nothing but positive and professional, and she could see herself becoming a permanent part of the force were she to make the move to Maine.

She turned on her phone and saw she had bars. Cell reception on the ocean was an iffy thing, but they were close enough to Portland to pick up reception. She could have used the ship's radio if necessary, but she preferred to keep the information private. She brought up Dent's number and put the call through.

He answered on the third ring. "Brie. I was just going to try to reach you to see how the search is going."

"Hi, Lieutenant. There's been a development."

"No good usually comes of that."

Brie smiled. "And this is no exception."

"Tell me."

"Turns out the Bendorff suicide was a ruse. A carefully planned one, I would say. Bendorff had disguised himself as one of the other passengers, one Paul Trasky. And to cut to the chase, we found Trasky, slash Bendorff, murdered in his cabin a short while ago."

"What's the cause of death?" Dent asked.

"Asphyxia due to suffocation. Doc Wolf will have to pin down the particulars, but Bendorff had a plastic bag over his head and a rope around his neck. Looks like a combination of suffocation and strangulation."

"Would have required the element of surprise," Dent said.

"Well, the killer struck in the wee hours, probably between three and five a.m. What's more, Bendorff liked his scotch. He'd been drinking earlier that night with his cronies, and he had a bottle in the cabin where I found him. I'd guess he was pretty far under when the killer struck."

"Which would make the job easier," Dent said.

"I'd guess the perp was planning on that."

"The autopsy will reveal COD and blood alcohol level," Dent said. There was a pause, and then he said, "I bet John's happy about this new development."

"That's a bet I wouldn't take," Brie said. "As master of the *Maine Wind*, John doesn't abide any funny business when it comes to his ship or crew. He wasn't happy last night, so you can just imagine this morning."

"I'm surprised you didn't pick up a sense of anything being off," Dent said. "I mean with Bendorff posing as two people."

"It was a very well executed disguise, and this guy Trasky, the alias, was seasick from the get go—spent most of his time in his cabin, missed meals. Now, you'd think that would set off some alarm bells, but the truth is, we get folks like that aboard. In fact, I asked John if it didn't seem odd a couple days ago, and he told me he's had people so seasick he's had to put into a port and let them off. And, truthfully, the other part of it is that the crew is quite busy when we're at sea. One tends to focus on shipboard duties. But that said, we'd all commented on the fact that this group had an odd feel to it."

"In what way?" Dent asked.

"Just not the normal level of enthusiasm we usually get. Some of them didn't seem to like the idea of being at sea."

"Huh." Dent was silent for a moment, processing that. "Do you think they were all in on this faked suicide plan?"

"I'd stake a lot on that supposition," Brie said. "The question is, will they cop to it, or will they claim ignorance of Bendorff's pseudocide? I'll get a better feel for the big picture once I start questioning them."

"No gut sense of who the killer might be?"

"Not a whiff. Although there are a couple of them I'd put at the top of the list, just based on physical capability."

"We'll run all of their names through NCIC," he said.

"I'll get the passenger manifest from John and call you back with the names and addresses."

"I'll need birth dates, too, and driver's license numbers if you can get them."

"Right. I'll do my best," Brie said. "I'll be eager to know if anything turns up on any of them."

"Where are you?" Dent asked.

"Underway. We left our anchorage at the Isles of Shoals a little over an hour ago. We're headed for Boothbay Harbor, where we plan to put in."

"When will you make port?"

"If conditions hold, John estimates around oh-six-hundred hours. If seas roughen up, it might be longer."

"I'll put Joe Wolf and the Evidence Response Team on notice," Dent said. "Let me know when you're an hour out."

"Roger that," Brie said.

"They'll be waiting for you at the town dock below the village," Dent said.

"Scott will motor in in the yawl boat and pick up the team and Doc Wolf."

"You've secured the crime scene?"

"Yes," Brie said. "The cabin is locked; John has the key. I plan to use the time between here and Boothbay to question the passengers."

"How many aboard?" Dent asked.

"Just five now. This was a charter—seven guys originally. Well, six, as it turns out, and now, of course, it's down to five."

"Well, you know what to do, Brie."

"I do."

"Put on your gun."

"Roger that, Dent—I mean Lieutenant."

"Dent's fine, Brie. We're not all that formal, remember?"

She imagined him smiling. They'd had this interchange before. Several times, in fact, and she could picture the intense blue eyes and heavy brow bone that lent a seriousness to his aspect.

"You want some help aboard? I could send Marty."

"That would be welcome. John will need to sleep when we make port, and I'd like to be below when they process the scene. Marty would be welcome as a presence on deck while that's going on—just so none of the suspects gets any funny ideas."

"I'll send him down there with the team," Dent said.

Brie had worked closely with Detective Marty Dupuis on two previous cases. He was a good egg and a good cop. She welcomed the thought of his coming aboard.

"That'll be great, Dent. I'll call you when we're an hour out." They ended the call.

Brie stepped out of John's cabin and looked around the passageway for a moment. The cabin forward of John's on the port side of the ship was occupied by Alexander Smith, history prof and author. Directly across the passageway was Lyle Jarvis' cabin and aft of that, Rusty Boardman's. The head was at the forward end of the passageway, between the port and starboard cabins and directly across from the companionway that led up to the deck. At the back of the compartment, tucked beside the ladder, were two crew berths where Scott and Ed slept.

Brie headed up the ladder and stepped over to the helm to talk to the captain. "I need to get my gun, John."

"Oh, right. I put the key in my pocket after we talked." He reached in the pocket of his rain jacket and produced the key to the lockbox. "I'm sorry about this morning," he said. "I know I acted a little distant. I'm struggling with what's happened here and also the fact of you leaving Maine."

"I'm struggling too, John. Maybe if we both accept that we're struggling, it won't drive us apart."

He shrugged. "I had visions of a different kind of cruise, that's all."

"Romantic visions?" Brie asked, a twinkle in her eye.

"Maybe," John mumbled. And even though they'd been together more than a few times, he seemed suddenly flustered and got very busy checking the ship's GPS.

"Do you have a copy of the passenger manifest up here?" Brie asked, changing the subject.

John foraged around in the cuddy that held the electronic equipment. He pulled out a piece of paper and handed it to her. There was a manifest made up for each cruise that contained passengers' names and addresses.

Brie took it and headed forward to get the rest of the information Dent needed to run the names. She found Boardman, Jarvis, and Alex Smith in the galley, playing what felt like a joyless game of poker. She handed the manifest to Boardman and asked them to put their dates of birth and driver's license numbers on the sheet under their names.

"Why do you need that?" Jarvis asked.

"She's going to run our names," Rusty Boardman said, as if it would be common knowledge.

"Why?" Jarvis asked, giving her a hooded look.

"I'd think that would be obvious," Smith said, regarding Jarvis. "She's looking for any criminal records we might have."

None of them looked particularly happy about it, especially Jarvis, but they took out their wallets and recorded the information on the sheet and handed it back to Brie. She nodded to them and headed for the ladder. George was busy concocting a large pot of soup, but he winked at her as she passed, letting her know he was keeping tabs on them.

Next, Brie descended into the amidships compartment. She was somewhat surprised that both Leo Dombello and Joe Callum had decided to return to their cabins, considering the gruesome reality lurking just across the passageway from them. But with the rough seas, it was definitely more comfortable back here amidships than up in the galley. Motion of the sea is always felt more below decks and is felt most in the bow of the ship.

She knocked on Joe Callum's cabin door.

"Who is it?" he asked, and Brie noted a thread of tension in his voice.

"It's Brie. I just need some information from you."

Callum opened the door. His flirtatious demeanor was gone—replaced by someone who looked and acted ten years older than the Joe Callum who had come aboard three days ago. Brie asked him to write his date of birth and driver's license number on the manifest. He studied her for a moment, then took the pen and paper and, using the door frame to write against, put his date of birth under his name and address. He took out his Maine state driver's license and asked Brie to read off the numbers as he wrote them down.

When done, Brie handed the license back to him and took the manifest. "I'll be starting the interviews with you, Joe. Would you come down to the captain's cabin in the aft compartment in ten minutes?"

"Should I bring anything?" Callum asked.

"Just yourself." She started to walk away but then turned back to him. "And the truth, Mr. Callum. I'd like you to bring the truth."

He nodded, but his expression was unreadable.

She stepped next door to Leo's cabin. It took a minute to raise him, and when he opened the door, he looked haggard and half asleep. She looked past him and noticed his cabin was in a complete state of disarray. All the paraphernalia he'd brought aboard—what she and Scott had joked was enough for a slow boat to China—now covered his berth and cabin floor, and she saw that he'd made a nest for himself on the berth in among his extra clothes, bags of snack food, and five or six books. The tiny floor was covered with many shoes and more books, and the upper berth had been given over to the suitcases, sachels, and boxes in which he'd lugged everything aboard. It was a hoarder's compact den—a hole in the wall, or rather, hole in the ship. But she quickly retracted that thought. After all, they'd had enough trouble.

She asked him for the information. He gave his date of birth but told her he'd left his driver's license ashore. *About the only thing he left ashore,* she thought.

"You may want to stay awake, Leo. I'll be interviewing you after I finish with Joe Callum."

He crossed his arms on his barrel-like chest and studied her with owlish eyes. "Okay," he said after a moment. And then, "This is a big mess."

Brie studied him. "Yes, it certainly is." She suppressed a smile as she glanced past him into his murky little man cave. *Does Leo know the meaning of the word mess?* she wondered.

She told him that was all she needed for now and headed for the companionway ladder. But she was thinking to herself that in her experience, killers tended to travel light. Leo just didn't seem like a fit for the job, but she marshaled that thought to the pigeonhole in her mind labeled *Don't Jump to Conclusions.*

On deck, the north wind sent a chill down her back. As she headed aft, she pulled up the hood on her rain jacket and snugged it down around the ball cap she liked to wear. If it started to rain, the cap kept the water out of her eyes, and the hood on the jacket, when tightened down, kept off the wind and spray and provided warmth. Warmth was always a concern for crew members who spent hours every day in the elements.

She stopped at the helm and leaned in close to be heard. "I'm starting the questioning with Joe Callum in a few minutes," she told John.

"Anything I should do?" he asked.

"Nope. Just keep us headed for Boothbay."

He nodded, and she started down the ladder. She stepped into John's cabin to port, took out her phone, and called Dent Fenton.

"Brie. Ready with those names and addresses?"

"Right here, Dent." She read off the names of the five suspects, followed by their birth dates, addresses, and driver's license numbers for all but Leo Dombello. "Leo said he didn't have his license with him."

"I'll check the Maine DMV for his name and address. I'll also run Peter Bendorff's name. I have his information here. Of course, nothing will show up in NCIC unless they've been convicted of a crime. But we can do some digging with Portland PD and anywhere else we find a connection."

"Roger that, Dent. Let me know if anything turns up." They ended the call.

She still had the key to John's lockbox, and it was time to retrieve her gun and put it on. The situation had escalated since the discovery of Bendorff's body. The gun was her protection, but also protection for everyone else aboard. A killer lurked among them; bold, desperate, maybe ruthless—he had murdered Bendorff knowing there was a cop aboard. That took some kind of balls. Or else it was the act of a desperate man. In either case, she had to do everything possible to keep the situation from escalating. She hadn't verbalized any of this, even to the crew. What was the point of scaring them? But the truth of the situation sat heavy on her.

She lifted several boards from the cabin sole next to the chart table, drew out the lock box from beneath the flooring, and unlocked it with the key John had given her. She took out her Glock 9 mm and clip-on holster and put them on, relocked the box, and placed it back beneath the cabin sole. She felt the weight of the gun on her right hip, and with it, the weight of responsibility to bring these shipmates safely back to home port.

Chapter 18

At ten minutes past ten, Brie heard a knock on the captain's cabin door.

"Come," she said.

Joe Callum opened the door tentatively and stepped inside.

"Please close the door, Joe."

He looked apprehensive, a feeling that seemed to sit uncomfortably on him. She thought about the brash and openly flirtatious Joe Callum who'd come aboard a few days ago. Self-confident, leaning toward arrogant. Qualities that would put him high on her list of suspects. Traits not uncommon in killers. Of course, there are two sides to every coin, and she was aware that those same traits can just as often mask a totally opposite personality—one that lacks self-confidence. *Human psychology is a funny old thing that way*, Brie thought.

"Take a seat, Joe, and we'll get started." Brie pulled the stool forward that John had brought from the galley, and Callum folded his long lanky body down onto it.

She placed her arm on the chart table to her left, leaned back in John's chair, and regarded him for a moment before starting. If he found this unnerving, he didn't let on but returned her searching look.

"I'll be recording this interview, Joe." She placed a small digital recorder, about the size of a pack of gum, on the edge of the chart table so the mic end faced him. She pushed the record button and spoke. "Please state your name, age, and date of birth for the record."

"Joseph Henry Callum. Age thirty-six. Birth date, April fifth, nineteen eighty."

Brie nodded. "What is your connection to Peter Bendorff?"

"I work for him. Or I guess I should say I worked for him."

"And the name of his business or company?"

"Bendorff Enterprises."

"In Portland, Maine, I assume." She knew the address on his driver's license was in Portland.

"That's right," Callum said.

"What does his company do?"

"Bendorff Enterprises and its subsidiaries do a number of things—primarily real estate and business acquisitions."

"Can you explain a bit more?" Brie asked.

"Peter was a genius at spotting a good opportunity. Businesses that had been poorly run—sometimes run into the ground. Same with real estate. He found people desperate to get out of whatever, and he presented them with an exit strategy."

"Would you say he took advantage of people?"

Callum smiled. "I'd say he took advantage of timing. There's a moment in such negotiations when a business or property owner is desperate to get out. And most of those folks are just happy to come out of the deal with something. A lot of them looked on Peter as some kind of savior."

"And the others?"

"The others were generally resentful. But that's business. Life too, you might say. It's eat or be eaten."

Brie studied him for a moment. "Interesting turn of phrase."

Callum gave her a level stare.

Not easily rattled, she thought.

"What do you do at the company?"

"I'm the head of accounting."

"How long have you worked for Bendorff enterprises?"

"Six years."

"And where were you employed before that?"

He hesitated for a moment and then said, "Holder Medical Technologies."

Brie opened her small notebook and wrote that down. "Same kind of job?"

"That's right."

"Why'd you change jobs?"

"I met Peter through a friend. He seemed to like me, and after I got to know him better, he told me if I ever thought about changing jobs, he'd be happy to find a place for me."

"So, based on that, you decided to go work for him?"

"It was time for a change."

"Why's that?" Brie asked.

Callum looked momentarily taken aback by her directness and seemed to fumble over his words. "I was . . . well . . . I was looking for a salary upgrade. Also, changing jobs can be a good thing—makes one look upwardly mobile. Companies like that. It's a brave new world. The days of staying with one company your whole career are long gone. Companies aren't particularly loyal to their employees anymore, so workers have learned to play the same game."

Not so in police work, Brie thought. She knew dozens of cops who'd spent their entire career with the same force. But she knew what he was saying about corporate America was true. Plenty of folks outside her realm had told her so.

She made another note in her small book, which gave her a moment to shift gears. Then she looked directly at Callum and said, "Did you know Peter Bendorff was planning to fake his own suicide?"

For the first time Callum acted a bit like a trapped animal. He glanced around the small cabin and finally back at her. "Yes," he said. He offered nothing beyond that.

"So you were part of the charade." She stated it as a fact, not a question. "A charade that led to a major Coast Guard search."

He looked nervous now. "I knew what he was planning, if that's what you mean."

"So, what were his reasons for such a radical choice?"

"I think he was terribly unhappy. He couldn't seem to find meaning in anything the past couple years. Even his passion for the business seemed to have faded."

"So you agreed to go along with the ruse," Brie said. "What was in it for you?"

"Nothing, really. I just felt I owed him."

"So, blind loyalty," Brie said.

Callum shrugged and looked down at the cabin sole, but not before she saw that same flicker of sadness she'd noticed before in his eyes.

In the silence Brie listened to the ship's timbers creaking and became aware of how clenched her leg muscles were from trying to stay seated in an environment where nothing was level.

After a few moments, she broke the silence. "Which of the others aboard knew about Bendorff's plan?"

He fixed his gaze on her. "You know what? I'd rather let them speak for themselves."

For whatever reason, the response surprised her. "Very well, Mr. Callum, then I'll ask you this," she said, and as she did, she watched him intently. "Did you kill Peter Bendorff?"

"No, God no. Why would I?"

"That's exactly what I'm wondering," she said, searching his face for any tells. There were none.

"So, who among you would have wanted Peter Bendorff dead, in your estimation?"

His response came immediately. "Lyle Jarvis."

The indelible nature of the response surprised Brie. Whatever she had expected from him, it wasn't this sudden revelation, and she put on her most practiced cop poker face. "Why?" she asked, and the word hung between them for a moment, stark and startlingly simple.

The response was equally stark. "Because Jarvis hated him," Callum said.

"Can you tell me why?" Brie asked.

"No, I can't," Callum said.

"Can't or won't?"

"Can't," Callum said. "I asked Peter about the tension between them plenty of times, but he wouldn't say anything. I know that Jarvis is Peter's nephew and that Peter kept a tight rein on him. More than that, I can't tell you."

Brie studied him, trying to divine if this were true, but got no read on it. She moved on. "Did Peter Bendorff like to drink at night?" She was thinking about that bottle of scotch he'd brought aboard. She'd seen another bottle—different brand—in Paul Trasky's cabin when she discovered the body.

"Pete liked his scotch."

"So, you think that even after he took on the persona of Paul Trasky, he would have been drinking before he turned in?"

"Maybe even more so," Callum said. "Probably would have needed it to calm his nerves. After all, he had to hope that none of you tumbled to his disguise on the voyage home. He'd even thought about leaving the ship if we went into a harbor. Telling the captain he was too sick to continue."

"Huh . . . did anyone else hear him say that?"

"He told me that in private, so I don't know if anyone else knew about his plan."

Brie was thinking it might be a reason why the killer had struck sooner rather than later. She jotted down the thought in her small notebook.

"Since you were Bendorff's accountant, do you know if he had a life insurance policy?"

"I have no idea. I was in charge of the business accounting. I didn't handle any part of his personal affairs."

Brie made a note about his answer. "Well, that's all for now, Mr. Callum," she said, looking up at him. "I ask you to keep anything we talked about here to yourself. Can you agree to that?"

"Sure," Callum said, and he seemed to let out a metaphorical sigh of relief, glad the interview was drawing to a close.

Brie reached over and stopped the recorder. "Would you tell Leo to come aft to the captain's cabin in ten minutes, please?"

"No problem." Callum stood and shook out his legs. He hesitated at the door and turned back to her. "I don't cotton to being trapped aboard this ship with a killer."

"No one does, Mr. Callum. You need to follow the protocols the captain and I have set up. If you do, you should be safe enough."

"Safe enough?" He looked like he wanted to say something confrontational. Instead, he turned and left the cabin.

Brie stared at the door for a few moments, thinking about the interview with Callum. She took out her phone and checked for reception. "Still good," she said to herself. She Googled Holder Medical Technologies, the company Callum said he had worked for prior to joining Bendorff Enterprises. She found a phone number and punched it in. She made her way through the phone bank and when she got to an actual person, asked for Human Resources. She spoke with a Sarah Campbell in Human Resources and told her she was with the Maine State Police, gave her badge number, and said she was checking dates of employment for one of their former workers, Joseph Henry Callum, who had worked in the accounting division and had left the company approximately six years ago.

Campbell put her on hold, and when she came back a full five minutes later, said. "I'm very sorry, Detective Beaumont, but our records don't show anyone of that name working for us during that period. I checked back farther in our records, but no sign of anyone by that name in or out of the accounting division."

"Thank you," Brie said and ended the call. *And so it begins,* she thought and wondered what else he might have lied about. Still, his visceral response to her question of who had killed Bendorff seemed strangely believable. She planned to be extra watchful of Lyle Jarvis from here on out and exercise caution when in his presence.

Before she had time to think more on the matter, someone knocked on the door.

"Come in," she said.

Leo Dombello opened the door and stepped in. He crossed his arms on his chest and looked around the small cabin like he might be deciding if it passed his approval.

"Hello, Leo," Brie said, always mildly amused by his behavior.

He clamped his lips together in a scowl and continued his inspection. "The captain doesn't have much more space than we do," he said.

"Space is at a premium on these ships," Brie said.

"Well, at least it's cozy."

Brie smiled at his choice of words and nodded toward the interrogation stool. "Have a seat, Leo. Not very comfortable, but the best we can do under the circumstances."

"I don't mind." Leo had a much lower center of gravity than Joe Callum, so the short stool seemed more suited to him. He sat carefully, compensating for the ship's motion, and placed his hands on his chunky thighs.

"I'll be recording this, Leo, if you don't mind."

He waved a hand. "Quite all right. Proceed."

She pushed the record button and, as she had with Joe Callum, asked him to state his full name, age, and date of birth.

"Leo Francis Dombello; sixty-seven; born June twelfth, nineteen forty-nine."

"Leo, this morning in the galley, when I asked who was closest to Peter Bendorff, you raised your hand. Can you tell me how you were connected to him? Did you work for him?"

Leo waved that away. "I'm retired. I moved to Maine two and a half years ago—Portland. I joined a local theatre group—had always wanted to act. You know, be in plays."

Brie nodded. Somehow it was a fit for Leo, who seemed to love a good story—either hearing one or telling one. And those hands, always in motion, always painting pictures. *He's a character*, she thought. *So why not be on the stage?*

"Anyway, that's where I met Peter," Leo said. "He was part of the group."

"Ahhh . . ." Like a clockwork, things began to mesh in Brie's mind: the quality and believability of the disguise in which Bendorff had become Paul Trasky, as well as his elaborate plan to act out his own death and then, like a magician's trick, to disappear to another life somewhere.

"So I'm guessing Peter Bendorff felt pretty confident about this ruse he was staging aboard our ship. I'm also guessing you knew about his plan to fake his own suicide."

Leo shrugged his shoulders and let out a puff of air through his nose, like he was disgusted about something. "Guilty as charged," he said.

"Why get involved?" Brie asked, leaning back in her chair, giving him her best cop stare. "You know all of you could be charged as accessories to a crime. A lot of government funds were expended in a bogus search. Not to mention the fact that one of you is a murderer."

Leo looked stricken. "You can't think I had anything to do with Peter's death."

"Why not?"

"Because we were friends. I cared about him."

Brie studied him, wondering if this were true or just part of the play. She moved on to her next question.

"You said you moved to Portland a few years ago. Where did you live before that?"

"North Boston."

That made sense to Brie, Leo being Italian. She didn't know much about eastern cities, but being a cop, she'd read plenty about North Boston—turf for the Italian mob since the early 1900s, and plenty of law-abiding Italians as well.

"I see what you're thinking," Leo said, jabbing an accusatory finger at her. "North Boston, Italian, Mafia."

Brie couldn't help smiling. "Well, it has a reputation. One you hear about even out in Minnesota when you're a cop."

"That's the past," Leo said, waving his hand like he was shooing away a fly. "The city's been clean since the nineties. The FBI did a good job of rounding up all the mob bosses."

Brie studied him but said nothing. What she knew as a cop was that organized crime was alive and well in every major city in the USA. The mob bosses had just been superseded by the drug cartels. But the ugly underbelly of organized crime stretched back in an unbroken line to the very beginnings of urban habitation. Man's inhumanity to man was alive and well and playing out in every urban core.

Brie pressed on with the interview. "So you're from North Boston. What did you do for work, Leo?"

"My family owned an Italian deli and bakery."

"There in North Boston?"

"That's right. Four generations now, it's been in the family." Leo held up four fingers just to drive the point home. "I worked in the bakery. Always liked making the bread."

It seemed a fit to Brie. Leo, with the hands always in motion, kneading and shaping the dough, baking the bread, showing it to people, telling them stories as he bagged it.

"So why not stay there?" Brie asked. "Show the next generation the ropes."

"I did. My two nephews run the place now, along with a bunch of the relatives—all ages." Leo held his hands apart in a wide gesture to show it was a big group effort. Then he circled back to her question. "I've always wanted to live in a smaller city away from all the noise and congestion. Now, the Mainers don't really like the Massachusetts folk, but I thought maybe if I became one of them . . ."

"How's that working out?" Brie asked.

"So far, so good."

"You could always open another bakery. Everyone loves a good bakery," Brie said, and her mind wandered to thoughts of a warm caramel roll. She had abandoned her meal when the question about Trasky's whereabouts hit her at breakfast.

Leo was talking again. "I *could* open another bakery, I guess. Hands are shot, though. Carpal tunnel." He held them up like they were Exhibit A. "So I'd have to hire someone to do the baking, and where's the fun in that? And I don't really need the money." He shrugged. But Brie was fixated on the words *carpal tunnel*, and she had good reason. If the condition was bad enough, he'd never have been able to strangle Peter Bendorff.

"So, the carpal tunnel. Does that mean you can't work with the dough, knead the bread and so on?"

"These hands are shot," he said again and held them up like she hadn't heard him the first time. "Three surgeries I had, and still they go numb. Doc says that's it. Nothing more they can do." Then a little gleam came into his eye. "Sure would like to help George make some bread, though, before we get back to port."

Brie smiled. "George would welcome that. Why don't you ask him?"

Leo blew out through his nose again and knit his brows. "Okay, I think I will."

Brie pictured the short Greek and the even shorter Italian down in the galley turning out Italian bread and maybe some amazing cannoli. Suddenly lunch seemed very far away.

She redirected the questioning. "So, are you married, Leo?"

Leo pursed his lips and shook his head. Then he looked at her. "I'm what they call the bachelor uncle. Lots of nieces and nephews to spoil, but no nagging wife to deal with. No offense . . . I mean . . ." He glanced sheepishly at Brie.

"None taken," she said. "I'm just a nagging detective." That got an actual smile from Leo.

But after another moment the emotional tide seemed to turn, and Leo looked suddenly quite sad. "How did he die?" he asked.

"I'm sorry, Leo, but I can't say anything about that. We're dealing with a murder here, so details of the crime and the scene need to be kept confidential for now."

Leo looked straight into her eyes. "Did he suffer?"

"It's hard to say." She actually felt bad for him and wanted to tell him Bendorff might not have suffered much, depending on the amount of alcohol he had consumed. But she said nothing.

"Do you know why anyone would want to do this to him?"

"Are you asking if I know who killed him?"

"Indirectly."

"No, I don't know."

"What *do* you know, Leo?"

The directness of the question seemed to surprise him. He studied her for a few moments, and finally a crooked smile crept onto his face. "I know Peter Bendorff was a genius at gathering information and knowing how to use it."

There was unmistakable admiration in Leo's voice, but along with it a trace of something more sinister, like looking through a nice clean window into a dark room and having only the dimmest sense of what dwelt within. And for whatever reason, her spine prickled.

"Let's talk plain here, Leo. You say Bendorff was a genius at gathering information. What kind of information?"

"All kinds." Leo made a big circle outward with his arms.

"Specifics?"

"I don't have specifics. But it's not too hard to find out what companies he acquired—what properties he bought. It's all a matter of public record."

"And people?" Brie asked. "You say Bendorff was a genius with information. What about people?"

Leo shrugged. "What about them?"

"Was he a genius there, too?"

Leo regarded her for a long time. Finally he nodded. "I like you," he said. "The rest of these guys . . . well, I could care less. So here it is. Peter had a gift for learning things about people and using those things to his advantage."

"Did that include you, Leo?"

He smiled an enigmatic smile, and Brie had the sense that she'd learned as much as she was going to. But she was beginning to flesh out a picture—maybe not a pretty one, but a picture nonetheless. Based on what Leo had said, there was gold to mine here: motives—the coin of the realm for detectives. It was possible every one of these guys had one. And she knew something else—knew it from experience. As the noose tightened on them, they would begin to turn on one another.

"Which of these men do you know personally, Leo?"

"Just Peter and Alex Smith."

"And the others? Callum, Jarvis, Boardman?"

Leo waved that away. "Don't know 'em. But that doesn't mean I don't know *about* them. Pete has told me plenty."

"Who do you think killed Peter Bendorff, Leo?"

"If I knew that, I'd tell you. It wasn't me." He looked straight at her. "You want my honest opinion?" He didn't wait for her to answer but made a sudden angry gesture with his arm as if sweeping trash off a surface. "I think it could have been any of them."

"What about Lyle Jarvis?"

Leo laughed out loud for the first time. "Maybe I spoke too soon. That spineless little weasel." He shook his head slowly. "I'd be very surprised."

"What about Joe Callum?" Brie asked.

"Joe Callum. Pete's right-hand man. Pete liked that boy. Talked about him almost like a son."

"Sons have been known to kill their fathers."

Leo's face darkened. "Yes, they have. Indeed they have," he said, and something about his tone sent a chill through her.

She was about to move on when suddenly his face changed.

"I heard them fighting the night we came aboard. Last Friday." He seemed surprised by the memory. "I didn't think much of it at the time, but that was before everything happened."

"About what time was that?" Brie asked, making a note in her notebook.

"Maybe eleven-thirty or twelve. It woke me up."

"Did you hear what they were saying?"

Leo shook his head. "It sounded angry . . . wait . . . I do remember something. I heard Peter say, 'Are you threatening me?' He said it in a loud voice."

"Did you hear anything else?" Brie asked.

"No, it was too muffled. I heard Joe's door close when he went back into his cabin."

"I'll follow up on that. And what about last night, Leo? Did anything wake you maybe in the hours between, say, three and five a.m.? Did you hear any noise coming from Paul Trasky's cabin?" She watched him for any response. "After the faked suicide, Peter had taken up residence in that cabin."

"Sorry, no. After we were finally allowed to go to bed, I slept straight through."

"Okay, Leo, just one more thing. I'll need the name of your hand surgeon."

He smiled at her. "I'd have been disappointed if you didn't ask."

Leo gave her the name, and Brie wrote it in her notebook. She reached over and shut off the recorder and told him he could go, but not to discuss their interview with anyone. Leo stood up and waddled to the door, compensating for the pitch of the cabin sole.

He turned before leaving. "Will Peter's body stay aboard till we get back to Camden?"

Brie looked up. "When we get to Boothbay, the crime lab team will come aboard. When they are done, the body will be taken off the ship."

He nodded solemnly and left the cabin, closing the door quietly after himself.

Chapter 19

After Leo left the cabin, Brie sat looking at the note she'd written, wondering what it might mean. *Callum threatens Bendorff.* What could they have been arguing about the night they had come aboard? She knew she would have to circle back around to Callum and question him about it. But before she did, she wanted to see if she could find out where he had worked before Bendorff Enterprises, and why he'd lied about that.

She was thinking about Jack LeBeau, a retired detective she'd met while working the case on Apparition Island in September. Maybe he'd do a little digging for her—see if he could unearth the reason Joe Callum had lied about his former employer. She was thinking about Angus, Jack's big, beautiful Newfoundland dog, when her phone rang. It was Dent Fenton.

"Hello, Lieutenant."

"You in the middle of anything, Brie?"

"Nope—in between. What's up?"

"Well, we're still waiting to hear on any hits at NCIC. I've got an officer at Troop D headquarters checking that out. In the meantime, we ran the names of your five suspects through the DMV. All but Leo have Maine state driver's licenses. Nothing but minor offenses on any of them. No record of a driver's license here in Maine for Leo Dombello."

"You might check Massachusetts. He lived in North Boston until a couple years ago, when he moved to Portland. I'll also get a Social Security number on him."

"We'll check that out. Marty and I are on the way to Portland now to interview Bendorff's widow. We're about forty-five minutes from there. We've got warrants for his computers, both home and business, as well as all phone records for both him and his wife."

"Who did the notification last night when we thought Bendorff had committed suicide?"

"Two deputies from Troop G and a chaplain were sent to his house."

"Have you seen the report?" Brie asked.

"This morning. They stated that Bendorff's widow, Rebecca, appeared genuinely shocked and grief stricken by the news. They got no indication that she knew anything about the plan. Marty and I will be informing her of the murder when we get there and questioning her about his history with the five men aboard the *Maine Wind* and any possible motives they might have had."

"I've interviewed the first two suspects," Brie said. "The first guy, Joe Callum, lied about his former employer. When I followed up with the company he named, they had no record of employment."

"Huh. Must be something there," Dent said.

"I thought I'd see if Jack Le Beau could do a little digging. The company Callum named was a medtech company, so maybe he worked for a different company in that sector, either here in Maine or the broader New England area."

"That's a good idea, Brie. Get Jack on that, and you press on with the questioning of the other three suspects. It'd be great if we could crack this thing before the ship gets back to Camden."

"That's my hope," Brie said.

"You're in a dangerous and potentially volatile situation there. Nowhere for the killer to go."

"I'm aware, Dent."

"Be careful."

"I will. Keep me posted." They ended the call, and Brie looked at her watch—eleven fifteen.

She put through a call to Jack Le Beau. The retired detective was in his mid-eighties, but still sharp as tacks. His connection with a cold case from the 1950s had been invaluable to her in solving a murder on Apparition Island in September. And beyond that, he was one of the most likeable cops she'd ever met. He answered on the third ring.

"Brie, is that you? Thought you'd gone back to Minnesota by now."

"Hey, Jack. Good to hear your voice. You know I wouldn't leave without saying goodbye. We got a charter group that extended the *Maine Wind's* season by one week."

She proceeded to tell him about the faked suicide and how the cruise had turned into a crime scene with five suspects now trapped together in close proximity.

"Good Lord. What a mess," Jack said. "Anything I can do at my end?"

She told him about the Callum interview and asked if he'd make some calls—see if he could track down his former employer. She gave him Callum's full name, date of birth, and the supposed year he had started working for Bendorff.

"Reception is sketchy out here on the ocean, Jack. If you can't get back to me, relay the information to Dent. We're making for Boothbay, where the Evidence Response Team will come aboard and process the scene."

"Copy that, Brie. I'll see what I can dig up."

There was a slight pause, and she heard Jack call out to Angus. "Angus, it's Brie. Come say hello."

She heard a pair of baritone woofs and pictured the big black giant lumbering up from the floor.

"Here he comes now, Brie."

"Hi Angus," she squeaked into the phone. She told him what a good boy he was and that she missed him.

He answered with one big joyful woof. They ended the call, and she noted she felt better than she had in several days.

It was time to check in with John to see if he needed her to help on deck. She tucked her small notebook into her back pocket, pulled on her rain jacket, and headed topside. It felt good to come up into the wind and sweep of the sea—to breathe in the salt air. She'd only finished two interviews, but already the tension aboard and the closed environment of the ship were making her feel claustrophobic, and for whatever reason the words *nowhere to run* played through her mind.

"Good timing, Brie," John said when he saw her. "We're about to come to a new heading. I'll need you and Scott to reset the jib."

"A welcome change of scene," Brie said.

"Looks like you've interviewed two of them. Any progress?"

"Well, according to Joe Callum, Bendorff liked his scotch at night. So if he'd been imbibing, it would have been quite possible for any of them to carry out the murder."

"Even Leo?" John asked.

"I'd say yes."

"Will you have to go ashore at all when we reach Boothbay?"

"It's possible, but Dent Fenton is planning to send Marty Dupuis aboard, at least while we're anchored, to keep watch over things. You'll be able to sleep, and if I should have to go ashore for any reason, there'll be police presence aboard."

John nodded. "That's good. I was wondering if I should give Ed a call and bring him aboard when we get to Boothbay. We could use an extra hand for the watch."

Ed Browning was the former mate on *Maine Wind*. He occasionally joined them for a cruise when they needed an extra deckhand or if Brie had to leave the ship due to a case.

"Let's see how the rest of the interviews go. I should know by then if I'll need to go ashore."

"Maybe I'll call and see if he's available—put him on notice, just in case," John said.

"Probably a good idea." She studied him for a moment. "I feel like I'm letting you down, John. Letting down my end."

"Hey, come here." He pulled her in front of him, circling his arm around her waist so they were a unit there behind the ship's wheel. Just them and the wind and the sea.

"You're not letting me down; you're doing your job. If you didn't do your job, you wouldn't be the person I care about." He paused and held her against him. "You wouldn't be the woman I've come to love."

Brie turned and tears came to her eyes.

"That's right, Brie. I love you." He looked straight into her eyes when he said it. "This wasn't the way I had planned to say it or the week I thought we'd be sharing, but it doesn't change the fact of it. And maybe in a way this is perfect. Just us and this moment and the ship." He kissed her forehead, and after a moment he chuckled softly.

". . . And a dead body," Brie said. "That's why you're laughing, right?"

"Part of the charm, Brie."

She laughed out loud at that.

"See, with you, life will always hold the unexpected."

"That's putting it mildly."

"I like the unexpected. I think it's why I go to sea."

At that moment, the wind huffed up. *Maine Wind* leaned into it, and her rigging hummed. There are very few perfect moments in this life, but over the past five months Brie had learned to recognize them. She added this one to her treasure chest of such moments, and just before closing the lid, she leaned back into him and spoke the words she'd been waiting to say. "I love you too, John."

Chapter 20

Bric moved toward the starboard bow, where the jib was made off. Scott was on lookout all the way forward. They'd been sailing along an arc since leaving the Isles of Shoals—an arc that, due to the curvature of the earth, was a shorter distance than sailing in what appeared, on a two-dimensional chart, to be a straight line from A to B. They'd been on a port tack beating close up into a north wind for the past few hours. Coming to the new heading would give them a slightly saner ride and a slightly more level deck.

"Prepare to come about," the captain called out from the helm.

Scott left his post and headed for the port side of the ship across the deck from Brie.

"Ready about," the captain shouted.

"Ready about," Brie and Scott called out.

"Hard alee," the captain called.

Back at the helm he spun the wheel, rotation after rotation, and as they began to cross the wind, he pulled harder on it. Brie released the sheet as they came across the wind, and across the deck, Scott hauled in on the port side sheet and made it off as they settled onto their new heading. As the ship moved from a port to a starboard tack, the pitch of the deck also shifted, the windward deck always being the higher side.

After the jib was sheeted in and made off, Brie went below to find Leo. She knocked on his cabin door.

"Who is it?" The voice held a combination of suspicion and irritation.

"It's Detective Beaumont." Brie decided to keep it businesslike.

"Just a minute."

She heard a bit of grunting and groaning as Leo extricated himself from his berth. In a few moments he opened the cabin door three or four inches and peered out.

"I just need a piece of information from you, Leo. Is your driver's license still active in Massachusetts?"

"That's right," he said, but Brie saw his eyes become hooded and decided she'd better play it cool—keep him off his guard if possible.

"Great. That's what I thought." She turned as if to leave. "Oh, almost forgot—what a scatterbrain. Could you write down your Social Security number? I'm thinking there might be other Leo Dombellos in the Massachusetts DMV."

Leo studied her for a moment, during which she gave him her best *oh-gosh-I'm-just-a-simple-minded-gal* smile. At this he puffed up like a turkey on the prowl, took the paper from her, and wrote down the number.

"Great. Thanks, Leo." She turned and smiled to herself. *Works every time*, she thought. She headed up on deck, pulled out her phone, and called Dent Fenton, but now it was his phone that went to voicemail. She sent him a text with Leo's Social Security number.

Brie turned from the rail and headed for the galley to find her next interviewee. She had decided to question Lyle Jarvis. He'd already been named by Joe Callum as the one most likely to have killed Bendorff. Leo didn't concur, but Brie had gotten a generally creepy vibe from Jarvis even before the murder.

When she stepped off the ladder, she saw that Jarvis and Alexander Smith were lying down on the bench seats behind the table.

"The motion up here in the bow was getting to those two," George said. "I told them to lie down."

Staying horizontal to the seas was the formula for keeping seasickness at bay. "We've come to a new heading—a little off the wind—so decks should be more level."

"That should help the situation down here and also make it easier to get lunch served. I think we should eat on deck, though, if the captain will allow it," George said. "These guys could use the fresh air."

Brie turned and looked at the three men. Boardman seemed unfazed by the motion of the ship. He sat upright against the bulkhead, legs stretched out along the bench seat. He was reading a copy of *Popular Mechanics*. The other two men looked the worse for wear, though.

"I'll talk to the captain and see if he'll okay it, George." She stuck her head over the big pot on the woodstove and sniffed. "What's cooking?"

"A hearty chicken and dumpling soup with lots of vegetables. Always a good choice for rough days at sea. It should sit well in the tummy. I'm serving grilled ham and cheese sandwiches with it."

Brie sniffed the pot again. "Do I have time to fit in one more interview before lunch?"

"Plenty of time. I'm just starting to assemble the sandwiches."

Brie turned from the stove. "Mr. Jarvis—Lyle—would you come with me?"

Jarvis lifted his head and then slowly sat up. Even in the dim light of the galley, there was a distinct greenish cast to his skin that spoke of *mal de mer*. Without saying a word, he stood up and went for his rain slicker that hung at the back of the galley. The slicker was yellow, which made him look even greener. He pulled it on and headed up the ladder. He looked miserable and angry, but there was something else there as well. To Brie it felt like fear. She followed him topside and told him to go aft.

Jarvis paused a few feet beyond the helm and stood, legs spread, mouth open, gulping in big breaths of sea air and staring off toward the horizon.

Brie stopped next to John and spoke to him. "George wants to know if he can serve the lunch on deck." She bobbed her head toward Jarvis. "A couple of these guys aren't doing so well down below."

John hesitated for a moment. "I wanted people below decks to keep the situation in hand. And, frankly, to keep them from talking too much to one another."

"I'm with you there, John. We don't want them cooking up anything else, and if they're alone in their cabins or with George in the galley, that can't happen."

"On the other hand, George doesn't need someone getting sick down in his galley. Tell him he can serve on deck, but I want you and Scott right in among these guys so you can hear anything they might be saying."

"Aye, Captain."

He smiled and turned to see if Jarvis was out of earshot. He was. "So formal, Brie," he said, holding her eyes.

She got it. After their proclamation of love, it did sound a little stiff, but Brie liked to stick to protocol. She'd been a cop for a long time. Sailor, too. She smiled and looked down at the deck. "I'll go tell George," she said.

She walked forward to the galley companionway and called down. "Capt'n says you can serve lunch topside."

"Thanks, Brie," came the reply.

She headed aft, taking her time, giving Jarvis a few more moments to pull himself together. When she got to the stern, she asked him to follow her down to the captain's cabin. "It's not so bad back here," she said, seeing the panicked look in his eyes at the thought of going below decks again. "If you get to feeling bad, we'll take a break." With that she ushered him down the companionway and followed him into John's cabin.

*   *   *

Joe Callum lay in his berth, angry at himself for giving out the wrong company name for his former employer. Why had he done such an idiotic thing? He told himself he'd been rattled—not expecting the question. He should have given the correct name. It had been quite a few years ago, and he'd never been charged with any wrongdoing. Even if she called to check on his story, chances were no red flags would have been raised.

"Idiot," he said under his breath. If she called the company he had named, she would find out he was lying. Then she'd be looking for the reason he had lied. Like a bloodhound, she'd go sniffing around his former company if she could find it. *Oh, she'd find it.* He could tell from the interview that Detective Beaumont was a force to be reckoned with.

Talk about dumb luck—picking a ship with a cop aboard. But maybe it was okay. She seemed to listen when he had named Lyle Jarvis as the killer. And why not? He hadn't lied about Jarvis' hatred of Peter. He was more than happy to stack the deck against Lyle the Weasel—a man he considered his personal nemesis.

Callum pulled the wool blanket over his shoulder and rolled over on his side. *May as well sleep,* he thought. *There's nothing else to do. We're trapped here.*

Chapter 21

Brie closed the door to John's cabin and turned to face Lyle Jarvis. He was busy looking around the cabin, his head moving in incremental jerks like a woodpecker listening for bugs inside a tree, his eyes barely resting on a particular thing before the head moved again. Finally, the eyes came to rest on the gun at her side and stayed riveted there as if it held some kind of fascination.

"Please sit down, Lyle, and we'll get started."

Jarvis sat his beanpole frame down on the small round stool. He fidgeted unmercifully, first crossing his arms on his chest and then trying to tuck his long feet up on the small rung of the stool, a maneuver that nearly sent him to the floor when *Maine Wind* rolled to port.

"Probably best to keep your feet down on the cabin sole," Brie said.

He gave a nod but never looked at her.

"I'll be recording our interview if that's okay." She didn't wait for him to respond since the words *if it's okay* were just a formality. He didn't actually have a say in the matter. She turned on the recorder.

"Please state your full name, age, and date of birth for the record."

He cleared his throat and spoke in a nervous voice. "Lyle Mark Jarvis. August ninth, nineteen eighty-six."

Brie jotted *30 yrs. old* in her notebook under his name. "Let's start with some background questions. I understand that you are Peter Bendorff's nephew." Remembering what Joe

Callum had told her about the animosity between them, she watched him closely for a reaction.

He darted a glance at her and nodded.

"The suspect has answered in the affirmative," Brie said, turning toward the small recorder.

"Suspect. Why am I a suspect?" He looked at her for the first time, and she saw anger and agitation in his eyes.

"At this point in time, all of you are suspects. No one has been eliminated. The fact of the matter is that you all had opportunity to commit the murder. Leo and Joe Callum had opportunity because they shared a compartment with Peter Bendorff. And due to the malfunctioning of the head in the aft compartment, all three of you back here also had the opportunity to commit the crime. The captain has told me you all went forward during the night to use the head in the amidships compartment." She wasn't trying to assuage his emotions but simply thought she might learn more if Jarvis didn't feel backed into a corner.

"So Peter Bendorff was your uncle, and you also worked for him. Is that right?"

Jarvis made a nondescript sound.

"Could you answer yes or no, Mr. Jarvis?"

"Yes," he said sullenly. "I was the IT guy for his company. Fixed all the nasty problems when his stupid employees screwed up their computers."

"Sounds like you didn't enjoy your work," Brie said.

"I don't like my work. I wanted to go into robotics, but my uncle made me go into IT instead."

"How was he able to do that?"

Jarvis became suddenly very quiet and darted his eyes around the room like a caged animal.

"Ever since my dad split when I was twelve, he thinks he can run my life."

"You mean your Uncle Peter?" Brie asked.

"That's right."

"Well, he won't be running it anymore, will he?"

"You think I killed him, don't you? Someone told you I did it, didn't they?"

"What makes you think that?" Brie asked.

"I just know it. They all hate me. They're all out to get me." His level of agitation had reached fever pitch.

Brie studied him silently, waiting for the pot to simmer down. The guy had a textbook persecution complex. She decided to take a different tack to try and diffuse some of his angst. "Tell me about your mother, Lyle."

The thing inside him that was wound too tight seemed to release, and for the first time his tone gentled. "Mom just lets men push her around—tell her what to do."

Brie wondered if he included himself in that generalization but didn't ask.

"Did that include your Uncle Peter?"

"Sure. I mean, he bullied everybody. Why not his sister?"

"So, he was your mom's brother?"

"Yup."

"Did he ever do anything good for you, Lyle?"

The question took him by surprise. He sat very still for a moment, as if translating a foreign language. Finally he shrugged. "I guess," he said.

"What did he do that was good for you?"

Now he looked trapped again. "I don't feel like saying."

"Okay. Let me ask you this. Did you kill your uncle?"

"No." He said it in a low, menacing voice, and Brie realized his eyes were fixed on her gun, and her hand went instinctively to the holster.

"Did you know about his plan to fake his own suicide?"

"We all did."

"If you disliked him so much, why did you agree to be part of the plan?"

"Didn't have a choice. I never have a choice. He tells me what to do, and I do it."

"Why don't you move away—take a different job?"

"Can't." The word was like the locking of a vault that Jarvis had withdrawn into.

"Did your uncle hold something over you?"

"What makes you think that?" The caged beast returned, but Brie could see she'd struck pay dirt. She knew he wouldn't tell her what it was Bendorff had held over him, but it didn't matter.

Suddenly Jarvis was talking fast. "He held something over everyone. It was his way."

"Do you know that for a fact—have any proof—or is that just a wild guess?" She suspected he was throwing up road blocks to divert attention from himself, and yet something Leo had said played in her mind. *Let's just say Peter was a genius at learning things about people and knowing how to use them.*

"It's not a guess at all. It's fact."

"Be specific."

"Okay. Let's take Callum. He's not the nice, stand-up guy he passes himself off as. He's got a past, and Uncle Pete used it to get what he wanted from him."

"And what was that?" Brie knew Jarvis hated Callum, so she listened but drew no conclusions about what she was hearing.

"He cooked the books for Uncle Pete. Hid income, assets."

"And how do you know that?"

"I have my ways, just like all the rest of them. And that's all I'm going to say."

"And what else do you know?"

"Leo acts all harmless with his disorganized curmudgeon act. Well, he's not all that innocent, believe me."

"Care to elaborate?"

Jarvis darted his eyes around the cabin. "No. Why should I do your job for you?"

Brie studied him. Beneath the self-absorbed, arrogant, jit-case exterior, Jarvis appeared to have the inside track on some of his shipmates. She wasn't sure what he was driving at with Leo, but she already knew Callum had lied to her—that there was a skeleton in his closet—so she put more credence in Jarvis' revelations than she might otherwise have done. The result was that she found Lyle Jarvis even more believable as the killer. He was smart and calculating. Maybe he'd decided to use his insider knowledge to deflect the focus from himself.

She trusted Jarvis about as far as she could have thrown him, but she had decided to ask each of the suspects the same question. Namely, who they each thought had killed Bendorff. Not that it meant a whole lot, but it was a window into the dynamics of the group—a way of stirring the pot to see what rose to the top.

She was pretty sure who Jarvis would name and was about to ask the question when he blurted out, "If I were you, I'd take a good hard look at Callum. I think he's your killer."

"Why's that?"

"They fought a lot. Anyone who worked for Bendorff Enterprises could tell you that. And he's my uncle's right-hand man. Anything happens to old P.B., Callum takes over."

"So he would have taken over either way. Why kill him?"

"Maybe he was tired of being told what to do, too. Maybe Bendorff planned to control him from a distance."

Brie didn't put much stock in anything Jarvis said, but his comment had her thinking about the two strikes Joe Callum already had against him. Callum had lied about his former employer, and Leo had overheard him arguing with Bendorff the night they had come aboard.

But juxtaposed with those facts was the sadness Brie had twice seen in Callum's eyes—what felt like genuine sadness over Bendorff's death. It begged the question: were the two of them arguing like enemies—rivals—or were they arguing like a father and son might?

One thing she knew—there was bad blood between Callum and Jarvis that bordered on hatred. Callum had flat-out accused Jarvis of committing the crime, and now here was Jarvis, returning the favor. She decided to shift gears.

"Who else aboard worked at Bendorff Enterprises?"

"Besides me and Callum, just Rusty Boardman."

"What does Boardman do at the company?"

"Cyber security."

Brie thought about that for a moment, and it fit. She already had him pegged as ex-military. She moved on to her next question.

"Where did you grow up, Lyle?"

He fidgeted on the stool and looked around the cabin and finally said, "Bangor." It was obvious he didn't want to tell her.

"And your mom? Does she live in Bangor, too?"

"Yeah. Why do you ask? What's she got to do with all this?"

"Just gathering information, that's all," Brie said, trying to smooth his feathers. "What's her first name?"

"Jane." Jarvis gave her a suspicious look, and Brie knew he could read between the lines. "You leave my mother out of all this, you hear? I mean it. I truly mean it."

It walked and talked like a threat, and Brie decided it was one. Thing is, you don't threaten a cop. In her book that put Jarvis, if not on the crazy train, at least waiting at the station. She decided she'd definitely be following up on his past, and soon. Metaphorically, she'd just placed a large "X" on Lyle Jarvis. And X marked the spot where she planned to dig.

"You know, your mother was Peter Bendorff's sister. I'm pretty sure she's going to find out about this, if she doesn't already know."

Jarvis' face soured, and he locked his arms across his chest. "I have nothing more to say."

Brie couldn't let that fly. "Actually, this is a police investigation, so I get to say when we are done, not you."

He huffed out a sigh. "Fine. What else?"

"Just a couple more questions. Where did you go to school?"

"Eastern Maine Community College."

Brie wrote the name in her notebook, and at that moment her phone rang. It was Dent. She let it go to voicemail.

"And high school?"

"Bangor High."

She studied him for a moment, trying to determine if he was lying. There were no tells.

"What time did you use the amidships head last night?"

"I have no idea. I didn't check a clock. All I know is it was pitch dark, and the captain was on deck."

She looked straight at him. "Did you tamper with the aft head, Lyle? Cause it to malfunction?"

"Hell no!" He straightened up, looked indignant, but then darted his eyes around the cabin.

Brie observed him for a moment. "All right, Mr. Jarvis. We're done here. Please don't discuss this interview with the others."

Jarvis bolted up from the stool, then seemed to regret the sudden move. His eyes got big. He covered his mouth and raced out the door, leaving it open. She heard him pound up the ladder and make for the side of the ship.

The captain's voice boomed out, "Downwind, Lyle— other side of the ship."

Brie heard Jarvis gallop over to port. "Oh my," she said.

She got up and closed the door and took out her phone. She had bars. She brought up Dent Fenton's voicemail. It was brief.

"The NCIC report came in. Call me."

She put through the call and drummed her fingers on John's chart table as she waited for Dent to pick up.

"Brie, glad you called back." His voice was staticky.

"You're breaking up, Dent."

"I'll keep it short. No criminal convictions on four of your suspects, but your boy Leo set off all the bells and whistles at NCIC. He's got a long and illustrious criminal record. Spent his early years under the tutelage of his uncle—one Francis Luigi—former Mafia capo and notorious drug trafficker."

The last two words came out *drug faker*, but Brie figured it for "trafficker."

"Did a stint in the federal pen at Allenwood, Pennsylvania, for racketeering."

"You're talking about Leo, right?"

"Right. After that, Leo—mister Mafia—must have found religion or something. He refined his skill set and specialized in money laundering and fencing stolen goods. He's been clean since 2007. Parole record shows he worked in the family bakery since then."

"That checks with what he told me. Seems he forgot to tell me about his other career."

"When you have a minute later on, you'll want to take a look at the link I sent you about the uncle. I think you'll find it interesting. These old Mafia dons never retire; they just slowly fade away."

"So Leo Dombello has had a hard time walking the straight and narrow," Brie said.

"Appears so."

The connection was suddenly filled with static. Brie waited till it cleared. "But no arrests or convictions for assault or connection to any homicides?"

"Nada," Dent said.

"So he gets involved in this faked suicide. Why? Why risk it?"

"Good question, Brie. I'm sure you'll dig up the answer."

"Sheesh, what a barrel of snakes we've got here. These guys run the gamut from mildly creepy to scary psychotic, and that's just the last one I interviewed."

That got a laugh from Dent.

"What's more, this last guy, Jarvis, seemed unhealthily fixated on my gun."

"Huh. You keep a weather eye on that guy, Brie. And keep digging. Eventually you'll come out on the other side. We're just pulling up to Bendorff's house. We'll see what we learn from his widow."

"We need to find out if there was life insurance on Bendorff. I asked Joe Callum, Bendorff's right-hand man, about it. He didn't know anything about a policy."

"We'll see what the wife knows about that."

Brie asked him to dig up a phone number and address on Jane Jarvis in Bangor and text her back with the info. Then they ended the call.

She sat thinking about Leo Dombello and his criminal record. It was time to track down his hand surgeon and get a statement from him.

She looked around John's cabin, a place that held great comfort for her—a safe place, filled with memories of their deep affection for one another. She closed her eyes and felt the motion of the ship and the sea. The old timbers whispered and creaked as they bent to the seas. She took a deep breath and then another and another. She opened her eyes after a couple of minutes and felt strangely renewed.

She brought up Joe Wolf's number and put a call through. Joe was the medical examiner she'd worked with on two cases during the summer. She figured he'd have a quick way of locating Leo's hand surgeon. He answered on the fourth ring, and they exchanged a few words of small talk. Then she gave him the doctor's name—Dr. David Andrews.

"He's an orthopedic surgeon, specializing in hands. His office is in Boston."

"Hang on, Brie. I'll look him up in the Physician Database."

Joe was back on the line in less than a minute with a phone number for Dr. Andrews' office.

"Thanks, Joe. You're coming down to Boothbay with the Evidence Response Team when we make port, right?"

"That's right."

"Great, see you then." They ended the call.

Brie punched in the number that Joe had given her, made her way through the phone bank, and in just a couple minutes got a live human on the line at Dr. Andrews' office. She identified herself, gave her badge number, and asked to speak to Dr. Andrews. Surprisingly, he was in the office and took her call right away. She told him about the circumstances of the case and that Leo Dombello was a suspect.

"I'd like to know, Doctor, if Leo Dombello would be physically able to strangle someone, considering his condition and the surgeries he has had on his hands for carpal tunnel syndrome?"

"If you give me a minute, I'll bring up his medical record."

Brie heard him typing on his keyboard and then heard silence as the doctor read the medical record.

"In my opinion, there's no way someone with a condition this severe could commit such a crime. Mr. Dombello has had three surgeries and, according to the record, suffers from numbness and tingling in his hands due to permanent nerve damage."

"So he wouldn't have the strength to strangle someone. Is that what you're saying?"

"That's exactly what I'm saying. He suffers from way too much impairment."

"Well, thank you, Doctor. That's all I need right now." She ended the call.

151

At least she could check one suspect off the list. She sat thinking for a minute. Leo seemed to know things about Peter. He had said they were friends. Maybe he knew things about the rest of these guys. Maybe he could be useful. Maybe it was time to make a deal of sorts. Considering Leo's criminal record and what he'd been foolish enough to involve himself in here on the ship, she decided to leverage the situation—see if she could make it work for her.

The case was heating up. Accusations were starting to fly. The closed environment of the ship felt like a crucible coming to a slow boil. *Keep stirring the pot,* she thought. It was a dangerous game, but she knew she had to keep turning up the heat if she hoped to smoke out a killer. She looked up a phone number for the Bangor Police. Time to start the excavation work on Lyle Jarvis' past. Right now he still topped her list of suspects.

Chapter 22

B rie punched in the number for the Bangor Police and sent the call. Dispatch answered, and she asked for the detective division.

"Detective James Wallace here."

Brie identified herself as Maine State Police and gave her badge number. She told Wallace they were investigating one Lyle Jarvis in a homicide case. "There's no record at NCIC, so he hasn't been convicted of a crime, but he grew up in Bangor, so we're checking to see if he's ever been brought in on anything."

"Let me see what I can pull up, and I'll call you right back."

Within five minutes her phone rang.

"You've hit pay dirt with this guy, Detective Beaumont. He was involved in a terrible crime twelve years ago. He was eighteen at the time. I'm patching you over to Detective Dan Branch, who was the lead on this case. He can fill you in."

Branch came on the line and greeted her. "So, Lyle Jarvis has resurfaced. I figured it was just a matter of time."

"I'll fill you in briefly, Detective Branch," Brie said. "It's an odd case, unfolding in an even odder location."

She told him about Peter Bendorff and his relation to Jarvis, and filled him in on the faked suicide and the subsequent murder aboard *Maine Wind*.

"Jarvis is the prime suspect. I'd say he's got BPD—Borderline Personality Disorder. He hated his uncle, and after interviewing him, I got the sense that something bad had happened in his past. Maybe something the uncle extricated him from. Since then, Peter Bendorff, the uncle, has kept a Nazi-like boot on Jarvis' life, and Jarvis hated him for it."

"Your instincts are good, Detective Beaumont. You've sized the situation up perfectly. Twelve years ago, Lyle Jarvis was a suspect in a truly heinous crime—a rape-slash-homicide. The uncle lawyered him up with a top-notch defense attorney. There were two juveniles involved. We never thought Jarvis had anything to do with the rape—we collected DNA evidence that led to the arrest of the other kid, but the manner of death was the real enigma.

"The girl drowned, but fortunately the current carried the body to shore, where it snagged and was spotted soon after she died. There was still DNA under her fingernails, which led to the arrest of the other guy, one Thomas Beloit.

"The girl had suffered blunt force trauma to the head, either from being struck or from falling and striking her head. But that head wound was not the cause of death, and when we located the crime scene, we found a rock near the shore with blood on it that matched the head trauma. Two theories unfolded. Either the girl got up, disoriented, and fell into the river —the case the defense made—or she struck or was struck on the head, rendering her unconscious, and either Beloit or Jarvis put her in the river."

"Did you check for DNA on that rock?"

"We did, but it was inconclusive."

Brie thought about Jarvis' professed hatred of the water, and she remembered his odd behavior on deck the first day they were under sail, when she found him frozen at the rail, staring down into the water racing past the hull. She wondered now if he'd been having a flashback that day—a flashback to another scene with water flowing by, water that would have been mixed with blood. If there was one thing she knew about, it was flashbacks and how unexpectedly they unfolded.

Detective Branch was talking again. "The other kid copped to the rape but said the girl got away from him at a point. He sent his henchman—Lyle Jarvis—after her to catch her. Jarvis denied it—said he was just a bystander, an observer. That his only crime was not trying harder to stop Beloit or to help the girl. We never bought it—thought he was in it up to his miserable neck. But there was the uncle and that goddamned lawyer, and you could tell Bendorff was determined to protect that miserable little delinquent. Turned out the kid's father had taken a hike when Jarvis was twelve. A lot of his worthless behavior got blamed on that. All bullshit, if you ask me."

Brie smiled to herself. She couldn't help liking Detective Dan Branch. And Lyle Jarvis was the poster boy for someone who'd had excuses made for him his whole life. She was beginning to think Peter Bendorff's tough love for his incorrigible nephew had been one of the victim's redeeming qualities in a sea of questionable ones.

"Anyway, I hope you nail the sonofabitch this time," Branch said.

"Well, sadly, he's not the only one with a motive. Of the five guys aboard, several of them could have a horse in this race."

"You mean they acted together?"

"Not that so much, but they have motive and opportunity. I'm not done gathering all the facts, but let's just say, if this were a movie script, they'd have to call it *Snakes on a Boat*."

Branch laughed. "Hell of a situation, Detective. You watch your back and call if I can do anything else."

"Thanks, Dan. I will." They ended the call, and Brie jotted down some notes in her notebook. Her stomach gave a loud protest. She looked at her watch. Lunch had to be imminent. She tucked her notes and recorder into the drawer of John's chart table and went topside to help get the lunch on deck.

Moving from the cloistered feel of the captain's cabin into the larger-than-life environment of the ship above decks was an awesome thing. *Maine Wind* heeled to port as the northeast wind raced over the windward rail and roared along the canvas at a steady twenty-five knots. Brie paused at the helm to talk to the captain.

John spoke over the noise of the wind. "Just had a call from Ed Browning. He said he can meet us in Boothbay and come aboard if we need him."

Brie leaned in close to be heard. "I think it's a good thing, John. I know I was a little hesitant before, but we can definitely use an extra deckhand. There's no way I can run the investigation and hold up my end."

"Not to worry, Brie. You're doing all you can. I told him to meet us in Boothbay this evening."

"That's great. I'm going to get the passengers on deck to form a food line. George should have lunch ready to go by now."

Brie headed forward and signaled to Scott in the bow that they needed to set up for lunch. She got the rubber mats out of the deck box and rolled them out on the amidships cabin top, where they would serve the lunch. With the tense situation aboard, it would do the shipmates good to get up from below decks and spend some time in the bracing wind.

She and Scott went below to check in with George.

"Good timing, mates. I was just going to come looking for you. Food's ready."

"Topside, you three," Scott told Jarvis, Boardman, and Smith, who had spent the morning here in the galley. They slid out from behind the table and made a beeline for the ladder, eager to leave the confines of the galley. Scott followed them up the ladder and called down the amidships companionway. "All hands on deck to form a food line."

Scott returned to the galley, and he and Brie started pulling together the dishes, mugs, silverware, napkins, and condiments and lining them up to be passed up the ladder. Brie heard the men gathering up on deck. What she couldn't hear were their thoughts, but nonetheless, those thoughts were shaping up like storm clouds on the horizon.

She's bound to find out I have a motive. Then what?

Seems cowardly, but I don't feel safe.

Just stay below the radar. Way below the radar.

Staying aboard—dangerous for me, but deadly for anyone who crosses me.

"I'll go topside and lay everything out as it comes down the line," Brie said. She disappeared up the ladder.

"Let's get a line going here," she said to the men on deck. "Food's coming up."

The men fell to, Scott took the middle of the ladder, George passed everything up from below, and Brie, at the far end of the line, arranged it all on the cabin top. George came up the ladder carrying the big soup pot, and Scott followed with a roasting pan filled with grilled sandwiches. There was salad too, which had been passed up the ladder with all the other stuff. And *voilà*, lunch was served. George went forward and rang the ship's bell just to make it official, and the men crowded into line to dish up.

Brie stepped aft and took the wheel, and the captain came forward and gave a brief summary of their progress, the forecasted weather and sea conditions, and what time they expected to make their anchorage in Boothbay Harbor. Then the five men spread out around the deck, each picking a spot away from the others, not a hard task on a large ship with so few shipmates.

So much for friendship, Brie thought. *If indeed any of them were ever truly friends.* The captain came back to relieve her, but she told him to go eat first. She was happy to put her mind in neutral for a little while and just be at one with the ship. Taking the helm of a sailing vessel is not a static activity. The sailor is in tune with every tug of the wheel, every vibration of timber, every nuance of movement in the sails that predicts a shift of wind, a need to fall off or head up to keep the ship sailing at maximum efficiency. For Brie, the experience was at once calming and exhilarating. So after a time, John had to pretty much coerce her to hand over the helm so she wouldn't go hungry.

Rusty Boardman and Joe Callum were headed back for thirds when Brie got to the food line. They ushered her to the front, where she claimed a large bowl of George's chicken dumpling soup and a grilled sandwich and sat down on the deck on the leeward side, out of the wind, next to Scott.

The captain had told her he wanted them right in among the passengers during lunch, but there was no "in among" to be had. Callum and Jarvis were a good thirty feet apart over on the starboard deck. Rusty Boardman was forward of them near the ship's windlass, sandwich and coffee in hand, on a kind of self-appointed bow watch. Leo was aft, sitting on the cabin top, shielded from the wind by the canvas dodger that covered the aft companionway. And Alex Smith was all the way astern, perched on the rail midway between port and starboard. He wore heavy wool socks under his Birkenstock sandals and sported a four-day scruff that gave him a salty air.

Brie polished off her soup, saving all the dumplings for last, and bit into the grilled ham and cheese. Not just any ham and cheese, mind you, but one worthy of George's reputation. The bread was marble rye, the cheese was Swiss, and there was something going on inside that involved honey and Dijon mustard. She'd just started into the second half, and Scott was rambling on about the haul-out of the *Maine Wind*, when all hell broke loose over on the starboard deck.

She and Scott bolted to their feet in time to see Joe Callum shove Lyle Jarvis away.

"I'm gonna kill you, Callum," Jarvis screamed.

In Brie's sensory-narrowed cop-focus, everything morphed into slow motion. She was aware of a convergence under way —she and Scott racing across the deck toward them, and Rusty Boardman bearing down on them from the starboard bow.

"Like you killed Peter?" Callum shouted as Jarvis charged him. Callum swung at him, attempting a right hook to the jaw, but Jarvis—beanpole that he was—went in low, like a wrestler, driving his head into Callum's gut. The posse was almost on them when Brie saw Jarvis lift Callum into the air and hurl him over the rail. She heard a disembodied gasp—hers or everyone's, she wasn't sure—and for a microsecond she froze, but no more.

"Man overboard," she yelled, racing toward the foremast that held the life ring.

Scott charged aft, and she turned with the ring to see him, in a two-step running stride, mount the rail and the heavy coiled lifeline and dive overboard.

John was hauling the wheel to port. "Prepare to jibe," he shouted, as Brie raced past him to the port rail and heaved the life ring overboard on a bead with Callum, who was flailing in the choppy seas already far abaft of the *Maine Wind*.

Boardman had come storming back from the bow to deal with Lyle-the-weasel Jarvis. He grabbed him by the jacket and delivered the right hook Callum had failed to land. Jarvis went flying backwards onto the deck. Hearing the fracas, George had stormed up the galley companionway and now appeared to revert to a Greek wrestler. As Jarvis staggered up from the deck, George took him down in one swift move, put a full nelson on him, and pinned him to the deck.

Alex Smith was recording the whole thing for posterity and most likely YouTube, but when he passed the captain at the helm, John, with one hand still cranking the wheel around, reached out and swiped the phone from Smith's hand and stuffed it in his pocket. Smith froze, shocked and embarrassed, and seeing the glare on John's face, retreated to his seat on the aft rail to take in the drama the old-fashioned way—with his eyes.

That left Leo, who stood frozen and bug-eyed, gripping the side of the canvas dodger for dear life and darting his head from one juicy tableau to the next.

Scott was making progress through the seas toward Callum, who—thank the Lord—had stayed afloat. As the ship came dead astern to the wind and began to fall off on the other side, the massive fore and mainsail booms came careening across the deck with head-rolling velocity.

"Jibe-oh!" the captain shouted. As if Zeus had blown down from on high, a gigantic whoosh of canvas, propelled by heavy spars, swept across the deck fore and aft and let out a bone-shuddering "BOOM" as the main and foresheets caught and held the sails.

Scott reached Callum a minute or so later as the ship bore down on the two men. Brie went forward to the deck box, pulled out the boarding ladder, and attached it under the starboard rail. George still had Jarvis pinned to the deck. John steered *Maine Wind* to port, keeping Scott and Callum to starboard, circling behind them and turning the ship upwind. Scott, towing Callum, who seemed to be in distress, waited as the captain circled *Maine Wind* to starboard and dead into the wind, where she stalled. Acting fast, Brie and Boardman lowered the ladder outboard, and Brie climbed over the rail and down the ladder. Scott swam to the ladder and brought Callum around in front of him and gave him a boost up toward the ladder. Brie grabbed his arm and pulled him up so he could gain purchase on the ladder. He was shaking badly, and she climbed backwards up the ladder, keeping an eye on him. She swung herself over the rail, and Boardman leaned over and got his hands under Callum's arms and steadied him as he climbed aboard.

He stood there, shedding water and shaking badly, as they helped Scott aboard. Scott headed below to get out of his wet clothes. Brie put an arm on Joe Callum and steered him toward the amidships companionway.

"Go below and shed these wet clothes. Dry off and get in your berth. I'll bring some extra blankets, and George will bring some hot broth and tea down once we get things sorted up here."

There was only one thing that needed to get sorted, and it was Lyle Jarvis. That would be the captain's job. She moved back to where George had him pinned on the deck. "I'll take it from here, George. And thanks."

George climbed off Jarvis and, with surprising ease, pulled him to his feet. "Don't you give Brie any trouble," he warned.

He started to talk back immediately. "Callum started it. He called me a coward. I guess I showed . . ."

"Shut up, Lyle," Brie snapped. "We'll let the captain deal with this." She gave him a nudge from behind. "March."

When they got to the helm, they halted, and John gave Lyle the stink eye. After letting it sit heavy on him for a moment, the captain said, "You have endangered both crew and passengers with your behavior."

Jarvis opened his mouth as if to argue, but John raised his hand to stop him. "I warn you: don't even think about speaking. Get below to your cabin, and don't come out till I tell you. We'll deal with you when we get to Boothbay Harbor."

Jarvis started to object again, proving he had no sense of the depth of John's anger.

The captain's voice descended to something like a growl. "Escort him below, Brie. Do it now."

She nudged Jarvis toward the companionway and followed him down the ladder. At his cabin door, she said, "I caution you not to test the captain any further. He abides no troublemakers aboard his ship, and make no mistake, when we're at sea, he has the ultimate authority."

Jarvis withered a little at that and turned and skulked into his cabin.

Brie climbed back up on deck and stood next to John, waiting for him to speak.

"You think he's Bendorff's killer?"

Brie stepped to John's other side, away from the companionway so there was no possibility of being heard by Jarvis. She leaned in so her head nearly touched his and spoke over the noise of the canvas.

"I think he's a lit match, and in this closed environment, there's plenty of fuel for an explosion. I could have Dent take him into custody at Boothbay. But they can only hold him for forty-eight hours before charging him. And while his crazy behavior makes him look like a good candidate for the murder, we have no proof. He had motive, but he's not the only one who did. I've still got to interview Boardman and Smith, and I'm waiting for information on Callum's past employment. Jack Le Beau's working on that."

"Well, for now, he stays below in solitary confinement."

"Fine by me," Brie said. "I need to go check on Callum. I'm going to pull the blood pressure cuff and thermometer from the first aid kit and get his BP and temperature. He was shaking badly when we got him aboard. We need to watch him closely—make sure he's not heading into hypothermia."

"Make sure George gets some hot liquids into him. I'll tell Scott to keep checking on him. I sent Leo and Alex to their cabins and told Boardman to wait for you down in the galley. Once you've checked out Callum, you go ahead with the other interviews. But you'll need to use the galley to make sure you're out of earshot of Jarvis."

"Aye, Capt'n. I'll check on Callum and then get started on the Boardman interview."

She headed below and stepped into the captain's cabin. In the far corner she spotted the large first aid kit in its red carrying case. She opened the case and took out the portable blood pressure cuff and, from the top tray, the thermometer and a disposable tip. She, John, and Scott all had Red Cross certification. Hers came from her police background, but on any of the ships in the windjammer fleet, the captain and mate always held such certifications.

Brie grabbed her notebook and pen out of the chart table and headed topside with the equipment. John had adjusted course back to their previous heading, and she made her way forward to the amidships companionway and descended the ladder. She saw Callum's cabin door was open, and George stood in the doorway. She crossed the passageway, and he stepped aside to let her in. Callum was sitting on his berth, two blankets around his shoulders, spooning in steaming chicken broth and drinking hot tea that George had brought him. He had on sweat pants and a heavy wool sweater and socks.

"How are you doing, Joe?" she asked.

"Better with these hot liquids, I think."

She noted the pile of wet clothes on the floor. "We can hang those up in the galley to dry for you."

He nodded.

"I'd like to take your temperature and blood pressure, if that's okay. I want to get a baseline temp on you to be sure it isn't dropping over the next couple of hours." She knew firsthand how insidious and incremental the descent into hypothermia can be. By the time you know you're in trouble, you're really in trouble.

Callum set his soup on the tray that sat on his berth and pulled his right arm out of his sweater. Brie put the BP cuff on and pumped it up and waited for the readout. It was 125 over 90. Slightly elevated, which wasn't surprising after the trauma he'd been through. She put the thermometer in his mouth and waited for it to beep. His temp read 97.5—about a degree below normal. She made a note of the numbers in her small pocket notebook.

"How do you feel, Joe? Are you still shaking?"

"Just now and then."

"Does your temperature usually run low?"

"I don't think so. But I almost never take it."

"How about blood pressure?" she asked.

"That seemed a little high," he said.

"That's not too surprising, but we'll keep checking that temp over the next three hours to make sure it doesn't go any lower. In the meantime, stay in your berth and stay warm."

"I'll keep the hot tea coming," George said. "It's more metabolic than coffee or other hot beverages."

"Thanks, George," Callum said.

"I'm going to get some tea to Scott up in the bow." George headed for the ladder.

Brie collected the equipment and was about to leave, but then she turned back to Callum. "What started the row with Jarvis?" she asked. "Did you say something to set him off?"

Callum looked sheepish. "Jarvis came up to me after he rinsed off his dishes in the bucket. Said from here on out, I'd better stay totally out of his life. I said I knew he'd killed Peter, and I was going to prove it. He started to come at me, and I shoved him back. That's when he screamed he was going to kill me and charged at me. You saw the rest."

"I'm going to give you some advice, Joe," Brie said. "In fact, stronger than advice. Consider it an order. You are not to engage Jarvis or anyone else for the rest of this voyage. And there will be no more accusations. Is that clear?"

"Crystal," he said. "Now, I think I'd like to lie down."

Brie and George left the cabin and headed up on deck. "Thanks, George," Brie said at the top of the ladder. "I'm gonna stow this stuff and grab my recorder from John's cabin. I'll be interviewing Boardman down in the galley. Don't want to be overheard by Jarvis."

"Do you want me to vacate the area?"

"Not necessary, George. Just try to keep a low profile."

"I'll be working at the back of the galley, out of earshot if you sit at the far end of the table."

"That's what I'll do." She turned and headed aft, thinking about the incident that had unfolded. Callum knew Lyle Jarvis was a ticking bomb, so why would he have goaded him like that? Was Joe Callum trying to make Jarvis look guilty? There was only one reason he'd do that. *Maybe he's not the "regular Joe" he pretends to be*, she thought.

When she reached the helm, she told John that Callum seemed okay, but she or George would check his temperature over the next couple of hours to be sure he wasn't becoming hypothermic.

"George gave him hot broth and tea, and he's resting in his berth with extra blankets."

"Thanks, Brie."

"I'm going to grab my recorder and start the Boardman interview."

John nodded, and she headed below and into his cabin, put the blood pressure cuff back in the first aid kit, retrieved her small recorder from the drawer of his chart table, and left the cabin. She walked across the passageway and knocked on Rusty Boardman's cabin door, just to be sure he'd gone forward to the galley as directed. No one answered her knock, so she headed up the ladder and moved along the starboard deck.

The *Maine Wind* was clipping along on a fast reach, her sails drawing at peak efficiency, the seas shooshing past her hull, slipping astern, leaving a white trail of foam that faded off into the distance, soon to vanish forever. Man leaves no mark upon the sea. Thousands of years, tens of thousands of crossings. The sea cares not, marks none of it, swallows those who perish there, and rolls on untouched, unmoved. *Why do we love her so?* Brie wondered. *Is it the beauty? Or do we only truly love what we cannot conquer? Is it only there we can find peace?*

She paused at the rail, feet spread wide—the sailor's stance —and turned to face the sea. There had been few moments on this cruise to commune with her. She emptied her mind, listened, breathed, felt the vibration of the lifeline in her hands, smelled the salt on the wind. She locked it all in her heart and then turned from the rail. Her mind felt clear—ready for the next round of interviews.

Chapter 23

When Brie reached the galley companionway, she met George coming up the ladder, carrying a board and a large bowl filled with sweet potatoes.

"What's up, George?" she asked, stepping out of his way.

"I'm headed back aft to peel and dice these potatoes and visit with the captain a bit. It's best if you have the galley to yourself to finish up the interviews."

"I appreciate that, George, but you need to have the run of your galley."

"Quite all right, Brie. These are odd circumstances. We need to accommodate one another."

"Well, truth be told, the interviews will go better if I have these guys all to myself. So thanks."

"No problem. And I get a little above-deck time out in the fresh air."

Brie continued down the ladder. Rusty Boardman sat at the far end of the galley on the bench behind the table. A brass hurricane lamp, hung from the side of the mast trunk, swung pendulum-like, casting its thin light around the galley. Boardman was reading a magazine by the lantern light, seemingly unfazed by the motion of the ship.

Brie sat on the opposite bench behind the table and slid two-thirds of the way in to where the table narrowed into the bow. She wanted to be close enough to look Boardman in the eye and read any tells he might display.

"How's Callum doing?" he asked.

"Okay, I think. George got some hot liquids into him. He's resting in his cabin. We'll keep an eye on him."

Boardman nodded but had nothing else to say. Whatever he was thinking about Lyle Jarvis and the whole donnybrook, he kept it to himself, and Brie decided to hold off discussing it any more right now. She'd wait to see what, if anything, came up in the interview about Jarvis.

"We'll get started, now, if that's all right."

He nodded, closed his magazine, and slid to his right so he was opposite her. She sensed he wanted to look her in the eye as well, and it occurred to her that since he had come aboard, she'd had virtually no face-to-face commerce with him. And while he had joined in the poker games with the other men, he seemed wary of too much contact with any of them either, keeping himself apart from the group, staying busy with his camera. Of everyone in the group, he had spent the most time up on deck and seemed comfortable out in the elements.

It was an icebreaker, so Brie said, "I've noticed you like being topside."

His eyes met hers. They were an unusually deep shade of blue. "I guess I like a big view."

It wasn't a flippant remark. Rather, it was said in a sincere way. She wasn't sure what she'd expected from him—maybe a monosyllabic grunt. She had thought he might be distant, un-engaged, but there was something magnetic about him, and it surprised her.

She took her recorder and small notebook out of her jacket pocket, set them on the table, and removed her ball cap and set it aside. She'd worked her hair into a quick French braid early that morning, and now numerous strands were making a break for it. She tucked them behind her ears and said, "I'll be recording our interview as I have all the others. We'll start with some basic information. Could you state your name, age, and date of birth for the record?"

Boardman leaned forward slightly. "Benjamin R. Boardman. Age 47. Born August twenty-eighth, nineteen sixty-nine."

Brie nodded. "So, where's the 'Rusty' come from? That your middle name?"

He smiled an easy smile. "No, middle name's Ray. But as a kid, I had this dark red hair. Pretty much the color of rust. My parents started calling me Rusty. When I got older, I realized it could have been Benji. Dodged a bullet there." He smiled again, and a dimple appeared below his right check. "Hair went to brown at adolescence, but the name stuck."

Brie smiled and flipped open her notebook, thinking, *totally not what I expected.* The ship creaked as it liked to do up here in the bow, and Boardman leaned back against the hull.

"I've been told you worked for Peter Bendorff," she said.

"That's right."

"For how long?"

"Two and a half years."

Brie made a note of that. "And before that?"

"Career military. Twenty-six years."

"I'm not surprised. I got that vibe from you when you first came aboard."

"You would, being a cop."

"What branch of the military?" Brie asked.

"Army. Special Forces. Did two combat tours."

Brie noticed Boardman's demeanor change, become more austere, more remote, as he spoke of his military service. He straightened up, almost like he was sitting at attention, and his aspect became guarded, like the barring of a fortress. *This guy was a soldier to the bone,* Brie thought. *He may be retired, but in his deepest self he will always be a soldier, just like I will always be a cop.*

Just then a strong gust whistled through the rigging. Boardman turned his head toward the companionway, and the light fell on the long white scar that ran from beneath his ear down the left side of his neck almost to his collarbone.

Undoubtedly a remnant of some very dark day on the battle-field. She decided not to ask him about it.

"What was your specialty?"

"Demolitions." Boardman looked back at her. "When I re-upped, I requested a change of MOS. Trained in cyber security. Eventually ended up stateside at the Pentagon my last five years."

"Impressive," Brie said. She sat back and studied him for a moment, fascinated by the two opposing natures that appeared to symbiotically exist in him. *He's complex*, she thought.

"In his interview, Lyle Jarvis said that you are in charge of cyber security at Bendorff Enterprises."

"That's right. Also physical security at Bendorff headquarters, and general building security for all the other properties and businesses owned by Bendorff Enterprises."

"So, metaphorically, you hold the keys to the kingdom," Brie said.

"Metaphorically and actually," Boardman said. "I'm the only one other than Peter who had access to all the properties."

"And that includes Callum, even though I've been told he was Peter's right-hand man."

"That's right. I told Pete it was best that way."

Brie nodded. It sounded exactly like what the security guy should say. She studied him for a moment. As far as who was most physically capable of committing the murder, Boardman topped the list. But with the exception of Leo, all the others were physically capable of the crime as well. It all boiled down to motive. No one but a psychopath murders without a motive.

Brie put on her best cop face and continued. "Mr. Board-man, did you go forward at all in the middle of the night last night?"

He paused, coolly assessing her. "I went forward to use the head. Apparently there was a problem with the one aft.

Someone had put a sign on the door to use the one in the amidships compartment."

"And what time was that?"

"Around four a.m., I think."

"And how long were you up there?"

"Five, ten minutes. Not long."

"Did you see anyone coming or going or hear anything unusual?"

"If I had, I would have checked it out."

Brie nodded.

And then as an aside, Boardman added, "I heard snoring coming from Leo's cabin, so I know he was asleep."

"All right." She made a note in her notebook and then looked him straight in the eye. "Did you intentionally disable the head aft?" She watched him carefully for tells, but if there were any, he had locked them behind an impenetrable exterior.

"No, I did not."

He held her gaze, never once blinking, but she was picking up some kind of emotion—maybe anger at being questioned — behind his highly trained military comportment. She decided to move on.

"Let's get back to Peter Bendorff. How did you end up working for Bendorff Enterprises?"

"After I mustered out, I came back home—Portland is home —and settled back into civilian life. It's an adjustment when you've spent your whole adult life in the military." He smiled and the dimple appeared. "I guess you could say I was married to it."

"The military?"

He nodded. "The whole way of life. The challenges. The adventure. The travel. It's intoxicating in a way—a lot like a love affair." He paused and looked at Brie, and she felt that magnetic pull again. It was the oddest thing, but he was actually quite charming.

"I know what you mean," she said. "Until the past year, I was pretty much married to my career as a cop."

"I've never been a cop, but I imagine it's a lot like the military. Your job is to protect and serve. If you take it seriously—do it right—that job can consume you, heart and soul."

Brie nodded. No words were necessary. They both got it.

"So back to Bendorff Enterprises and how you ended up there?"

"Long story short, I had a friend from high school who went on to become a journalist—works at the Portland *Press Herald*. He wanted to do a story on me for the paper. You know, small town boy makes good."

"Comes home a decorated soldier with a distinguished service record."

Boardman shrugged. "Something like that, I guess."

Brie guessed the same part of him that shied away from the limelight was just as uncomfortable with praise of his military record. She gave him points for that. He fit the profile for the personality type the military seeks out for Special Forces. As a group, they are *not* about bravado.

Boardman was talking again. "Anyway, Peter Bendorff read that article. He was in the process of looking for security personnel to hire. He tracked me down and offered me a job as head of security."

"Just you?" Brie asked.

"He was willing to hire more men if necessary. I thought I could handle the job myself, but I told him once I had gotten the logistics in place, I'd assess the situation again."

Brie noted the military speak that was second nature to him.

"I've been told that Peter Bendorff acquired companies that were in trouble. Were you ever part of any of that? For example, acquisition of information on any of those companies?"

"Are you asking if I hacked those companies to get information?"

"It would have been within your skill set."

"Yes, it would have, but I never did any of that." He studied her for a moment. "Doesn't mean it didn't go on, though."

"Explain, please," Brie said.

Boardman looked uncomfortable, and she guessed what he was about to tell her fell under the heading of ratting out a co-worker.

"Normally, I wouldn't reveal any of this, but Pete's dead and someone's responsible, and who knows what or whom it's all tied to?" He paused and straightened up, as if girding himself for battle. "There was hacking going on, and Lyle Jarvis was the guy who carried it out, no doubt under Peter's orders. Bendorff ran him like the proverbial dog, but I also think Jarvis liked the work. I think it made him feel important."

"Jarvis told me he was the IT guy at the company. That he fixed everyone's computers when they went on the fritz and that he hated it."

Boardman smiled. "You're a cop. He wouldn't have admitted carrying on an illegal activity to a cop."

"Okay . . ." Brie said.

"Listen," Boardman said. "That kid is smart as a whip. He's a computer whiz. I was trained to do what I do. He's a natural."

"Interesting," Brie said.

"What he needs, probably what he's always needed, is discipline."

She couldn't argue with that. Discipline builds character, and Jarvis sure could have used some of that. "I've been told he hated Bendorff because Bendorff kept such a tight rein on him."

"More like a stranglehold, I'd say."

Interesting choice of words, Brie thought, picturing the body —the plastic bag over the head and the rope around the neck.

"He hated Bendorff's tough love. He'd never had to deal with anything like that. But you know, deep down, I think he knew well and good that he'd have been lost without his uncle."

"So you don't think he could have committed the murder."

"Maybe not in his right mind. But believe me, I know about explosives, and that kid is nitro. Look at what just happened up on deck. He's not one you want to cross."

Brie sat thinking for a moment. Jarvis was an enigma. He was also a lodestone—his outrageous behavior drawing all the attention and suspicion to him like a magnetic force. If he hadn't killed Bendorff, he certainly had created the perfect cover for one of the others to fly under the radar. On the other hand, sometimes things are exactly as they appear to be. That's why most murders are committed by a spouse or someone very close to the victim.

"Getting back to Jarvis' job at the company. You say Peter Bendorff tasked him with hacking into companies he thought might be in trouble. And by the way, you're right—that is illegal. The troubling question is this: if Bendorff was trying to keep his nephew on the straight and narrow, why would he do that? If the FBI got wind of the activity and came sniffing around, Jarvis would take the fall."

Boardman shrugged, but she could see it bothered him. "If that were the case, it would be pretty cold." He grew silent, and in that silence, all the sounds of the ship seemed exaggerated. The timbers creaked under the pressure of the seas, and the roar of the wind in the canvas, always muffled below decks, grew more audible.

"Here's what I think," Boardman said. "Like a lot of people who blur the lines between legal and illegal activities, I think Peter Bendorff had a way of hiding from the truth of what he was doing."

"So, denial," Brie said.

"Or some brand of magical thinking. Either he'd found a way to justify his actions in his mind or to hide from the potential consequences—denial, as you say."

"Sounds a bit like you're defending his actions." Brie said.

"Maybe just trying to understand them."

"Tell me this," Brie said. "If you do bad things, does that make you a bad man?"

Boardman looked almost surprised before locking that expression in the military-grade vault where he stored his emotions. His eyes morphed to an even deeper shade of blue, like the sea ahead of a storm.

"That's a question for the philosophers. I'm just a soldier."

He'd taken refuge in his military persona. She decided it was time to move on.

"So, since you're the security guy at Bendorff Enterprises, based on everything we've discussed, did you ever think Peter Bendorff was in danger or afraid of anyone? Could that be why he decided to disappear and start a new life? Could he have been in any kind of trouble?"

"Are you asking if someone might have hired one of these guys to kill him?"

"It's not beyond the realm of possibility," Brie said. "Money is a great motivator."

Boardman sat stony-faced. "Peter certainly was in a position to make enemies. If someone really wanted him dead, that person would not want him to escape into another life, scot-free."

Brie considered the fact that these five men, with the possible exception of Lyle Jarvis, were probably the closest thing Bendorff had to a group of friends. But sadly, friends can sometimes be bought—and sold, for that matter. Clearly, one of them had committed the murder, had a motive that drove him to act. She didn't dismiss the possibility of gun-for-hire, and Leo, with his Mafia background, came momentarily to mind.

But, based on her cop experience, if you are going to hire someone to off someone, you're either going to hire a professional hit man or look for a person who has a reason to want that individual dead. Detective work is circular—it all comes back around to motive.

She checked her watch. She had started the interview right around two o'clock. It was now two thirty. The interviews were getting longer—the natural progression of things as the investigation drew out more facts.

"Do you know anything about where Joe Callum worked before coming to Bendorff Enterprises?"

"No, I don't. He was already at the company when I came on board. Why?"

"Just trying to follow up on his former employer." She didn't tell him Callum had given her false information, but she could see by his expression that he was reading between the lines.

"Pete said one time that he'd worked for a bio-tech company."

Brie nodded and moved on. "What do you know about Alexander Smith?"

Boardman shrugged. "Not much. He's some kind of academic. Personal friend of Pete's—nothing to do with the company." He turned his head and looked toward the companionway, and the lightning bolt scar seemed to pulse like a living thing. "There's something about the guy, though." He slowly turned his head and looked back at Brie. "Something below the surface. He's hiding something."

He said it with a kind of certitude that made Brie a believer. But with the possible exception of Boardman himself, that described everyone she had interviewed so far. And more troubling was the fact that she believed Peter Bendorff had had a very specific and very intentional reason for bringing each of these men into his inner circle.

"So did you ever check out Smith in any way?" she asked him.

"Had no reason to. I did what Pete requested, and that kind of background check usually involved a potential employee."

"Usually, but not always? Can you tell me who he had you check out that wasn't with the company?"

"Not offhand, but it happened occasionally." He looked away, and Brie had the sense that he was being evasive. She tried to press him on the issue but got stonewalled. It was time to move on to the last suspect: Alexander Smith, author and former professor. She closed her notebook and turned off the recorder. "That will be all, Mr. Boardman. You can return to your cabin."

He slid out from behind the table and headed up the ladder, leaving Brie to her thoughts. Leo had said that Bendorff was a genius at learning things about people and knowing how to use that knowledge. Jarvis, Callum, and Leo had all hidden damning information about themselves from her. She didn't know yet what Callum was hiding, but obviously it had to do with his former place of employment. Had Bendorff held something over the other two as well? She planned to have Dent Fenton look up Boardman's military record. Maybe Boardman was in the same boat with the others—*no pun intended*.

She stood up and stretched her arms above her head and leaned from left to right, trying to get the blood flowing. She got a cup of coffee for John and headed up the ladder to talk to him. She paused on deck, gripped the lifeline, felt the sea surging past the hull. The sun had temporarily broken through the clouds, and she stood with her face turned towards it, soaking in its diminished warmth here in the northern latitudes in mid-October. Far off on the eastern horizon, trouble was brewing; dark thunderheads were just becoming visible, boiling up as if spit forth from the sea. She pulled out her phone and called the lieutenant. Dent Fenton answered and asked her for an update.

"I've got one more interview to go. Could you check a military record on one Benjamin Ray Boardman?" She flipped open her notebook and gave him the birth date.

"Anything else?"

Brie considered the question for a couple moments. "I think you should get a warrant for all of the phone records for the five suspects onboard the ship, in case we need to dig into them."

"Already done. We should have access to them later in the day."

"Thanks, Dent. I'll call you back after I finish this last interview. I need to know what you learned from Bendorff's wife."

"I'll see what I can find out about Boardman's time in the military."

"Roger that." They signed off, and she walked aft with the coffee for John.

Chapter 24

When Brie got to the helm, George and John were engrossed in conversation. She handed the coffee to John.

"Do I have time to go below and put the meat in the stove before your next interview?" George asked, leaning in so Brie could hear over the wind in the canvas.

"By all means," Brie said. "What's on the menu?"

"I've got a large beef roast I thought I'd cook since we may have a few extras on hand, what with the guys from the Maine State Police coming aboard at Boothbay and Ed Browning joining the crew for the rest of the trip. I want to be sure there's plenty of food in case any of them wants some dinner."

"That's thoughtful of you, George," the captain said.

George headed forward, and Brie asked John for an update on their progress.

"We've made up the time we lost with our man overboard drill."

Brie smiled at that. "At least we didn't have to call the Coast Guard again to report someone lost at sea."

"Thank God for that," John said. "The Coasties will start thinking there's a curse on this ship."

"Well, the season's almost over. Next year we can start fresh."

John seemed to brighten up at the reference to next year and her use of "we." They stood together for a moment, listening to the sound of *Maine Wind* slicing through the seas.

"The wind's picked up some more," John said. "If it stays steady, we should make harbor ahead of schedule."

"That's good." She nodded toward the eastern horizon. "Something brewing there."

John looked over his right shoulder. "Squall line. We should outrun it." He paused. "You can feel the tension aboard. No way to outrun that."

"I know." She sensed there was more he wanted to say but that he was holding back. At that moment the wind huffed up and the rigging creaked.

"Any progress?" he asked finally.

"There are motives here. And no shortage of blighted pasts. It makes for good camouflage. I think our killer knows that and is using it to his advantage. We need to be watchful of these guys once we anchor."

"You think the killer might try to jump ship?"

"After what happened during lunch, I think anything is possible. We need to keep our guard up."

John looked at her, and she saw the concern in his eyes. "What can you do?" he asked.

"Work the case, John. Trust the process and work the case. Every crime leaves a trail of evidence. That trail often starts long before the crime is committed. My gut tells me that's the case here. I need to keep digging." She gave his shoulder a squeeze and headed below to get Alexander Smith. His cabin was on the port side of the ship just forward of John's.

She knocked on his cabin door, and within seconds he opened it. "Could you come forward to the galley, Alex? I need to interview you."

"Sure, I'll get my shoes on and be right there."

Brie headed back up the ladder and made her way along the pitch of the windward deck, the wind strong on her right side. She descended the ladder and found George next to the stove, tidying up the area.

"Everything's shipshape down here," he said. "I think I'll hit my berth for a few winks while you finish your questioning." He paused suddenly and became quite serious. "Is everything okay, Brie?"

She was used to carrying the concerns of those on the periphery of her investigations, and she knew what a helpless feeling it could be for them. She also knew that the crew was like a family, and that they wanted to help.

"Everything's okay, George. Go grab a nap. I should be done in a half hour or so."

He nodded and headed for his berth, and within a few seconds Smith descended the ladder. Brie saw the baggy wool socks and Birkenstocks first, followed by cargo khakis. At the bottom of the ladder, Smith turned and pulled the watch cap off his head. His wire-rim glasses were speckled from the salt spray, and he wore a heavy wool cowl-neck sweater. Brie noted his hands were the color of icebergs.

"Would you like a cup of coffee?" she asked.

He looked surprised at the offer. "That would be lovely and most welcome."

Brie gestured toward the pot that held the coffee, and Smith poured himself a mug.

"Please sit down, Mr. Smith, and we'll get started. I'll be recording our interview."

She slid onto the starboard-side bench, and Alex sat across from her as Boardman had. He took off his glasses and started polishing them with the bottom of his sweater. Brie turned on the recorder and asked him to state his full name and date of birth for the record.

"Alexander Barrett Hayes Smith. February third, nineteen fifty-nine." He wrapped his hands around the mug and took a sip of the hot coffee. "My family was into last names."

"I can see that," Brie said. *Maine Wind* was rolling a little now, which told Brie they'd come to a new heading with the wind on their starboard quarter. She did the math on his birth date and determined that he was fifty-seven.

"This morning when I asked which of you was closest to Peter Bendorff, you raised your hand. I've learned from interviewing the others that you don't work for Bendorff Enterprises. So how did you meet Peter Bendorff, and how long have you known him?"

"I've known him for about seven years. I told you I'm a former history professor. Now retired."

"Yes, I remember," Brie said. "You wrote a book."

"Yes. But back to Peter. I used to teach some classes at a community college in Portland. Just moonlighting, you understand." He said it like maybe he considered himself too good for such a position. "Anyway, that's where I met Peter. He took several of my classes."

"So where was your main job?"

"I was a professor of history at Nathaniel Bowditch College in Brunswick."

"A very good school," Brie said.

"Yes. We get a lot of top-notch students who don't quite make the cut at the Ivys." He brushed something imaginary off his sweater and regarded Brie. His look said, *You wouldn't make the cut.*

Brie knew jolly well she would. "So I suppose, to you, teaching at the community college felt a bit like slumming."

Smith shrugged. "One does what one must."

"So you needed the money?"

He shrugged again but looked distinctly uncomfortable.

Brie pressed on. "I'd think a top-notch school like Bowditch would pay a very good salary."

"I was going through a divorce. I needed extra money." His eyes shifted up and to the left, and Brie knew there was more to the story than that. Then he was talking again. "Edward said I shouldn't do it—that I'd burn out."

"Who's Edward?" Brie asked.

Smith looked momentarily surprised—in fact, almost startled. "Just a colleague—no one important."

But, for whatever reason, Brie got the feeling it *was* important, and Rusty Boardman's words came back to her. "There's something about that guy . . . He's hiding something." She made a note in her notebook.

Smith must have picked up the vibe, because he suddenly plunged headlong into a narrative about Peter Bendorff and his deepest longings. "I was closer to Peter than any of these other guys were. I can tell you that. What Peter really wanted but never got was an education. He'd made money—plenty of it—but he knew he lacked something that set him apart from a lot of people in his economic class."

"And that was education?"

"Exactly."

"Leo told me he loved theater—that he wanted to act."

"That's right. The first class he took from me was history of theater. Peter used to hang around after class and talk to me. Eventually we started going out for a drink or dinner. Pete always insisted on picking up the tab, which was nice. I was part of a community theater group in Bath. I introduced him to the group, and we even found some minor roles for him in the plays. When he found out about my divorce, he got me a really good attorney. I would have lost my shirt otherwise. So as you can see, we were the best of friends. I'd have no reason to ever hurt him. I was sad that he was planning to leave the country—disappear."

"So why was he?" Brie asked. She'd gotten some opinions from the others, but one more couldn't hurt.

"I got the sense some of what he was doing with Bendorff Enterprises wasn't strictly legal."

"So he leaves the others at the company to take the fall?"

"I don't think they could be blamed for decisions that were his alone."

Brie had to wonder about Jarvis, though. Why would the uncle who had protected him leave him holding the bag, so to speak? Bendorff must have known he'd be arrested for hacking if there was ever an investigation. Maybe he'd finally realized that Lyle Jarvis was a hopeless cause, that he would always find a way to get into trouble. She thought about him throwing Callum overboard. Maybe it was like Rusty Boardman had said—that Bendorff was just tired of it all.

The whole scenario wasn't too hard for Brie to believe. After all, she'd run away in a sense. Yes, it was a leave, and yes, she had always planned to go home once she got her head straight, but she certainly knew what desperation felt like.

She returned her focus to Smith. "You say you were his best friend."

"I think I probably was," Smith said.

He seemed completely calm when he said it, and Brie decided he was telling the truth.

"And he was your best friend?"

"Of course," he snapped. But he became anxious, and Brie could hear his foot tapping beneath the table, so she suspected it wasn't true. She wondered what Bendorff had learned about the professor, because a pattern was developing—one she found fascinating. Peter Bendorff kept people close not through the bonds of friendship alone, but because he had learned things about them he could use against them. She figured he had held some or maybe all of these men captive in this way. If he knew something damning about each of them, that would have given him considerable power over their fates. It also could have given some of them compelling reasons to want him dead.

She knew for certain Jarvis fell into this category, and she suspected Callum did too, and maybe Smith here. Leo had a sketchy past, but he'd done time, so it was all a matter of public record. What was more, he wasn't physically capable of committing the murder. And Boardman—he seemed like an outlier. Bendorff needed a topnotch cyber security guy, and Boardman fit the bill with his military past. She'd see what Dent turned up in the military records, but somehow Boardman stood apart from the others, both literally and figuratively.

There was more information she hoped to obtain from the professor, so she pressed on with the interview.

She looked him in the eye. "Did you tamper with the aft head in any way last night?"

Smith became very still and gave her a penetrating look. "No, I did not. But when I got up to use the head in the wee hours, there was a sign there that said to use the forward head. So I did."

"And what time was that?"

"About four twenty."

"And did you see or hear anyone moving about in the amidships compartment or the aft compartment?"

Smith thought for a moment. "It sounded like Leo was moving around in his cabin. I figured he'd just gotten up to relieve himself and was settling back in."

Brie made a note in her notebook. "But you didn't see or hear anyone else?"

"Just the captain up on deck."

"Getting back to Peter Bendorff. Did he ever talk about life insurance?"

"Funny you should ask about that. Peter had a lot of weird superstitions. He told me once he'd never buy life insurance. He thought it was asking for trouble—you know, gambling with your own life. As he explained it, you're gambling that you are going to die and they, the company, are gambling that you're not."

"Wasn't he worried about his family?"

"He said he had other ways of providing for them."

"Did you know his wife?"

"I only met her once, briefly. Pete didn't mix his family and friends. For whatever reason, he kept them quite separate."

That actually made sense to Brie, especially if Bendorff was holding something over each of those so-called friends. She decided to move on.

"Leo Dombello said he moved to Portland two and a half years ago. He also told me he met Peter in a theater group. Apparently Leo liked to tread the boards, too. That seems to be the thread that tied the three of you together, so I assume it's this same theater group you've been describing."

Smith seemed to grow anxious. *He certainly is easy to read,* Brie thought. *Push a button, get an immediate response.* The topic of Leo seemed to be a button, so she decided to keep going. But suddenly Smith was talking again, unprompted.

"Good old Leo. Life of the party. Sure knows how to insert himself into any situation."

"Meaning?"

Smith sighed. "You're right. A couple years ago Leo joined the theater group in Bath. I thought it was odd, being so far from Portland and all."

Brie knew the drive from Portland to Bath took about forty minutes, which didn't seem long to her. But then she hailed from a large metropolis where one could easily spend forty minutes driving from one end of the city to the other, and that was without traffic.

"You know Leo lived in Boston, where it can take forty minutes to get from one freeway exit to the next."

"Okay, maybe you're right. I guess I have a different perspective. I just thought it was odd. Anyway, right from the get go, he was befriending Pete. Hanging around, telling him stories. He made a big show of entertaining Pete, and Pete just seemed to lap it up."

"Leo is larger than life, somehow," Brie said. "Maybe that's how he compensates for his small stature. He's a character."

Smith shrugged. "Maybe that's what charmed Pete. Maybe Leo made life seem more interesting—like some zany farce he'd stumbled into."

Brie thought Smith sounded almost jealous. Maybe he had felt threatened. After all, Peter Bendorff had been his meal ticket in more ways than one. "Sounds like you weren't thrilled about their friendship."

Smith shrugged. "I don't know. It just seemed like he was after something."

"Maybe that was a quality Bendorff could resonate with," Brie said.

Smith opened his mouth in apparent surprise, but nothing came out. He closed it again.

Does he really think I've learned nothing about Bendorff? she thought to herself. She found it ironic that it was Leo who had given her the most revealing piece of information about the victim—namely, that he was a master at learning things about people. So far that was turning out to be true and had provided a framework of potential motives in the murder. A sudden gust rolled the ship to port, rattling the dishes behind the rails and clanging the pots together that hung above the woodstove. She studied Smith. Her original assessment of him still rang true. Slightly arrogant; definitely insecure. Was he hiding something, as Rusty Boardman had suggested? Had Peter Bendorff found out what that something was and somehow used it against Smith, or if nothing else, used it to buy his loyalty? Brie knew what her next move was.

It was time to end the interview, but first she circled back to his comment about Leo. "You said it seemed like Leo was after something when he met Peter."

Smith shrugged. "Seemed like it."

"What do you think he was after?"

"I have no idea. It was just a feeling."

"Maybe he was looking for a friend. He'd just moved to Maine from Boston."

"Maybe," Smith said with a nonchalant shrug. He fidgeted on the bench like the interview was wearing thin.

Brie regarded him for a moment, which made him more anxious. "That's all for now, Mr. Smith. You can return to your cabin."

He slid out from behind the table, crossed the galley, and climbed the ladder. Brie sat thinking about the interview and looked back through the notes she had made. She decided she had to call the college where Smith had taught and see if she could gather some information about his time there.

She pulled out her phone. There were no bars, but maybe up on deck. She slid out from behind the table and climbed the ladder, nearly colliding with George at the top.

"Are you done, Brie?"

"All done. I'm going to work on my reports in the captain's cabin. The galley is all yours."

George nodded and headed down the companionway. Brie walked forward toward the bow and checked her phone. She had bars. She looked up the number for the administrative office at Bowditch College and punched it in. When a woman answered, Brie identified herself and asked who the chair of the history department was.

"That would be Dr. Whitmore," the woman said.

"Can you tell me if he is on campus today?" Brie asked.

"Let me check his schedule, Detective." A little key tapping followed, and then she was back. "He's in class until five thirty, and then it shows he will be in his campus office until six thirty."

"Does he have any meetings scheduled during that time?" Brie asked.

"Not at this time."

"I need to speak to Dr. Whitmore about a case I'm working on. Could you put me on his schedule at six o'clock? The meeting shouldn't take more than a half hour."

"I'm typing you into his schedule now, Detective. I'll also leave him a text message giving him a heads up about the meeting."

"Thank you, Ms. . . . ."

"It's Mrs. Robbins."

"Thank you for your help, Mrs. Robbins."

"Dr. Whitmore's office is in the humanities building—Cabot Hall. There's a campus map on our website."

"I'll find it. Thank you again." Brie ended the call.

She knew the drive from Boothbay Harbor to Brunswick would take forty to forty-five minutes. John had said they were ahead of schedule. If they anchored between four thirty and five o'clock, she'd have enough time to turn the crime scene over to the Evidence Response Team and still get ashore and up to the college in time for the meeting. She put her phone in her pocket and headed below to get her laptop.

*   *   *

Alexander Smith lay in his berth, glaring at the underside of the bunk above him. The phrase *Freudian slip* kept playing through his mind. How had he let Edward's name enter the discussion—the questioning? He was appalled at himself and angry. That mistake put Detective Beaumont too close to the truth of his life. Dangerously close. He wondered if there was a way to get off the ship. He desperately wanted to escape. That would be the wrong move, though. He knew that. That would make him look guilty for sure.

He took a couple of deep breaths, trying to calm himself. *If I run now, they will believe I did it, and they will arrest me.* He guessed it was just a matter of time now before the rest of it came out, before his life was ruined. He felt like he had nothing more to live for.

He crawled out of his berth and, balancing on the listing cabin sole, dug a bottle of sleeping pills out of his dopp kit. He stood looking at them, weighing them in his hand. Finally, he shoved them back into the dopp kit and climbed back into his berth. He turned over on his side and curled into a fetal position. He let the tears flow, let them carry him down, down into the depths of self-pity.

Chapter 25

Below decks, Brie made her way through the galley, where George was in full battle mode, preparing to attack a huge pile of vegetables. There were carrots, parsnips, rutabagas, beets, and sweet potatoes. George liked to roast vegetables in the woodstove, and she guessed that was part of his strategy for taming the hungry hordes tonight.

She slipped back to her berth behind the galley and located her laptop in the bottom of her sea bag. It was nothing fancy—Maine State Police issue, given to her when she had been deputized and worked the case in Tucker Harbor in August. She never used it except when she was on a case. In her mind, laptops and historic schooners were two things that should never be allowed to get together. So her phone and the computer stayed at the bottom of her sea bag unless she was tasked with using them.

She zipped up her bag, stowed it, and headed topside and made her way along the starboard deck. The wind had picked up again, and *Maine Wind* drove forward at what felt like eight to eight and a half knots.

As she approached the helm, she thought John looked amazingly alert, considering he hadn't slept the night before. She stopped next to him and told him she had finished the interviews.

"Do you want me to spell you at the helm?" she asked.

"We're only an hour out, Brie. I'm okay. Anyway, I need to be at the helm as we make the approach to Boothbay."

Brie nodded. "In that case, mind if I use your cabin to type up my reports and make some notes?"

"By all means," John said.

"Shout out when you need me on deck for lowering sail."

"Will do."

Brie headed down the aft companionway, stepped into the captain's cabin, and shut the door. She set her laptop, notebook, and recorder on the chart table. It was warmer below decks, and she took off her foul weather jacket. She still had two layers underneath—a silk long-sleeved thermal shirt and her heavy gray wool sweater.

She sat down in the chair in front of the chart table. It was bolted to the cabin sole so it couldn't go flying around when the seas got wild. The wood chair rocked on its base, and Brie leaned back and stared up at the overhead, trying to clear her mind. Trying to think anew about the case, now that she'd finished the interviews. She ticked off the suspects in her mind.

Leo Dombello. Criminal past but no apparent motive to kill Bendorff. Also physically incapable of committing the murder.

Rusty Boardman. No apparent motive. Solid military background. Bendorff needed a good cyber security guy. Boardman was it. An outlier in a group where everyone seemed to be hiding something.

Alexander Smith. Claimed to be Bendorff's closest friend. Was *he* hiding something? Boardman thought so. She'd see if her visit to the college shook loose any skeletons. If he *was* hiding something, had Bendorff learned about it and used it to control him in some way? Did that create a motive for Smith?

Joe Callum. Where had he worked before? Why had he lied about it? What was *he* hiding? Jarvis had said he cooked the books for Bendorff. If so, why? How might that relate to his previous job? Had Bendorff used something in Callum's past to manipulate him?

And finally, Lyle Jarvis. Peter Bendorff's nephew and most likely fit for the title of Perpetrator. Under Peter Bendorff's heel since he was eighteen, and probably long before that. Involved in a heinous crime—maybe got away with murder. Would he again? Not if Brie could help it.

She plugged her laptop into the ship's auxiliary power, turned it on, and brought up a Word document. She planned to type her reports into the Word doc and transfer them to the Maine State Police site later on tonight, after they reached Boothbay Harbor. She flipped open her notebook to the first interview, turned on her digital recorder, and started typing in the pertinent information from the interview with Joe Callum. She hadn't gotten far when her phone rang. She picked it up from the chart table and checked to see who was calling. Jack LeBeau. *What timing*, she thought.

"Hello, Jack. Good timing."

"Why's that?" he asked.

"Well, I just finished the interviews and am writing up reports. Any luck on the Joe Callum inquiry?"

"As a matter of fact, yes. I located the company where Joseph Callum previously worked. You were right in your guess. It was a med tech company—Hopkins Lilliwell in Boston. Callum worked in the accounting department there for almost eight years. He left the company seven years ago. But here's the thing. A few months after Callum left the company, there was a major shakeup. An employee in the accounting department was arrested for embezzling funds—over two hundred thousand dollars—from the company accounts. Primarily the travel and expense accounts. The man who was arrested—one Jeffrey McCormick—swore he hadn't stolen the money, even though the transactions were performed on his computer. McCormick was going through a divorce at the time, and that fact worked heavily against him."

"What did the money trail show?" Brie asked.

"It showed the money was moved through two shell corporations into an offshore account with McCormick's name on it. By the time they tracked down the account, the funds had been withdrawn and the account closed. The money was never recovered, and McCormick went to prison, disclaiming the charges—saying that Joseph Callum was behind the theft. And while they investigated Callum aggressively, they were never able to connect him to any part of it."

"Wow." Brie was thinking how easy it would have been for Peter Bendorff to have gotten wind of the crime. It would have been big news throughout New England. Not surprising that he had decided to track Callum down and hire him. Lyle Jarvis had said Callum "cooked the books" for his uncle. How Peter Bendorff had leveraged him into falsifying the accounts for Bendorff Enterprises was not too hard to imagine.

In Brie's mind, cunning and unscrupulous were the words that defined Peter Bendorff and some of his employees. She thought about him now, lying dead in the forward compartment. A study in futility. He would be well into the throes of rigor mortis. *No way to manipulate your way out of that*, she thought. And yet the people around him were loyal to him, cared about him. The whole thing reminded her a little of Stockholm Syndrome, where the captive forms an attachment to the captor. She wondered if somehow there was another side to Peter Bendorff she'd never get to see. She thought about the suicide note that had seemed almost tender. But then she remembered it was all a lie.

"You know, Jack, this case is such a maze of Machiavellian twists and turns, I feel like I might get trapped in it and never find my way out."

"Don't let that happen, Brie. We might need you down the line."

"It's like a confused sea that comes at you from all directions." She paused, rocked back in the chair, and felt the motion of the ship. It calmed her. "I have to admit, the detective in me is fascinated by the case, but the cop in me is alarmed." She was quiet for a moment. "Jack, you were in this business a long time."

"I was."

"I've been a cop for twelve years, but I'm still baffled by why people do the things they do. Why do they set themselves up for trouble?"

She heard a sigh at the other end of the phone. "I know how you feel, Brie. Not sure I've got the answers, but here's what I think, for what it's worth. First off, people believe or convince themselves that they won't get caught. And some don't. Those are the cold cases."

"But those folks spend the rest of their lives looking over their shoulders."

"That's right. And that has to be its own kind of punishment."

"What else, Jack? Enlighten me."

"Sounds like this case is getting to you, Brie."

"I'm just astounded at the ways people find to ruin their lives."

"Certain people want power, and they want money. It can bend them pretty bad. Sometimes those people gravitate together—feed off each other. Sounds like that may be what you're dealing with. You've probably got a clever metaphor."

"I've got nothing, Jack. Actually, I'm really angry at this bunch for getting on our ship and spoiling my last cruise with John."

"You need to come over and pet Angus. It's therapy, you know."

"I know. I miss that furry giant. You know, Jack, not to sound all cliché and hippy like my friend Ariel, but maybe the song is right. *All you need is love.*"

"Well, that and enough money to get by, but folks sure are mixed up about what brings happiness. And by the way, don't say 'last cruise.' We're all hoping you'll be back once you settle your affairs in Minnesota. Captain John needs you. You'll keep that boy on an even keel."

"He's hardly a boy."

"From my vantage point he is."

"Fair enough, Jack." She wondered what forty would look like to her when she reached the age of eighty-five. She wondered if John would be there with her.

"Let me know if there's anything else I can do."

"I will. Thanks."

"Steady as she goes, Brie."

"You too, Jack."

She hung up and noted that she felt better. Something about the old retired detective and his big Newfoundland dog had a steadying effect on her. She felt isolated here on the ship, surrounded by this case, but she reminded herself that she had support. Dent Fenton and Marty Dupuis were working their end, and as soon as they anchored, Doc Wolf and the Evidence Response Team would come aboard. Not that she had much hope for a forensic solution. Since the suspects had been in and out of each other's cabins a lot during the first three days of the voyage, the crime scene would be thoroughly contaminated.

She leaned back in the chair, thinking about what she had just learned; thinking about Callum and Jarvis, whom she considered the chief suspects in the murder. But something didn't compute. Bendorff may have used their checkered pasts against them to secure their loyalty and possibly coerce them into carrying out illegal activities for Bendorff Enterprises. But he had also helped them—put Lyle Jarvis on an even keel and given Callum a job when it was certain no one else would have—not with embezzling allegations floating around out there. And two hundred thousand dollars doesn't go all that far in this day and age.

So why would Jarvis or Callum want to rock the boat? They were both secure within the structure of Bendorff Enterprises. Callum was set to take over. Jarvis was important to the success of the company and, according to Rusty Boardman, liked what he did. Why would either of them risk shining a light on the company by murdering Bendorff? It didn't make sense.

Of course, there was always Alexander Smith to consider, and she'd see what she could learn up at Nathaniel Bowditch College, where he'd been a professor. Smith didn't work for Bendorff; they were friends, which begged the question: Had Bendorff put the same dynamic into play with his friends? Had he learned nefarious things about them, then held those things over them when he needed something from them, something like help faking his own suicide? Were the bonds of friendship more like bondage? Or had he simply bought Smith's loyalty? Bendorff had found him a topflight divorce attorney, and while Smith hadn't said so, Bendorff must have paid for the attorney, since Smith had admitted to moonlighting at the community college because he needed money.

Brie finished the report she'd started on Joe Callum before Jack had called. She checked her watch. Dent had said to call him when they were an hour out of Boothbay. She picked up her phone, brought up his number and sent the call. He answered on the third ring.

"Hello, Brie. I was just going to check in with you."

"We're ahead of schedule, Dent. You said to call when we're an hour out. Right now, we're about forty-five minutes out, and making our way into the harbor and anchoring will take another fifteen minutes."

"In that case I'll round up Marty and the team and start down there. I'll give Doc Wolf a call too."

"After we anchor, I have to drive to Bowditch College to follow up on a lead. Do you have a couple minutes now to fill me in on the interview with Bendorff's widow?"

"Let me call Marty and Joe Wolf and give them a heads up. I'll call you back from my car."

"Roger that, Dent." She hung up and started her report on Leo Dombello. Ten minutes later her phone rang, and she answered it.

"Okay, Brie," Dent said. "Let's talk about the interview with Rebecca Bendorff."

"Go ahead, Dent."

"As I told you before, the officers who gave the initial notification of Bendorff's suicide reported that Rebecca Bendorff seemed genuinely shocked and grieved at the news of the suicide. As you know, officers are trained to carefully note the reaction of spouses in a murder investigation, but since the officers dispatched in the middle of the night were reporting on a suicide, there was no reason for a laser-like focus on the wife."

"So what kind of a read did you and Marty get today when you reported the murder to her?"

"Rebecca Bendorff wasn't looking good when we got there, but when we revealed what had unfolded aboard the ship, she completely fell apart. Said it was more that she could bear—first thinking about why he would kill himself, and then learning that not only had he intended to disappear forever, but that one of his friends or colleagues would murder him. She was literally sick with shock and grief, to the point she had to excuse herself and rush for the bathroom. I've dealt with quite a few murderous spouses in my time in homicide, and she does *not* fit the profile. Whatever crazy plan these six guys had cooked up, I don't think she had any part in it."

It troubled Brie slightly that she had no picture in her mind nor sense of Rebecca Bendorff. As the wife of the victim, she was a factor in the unfolding case. But being on the ship, Brie had no recourse but to get some of her information from Dent Fenton. Such was the odd nature of this case.

"Did you ask about life insurance?" she asked.

"Yes, and as far as Mrs. Bendorff knew, there wasn't any policy. She said she had asked her husband for years to purchase life insurance and that he had refused every time. Something about some ridiculous superstition he had about life insurance. Apparently Bendorff thought it was like betting you'd die."

"I got the same weird story from Bendorff's friend, Alex Smith."

"Huh," Dent said.

"So, did Rebecca Bendorff work—have some kind of a career?"

"We asked that, and she said she worked with the residential properties her husband acquired. Made decisions about updates and repairs. Hired workmen and generally oversaw the work. We asked if she would become more involved with Bendorff Enterprises now that her husband was gone, and she said no—that she'd never had anything to do with the running of the company. She said she thought it odd when Peter told her one day, out of the blue, that Joe Callum would take over as CEO if anything ever happened to him."

"Doubly odd when you consider his aversion to life insurance. Did she ask him what he meant by that?"

"She did, but he told her there was nothing to worry about, that he was drawing up some legal documents, that he had promoted Callum to COO—Chief Operating Officer."

"When did all this take place?" Brie asked.

"Within the past month, according to Rebecca Bendorff."

Brie drummed her fingers on the chart table. "I don't know if Bendorff Enterprises has much of a future considering what I've learned about some of the goings-on within the company. Rusty Boardman, Bendorff's cyber security guy, revealed some troubling information about how Bendorff Enterprises gathered information on companies it was looking to buy out."

"Did it involve hacking those companies?" Dent asked.

"Apparently so."

"I'm surprised he'd reveal that," Dent said. "Puts his job in jeopardy along with all the rest."

"Maybe he doesn't care. Maybe he plans to move on. Seems like too straight an arrow to be mixed up with Bendorff's shenanigans."

"That's what his military record showed. He's a decorated combat vet with a solid gold military pedigree. I can't imagine a guy like that getting mixed up with any kind of shady operation."

"I suspect Bendorff paid him very well. And as far as we know, he had nothing to do with the acquisitions part of Bendorff Enterprises. His job was security—cyber and physical site security."

Brie waited for a response from Dent, but he said nothing. "Getting back to Bendorff and his wife, what kind of lifestyle did they have?"

"Seems they were living pretty high on the hog. Big brick colonial on Baxter Boulevard, right on Back Cove."

"Doesn't mean a lot to me, since I don't know Portland very well. Again, not to harp on a point, but you'd think a guy who owns a home like that would want life insurance. But then again, Alexander Smith, the professor slash author, said Bendorff had told him he had other ways of taking care of his wife and family, whatever that meant."

"Huh," Dent said. "Well, I did ask if they had a mortgage. The wife said yes. Guess we could check and see if there was mortgage insurance."

"My guess is that would have felt too much like life insurance to Bendorff."

"You're probably right," Dent said. "You know, it's possible Bendorff had been thinking of disappearing for quite a while. Maybe he thought the existence of life insurance would just muddy the water."

"How so?"

"Insurance companies are bloodhounds when it comes to tracking evidence. I'm sure Bendorff didn't want anyone to come looking for him if he was planning to drop off the map."

"But insurance doesn't pay out on a suicide."

"That's right, but what if questions arose?"

"I see what you mean," Brie said. "How well did Rebecca Bendorff know these five men—the five suspects currently aboard the *Maine Wind*?"

"The only one she seemed to know much about was Lyle Jarvis, Peter Bendorff's nephew, and I can tell you she believes he killed her husband."

"She's not alone there."

"Said she always knew Jarvis was a bad apple—'completely unstable' were her words. Said she warned her husband many times not to get involved with him, but that Peter seemed to have some misguided sense of responsibility when it came to Jarvis. She thought her husband always felt guilty that he hadn't set his sister up in a better life. Thought it might have made a difference for his wayward nephew."

There was static on the connection, and Dent was getting harder to hear. "You're breaking up a little, Dent."

"I'll send you the transcript of the whole interview so you can read through it." There was silence for a moment. "What's your gut telling you, Brie?"

She rocked back in John's chair. "It's telling me there's more to learn. I need to keep digging. When you get the phone records, could you cross reference the phone numbers of these five guys, see what comes up?" She thought for a moment. "And add Rebecca Bendorff's cell phone and landline to the list, too. See if you come up with any connections."

"We'll get to work on that as soon as we receive the phone records."

"See you in Boothbay then, Dent."

"Roger that." They ended the call.

She went back to writing her report on Leo Dombello. Now and then she turned on the recorder to check for details as she proceeded through the report. As she typed, she debated about whether or not to reinterview Joe Callum about his time at Hopkins Lilliwell. But to what avail? If a thorough investigation of him at the time had turned up nothing, he certainly wasn't going to cop to anything now. For the time being, she tabled the question of whether or not to re-interview him. The question in her mind after talking to Jack Le Beau was, *Would he try the same thing again? Was it possible he had embezzled funds from Bendorff Enterprises?* She'd gotten the sense that Callum was genuinely attached to Bendorff. Genuinely sad at the loss of him. But then again, they had argued about something the night the group had come aboard. Leo had heard them but couldn't say what it was about. She *would* have to follow up on that. But for whatever reason, right now, she just didn't make Callum as the killer. She left the door open, though, knowing that in an open investigation, things can change.

She finished up her report on Leo and had just started her report on Lyle Jarvis when she heard the captain's order shouted topside.

"All hands on deck. Prepare to lower sail!"

Brie saved her file, shut down the laptop, and stowed it in John's chart table. She grabbed her jacket and headed topside.

Chapter 26

When Brie gained the quarterdeck, the captain was radioing the Boothbay harbormaster to alert him of their approach and receive any last-minute anchoring instructions. Scott was already over to port, muscling the mainsail halyard down from the rigging, and George had abandoned his galley to help on the lines. She headed over to starboard to take down the throat halyard for ballantining.

The squall line lay astern in the distance, still a long way off but advancing, and an oily sea was making up. She guessed the storms would arrive sometime in the middle of the night. At least they'd be safely anchored. She could see Boothbay Harbor in the distance. They were on a bead with Squirrel Island that marked the approach to the harbor, and Cape Newagen and the Cuckolds Light lay ahead off their port bow.

Putting her shoulder under the heavy coil of halyard, she lifted it to the deck and began working the line into the familiar three-leaf-clover formation that kept it from fouling as the mainsail was lowered. Rusty Boardman and Alex Smith had come on deck aft, and soon enough, Joe Callum and Leo appeared forward. There was no sign of Lyle Jarvis. Brie figured he was sulking in his cabin and ignoring the captain's order for all to come topside. Or maybe he was just afraid of Captain DuLac. *He should be,* she thought. *John's pretty much reached the end of his rope.*

She finished working her line, and she and Scott walked aft to the helm. "What's the plan, Captain?" Scott asked.

"Will we need to transport the team from the Maine State Police?" he asked Brie.

"I think they're planning on that."

"Then we need to lower the yawl boat. North of Squirrel Island, we'll head up, lower and furl sail, and drop the yawl. This time of year there'll be plenty of room to anchor due north of Tumbler Island. You two head forward and keep a lookout for red nun four as we enter the passage."

They headed forward to watch for ATONs—nav aids—as they entered the passage. Brie had visited the harbor in mid-June, when the Maine windjammer fleet crowds into Boothbay Harbor for Windjammer Days, the village's annual festival. During the festival, the village swims with tourists, and schooner crews and shipmates party in the local establishments or climb aboard neighboring schooners for a gam—a nautical term for a social visit to another ship either at sea or at anchor. For the duration of their brief time there, Brie recalled simply wanting to escape back to the peace of the sea.

By this time of year, though, Maine villages lie quiet— unhurried and unharried, the tourists largely gone. But the villagers, in their industrious Yankee way, are already battening down for the long New England winter.

Within fifteen minutes they made their approach, passing Cape Newagen on their port side. Squirrel Island lay to starboard, and dead ahead, the snow white, granite rubble stone tower of Burnt Island Light—second oldest surviving lighthouse on the Maine coast. John had told her Burnt Island got its name from the practice of burning the island's vegetation to keep the island clear for sheep grazing.

Northwest of Squirrel Island, they kept red nun 4 to starboard and steered northeast, picking up speed, starting to make their turn upwind. The captain cranked hard on the wheel, and the *Maine Wind* clawed her way slowly to starboard and upwind. Brie and Scott headed forward to man the peak halyard on the foresail.

When the ship lay dead into the wind, the captain called out, "Scandalize the forepeak." They eased the halyard, lowering the peak of the sail—a maneuver that stopped the ship's headway. Then with George's, help they repeated the maneuver with the mainsail.

"Prepare to furl sail," DuLac called out, and seeing that Lyle Jarvis was absent, stepped to the aft companionway. "Jarvis, topside now! We need all hands." Within moments Jarvis came skulking up the ladder.

Everyone climbed atop the cabin and took their places to port and starboard along the boom to furl sail as it was lowered. Brie and Scott manned the halyard as the mainsail crept down the mast to be folded and lashed off. Next they furled the foresail and staysail and doused the jib. Then all hands lined up aft for the grueling task of lowering the yawl boat from the stern of the ship.

Within minutes Scott climbed down the ladder, fired up the yawl and began pushing the *Maine Wind* toward their anchorage with the captain at the helm, steering the ship. North of Tumbler Island, Scott slowed the yawl, and Brie and George manned the starboard anchor, waiting for the captain's order to "drop the hook," which came a few minutes later.

As the ship coasted to a near stop, they let go the anchor. The chain rumbled through the starboard hull like a fast-moving freight train, and the quarter-ton anchor found purchase. The *Maine Wind* rounded up into the wind, and they laid out plenty of anchor chain, known as "road." Then followed that oddly disorienting moment of transition from constant movement to stillness. To Brie it was always a letdown— a pause in the normal routine of being at sea and the heady exhilaration of being underway.

In Boothbay Harbor, large ships anchor south and west of the inner harbor, where the village of Boothbay lies. The *Maine Wind* had spun at anchor to face into the wind, and now the five passengers lined up along the port side of the ship, surveying the shoreline. For whatever reason, her lineup of suspects suddenly reminded Brie of targets in a shooting gallery, except that they were facing the wrong way. She took it as a sign it was time for some shore leave. She was about to get some on her drive up to Bowditch College.

As she watched the five men, she was glad the ship lay a good ways off shore. She didn't want any of them contemplating leaving the ship. Her gaze stopped on Alex Smith, who stood apart from the others, scanning the shore through a pair of ship's binoculars. The vibe coming from him felt off—desperate somehow. Was he looking for an escape route? If so, there were only two reasons. He was afraid to remain on the ship, or he was guilty of the murder. Initially he wouldn't have been her first choice for perp, but now she was pretty certain he was hiding something. That made her eager to get ashore and head to that meeting she'd scheduled with Dr. Whitmore at the college.

First things first, though. They needed to get the Evidence Response Team aboard to process the crime scene and remove Bendorff's body. She took out her phone and put through a call to Dent Fenton. When he answered she said, "Hi, Lieutenant, we just anchored. What's your ETA?"

"We're all assembled on the town dock. Doc Wolf and the evidence team are here along with Marty and me. Total of six people, and one litter to transport the body."

"The yawl boat's in the water. We'll head in for you right away." Brie walked aft and told the captain the team was waiting for them ashore. She signaled Scott to bring the yawl over to the starboard side.

"I think it would be best if you sent everyone below to their cabins, John, before I get back with the team."

"I'm on it, Brie. Just letting them have a few minutes above decks, then down they go till George serves dinner." He paused and looked at her. "I'd prefer if you stay aboard and let George go with Scott to collect the group."

Brie nodded. "Probably a good idea. Dent and Marty are coming aboard with the crime lab team to keep watch over things. You can get some much-needed sleep. I have to drive up to Bowditch College to check out some information. But the ship will be safe and sound with Dent and Marty on tap. Any word from Ed Browning?"

"He's on his way down. Scott will run the yawl in and pick him up when he gets to the dock."

"That's good. That'll be one extra crew to stand watch."

Brie walked forward and called down to George in the galley that the captain wanted him to go with Scott to collect the team from the Maine State Police. Her announcement caused a stir over at the port rail, and her five suspects shape-shifted into a kind of tightly-knit formation in which no one of them seemed overly conspicuous.

George was on deck in a few moments and climbed over the starboard rail and down the boarding ladder to the yawl boat. He clambered aboard the yawl and pushed it off from the side of the ship, and Scott headed the boat northeast across the water toward the inner harbor.

Chapter 27

Abaft of where the five shipmates had stationed themselves, the captain and Brie rolled up the charts they'd used in the day's voyage and listened to the Coast Guard forecast. Before going below, John walked forward and asked the men to return to their cabins until dinner was served. The five of them dispersed quickly and headed below, and John came aft and asked if he should wait for the team to board. Brie shooed him below to his cabin.

"You haven't slept in over twenty-four hours. I'm relieving you of duty."

"Just like that?" John smiled.

"Just like that. You need to lie down before you fall down."

"I guess we'll have plenty of sentries aboard."

"Like I said, Dent Fenton and Marty are with the team. Once I turn the crime scene over to the evidence team, I'm heading ashore."

"You using Dent's vehicle to get up to Brunswick?"

"Dent's or Marty's. So, go. Sleep. I'll tell Scott to wake you when dinner's on. I won't be back by then."

John nodded. "Okay then. Drive safely." They were totally alone on deck, and he pulled her into his arms and held her there for a moment till he felt her duty-charged muscles relax a bit. Then he headed down the companionway.

*　　*　　*

Down below, he stowed his sea boots next to the cabin door in the corner of the passageway and hung his foul weather jacket on the wood peg above them. He stepped into his cabin, locked the door, and crossed to his berth. It took one and a half steps across the cabin sole to get there. He pulled off his wool socks, threw back the wool blanket—wool being the fabric that goes to sea due to its warmth and wicking ability—and sheet and crawled into his berth. He stretched his legs, flopped over on his back, and stretched his spine.

That's when he made the mistake of turning his head. He immediately saw something amiss over on the chart table. Amiss and disturbing. He threw back the blanket, rolled out of the berth, and crossed to the table, where he saw that one of his charts had been torn into pieces and impaled with what looked like one of George's knives from the galley. He stared at it, shocked by the audacity of the act, and his sleep-deprived mind tried to sort out what to do. If he called Brie's attention to this, it was just one more thing she'd have to deal with, and he knew she needed to get ashore for that interview. But if he'd been honest with himself, his true motivation was exhaustion—being too dog-tired to deal with one more thing. He headed back to his berth and crawled in. Next to him, in a concave arc, the hull of the ship curved up to the deck that ran overhead, enclosing him in a kind of maritime cocoon—the place in this troubled world he felt safest.

*　　*　　*

Within twenty minutes of Scott's departure, Brie heard the yawl boat approaching. She crossed the deck to the port rail and could see the boat filled with people and equipment. Scott made his approach, circling around the stern of the ship and up to the starboard side. George got hold of the boarding ladder and sent the two women and one man from the Evidence

Response Team up the ladder first. Then their kits were passed up to them. Next came Joe Wolf, the medical examiner. Brie hadn't seen Joe since August, when they'd worked on a deeply sinister and complicated case in Tucker Harbor, Maine. His dark eyes flared with affection as he stepped over and gave her a hug.

"Hey, Joe. Really good to see you."

"About to leave the womb of the sea, I hear, and travel back to the deep woods and clear lakes of Minnesota."

There was something poetic about Joe that Brie attributed to his Penobscot Nation roots. "Well, yes," she said simply. "Decisions need to be made—things set in order back home."

"You'll find a straight and true path through it, Brie. I've seen what you're made of."

Next up the ladder was Lieutenant Dent Fenton, Major Crimes Unit. He wore a Maine State Police ball cap that accentuated his heavy brow bone and arctic blue eyes.

"Good to see you, Brie." He clasped her hand and pulled her into a half hug, half shoulder bump greeting.

Then Detective Marty Dupuis was climbing over the gunwale and giving her what could only be described as a friendly bear hug. Marty wasn't of grizzly or even black bear proportions; nonetheless, there was a solid bear-like quality about him. Built like a granite block house, his dark eyes twinkled, letting you know block houses can be mighty friendly. His curly black hair and mustache testified to his French Canadian lineage.

Below in the yawl boat, Scott stepped onto one of the thwarts, and he and George passed the litter up to Dent and Marty on the deck. Then George shinnied up the ladder, and Brie leaned over the side and asked Scott to wait in the yawl, as she'd be ready to go ashore within a few minutes.

Brie told Dent the captain had gone below to sleep and described the lay of the aft compartment. Dent posted Marty to stand watch on deck and also cover the aft compartment where the captain and three of the suspects had their cabins. Then Brie led Dent and the team below into the amidships passageway. As they were congregating and pulling on booties and latex gloves, Leo opened his cabin door and poked his head out, surveying the scene. He looked like a turtle just ventured forth from the safety of his shell into a dangerous world. Brie stepped over and told him he needed to stay in his cabin.

She moved back across the passageway and unlocked the door to what had been Paul Trasky's, alias Peter Bendorff's, cabin. She gave Joe Wolf a brief account of discovering the body and the time period they estimated the murder had taken place, based on the comings and goings aboard the ship after she and Scott had been relieved of duty and gone to sleep. She stayed outside while Dent Fenton and Doc Wolf entered the cabin. One of the evidence response team passed in a light that Dent plugged into the ship's auxiliary power and turned on. They did a preliminary examination of the body, and then Dent stepped out to talk to Brie.

"The victim is still in rigor, which will make it more difficult to move him. I'll let Doc Wolf and the team take over from here, and I'll stand watch in the passageway." The three techs had already consulted, and the two women went into the cabin, leaving the man outside to process and categorize the items that were passed to him.

"I have to head ashore and follow up on something that arose in questioning one of the suspects, Alexander Smith."

"You told me you had to drive to Bowditch College."

"Smith taught at the college until a couple of years ago. I've got an appointment with the chair of the History Department to gather information about his time there."

"You can use my vehicle to drive up there," Dent offered.

"Thanks, Dent." She checked her watch. "If you've got things in hand here, I need to head ashore and get on the road."

Dent fished out his keys. "You'll find my SUV next to the evidence team's van in the parking lot above the town dock."

Brie took the keys. "I'll see you later." She started up the ladder and then turned. "George said he's cooking plenty of extra dinner for you guys and the team if you need to eat."

"That's great. Thanks, Brie." He hooked his thumbs in his belt and stepped to parade rest, and Brie continued up the ladder.

She ducked down to her berth behind the galley to collect her badge and ID for the Maine State Police, patted her pockets to be sure she had her phone, small notebook, and recorder, and headed topside. Scott was waiting below in the yawl boat; she swung a leg over the gunwale and climbed down to the yawl, released the bow line, and sat in the bow. Scott, steering with the tiller on the yawl, motored away from the ship and then opened up the powerful diesel engine.

The *Maine Wind* was anchored in about forty feet of water, lying due east of McKown Point and about a half mile from the village. They cut across the water, skirting south of McFarland Island, and soon entered the inner harbor. Restaurants, marinas, lobster pounds, and inns jockeyed for position along the crowded shore in an attempt to lure boaters and tourists.

The village of Boothbay comes to a bustling head at the end of Route 27 that runs down the long, rolling Boothbay Peninsula between the Sheepscot and Damariscotta Rivers. Ahead, off their starboard bow, Brie saw Cap'n Fish's Inn and the Rocktide Inn, and up the hill in East Boothbay, the village's white steeple church sat like a peaceful dove in the early evening light. Straight off their bow, a quarter mile in the distance, the thousand-foot-long pedestrian bridge spanned the inner harbor, connecting Boothbay Harbor with East Boothbay.

Scott steered northwest past the Tugboat Inn Marina and the yacht club, where just a handful of boats still lay at their moorings, and cut the motor to a crawl as they approached the town dock. He idled the motor as they came alongside, and Brie stepped up onto the dock.

"I'll call you when I get back," she yelled to Scott over the engine noise.

"Call when you're fifteen minutes out." He pulled out his phone. "Think I'll try Ed Browning since I'm here, see if he's nearby—save myself another trip in from the ship."

"Good idea. Want me to tie you off?"

"Sure."

Brie climbed back aboard, grabbed the bow line, and ran a clove hitch around the docking cleat. Scott killed the engine, and she stepped back onto the dock. "See you in a couple hours."

He gave her a wave, and she headed along the dock and up the stairs to the parking lot. She immediately spotted the large panel van the evidence response team used. Dent's black SUV sat next to it, and she walked toward it. She felt like she was wearing cement galoshes—the result of being at sea for an uninterrupted period of days, which affects both muscles and equilibrium.

Suddenly she had a thought. There was a bookstore here in the village, Sherman's Books and Stationery. Now there was a name out of the past, a name that attested to the book vendor's long history here in Maine. She remembered St. Paul Book and Stationery—long gone now—in her home town of St. Paul, Minnesota, where she'd grown up. The Mainers held fast to tradition and their connection to an earlier, simpler time. Brie liked that.

She headed up Commercial Street, where imposing brick buildings rubbed shoulders with colorfully shuttered board and batten structures to house shops and restaurants. She'd visited the bookstore in June when they'd anchored here for Windjammer Days, and she remembered where it was. A short ways up the hill, she spotted it over on the left-hand side of the street, crossed over, and walked in the door at the far end of the store. Inside was an open, airy space filled with books and gifts, a space geared for both readers in the village and tourists passing through. In the center of the store, a wide stairway ascended to an open balcony-like second level. Brie headed over to the register on her left and asked the woman there if they had a copy of *Jumping Ship* by Alexander Smith. The woman clicked in the title on her keyboard and searched her monitor.

"We have that in stock," she said, looking up. "Would you like me to get it for you?"

"Please," Brie said. She browsed a tee-shirt rack while she waited, and in a few minutes the woman reappeared with the book and rang it up. Brie paid, thanked the book vendor, and headed out of the store. She checked her watch—enough time to reach the college before her meeting at six, but it would be close.

She jogged down the hill to Dent's SUV, popped the lock with the remote, climbed in, and turned on the engine. She adjusted the seat and mirrors, plugged her destination into the GPS, and rolled north out of the village along Townsend Avenue, passing the savings and loan and Grover's Hardware. On the outskirts, Townsend Avenue became Route 27 as it climbed north along the Boothbay Peninsula.

The land rose and fell like a stormy sea as it climbed through rolling, granite-intruded Maine landscape punctuated with stone walls and tall clapboard houses with their attached barns—an architecture of practicality designed for bitter New England winters.

Details of the Bendorff case rolled like the landscape through Brie's mind. Joe Callum and the embezzling allegations; Lyle Jarvis and his involvement with the decade-old rape case in Bangor; Leo Dombello and his criminal past and Mafia connections; and Alexander Smith, professor emeritus, whom she sensed was hiding something. Finally, Rusty Boardman, the outlier. Former military. Straight arrow. Bendorff's security guy.

All of them closeted together on a cruise that was about any-thing but pleasure. A cruise with an ulterior motive—one that had turned deadly.

And the murdered man, Peter Bendorff, collecting this nifty cabal of players, knowing damning things about each of them —using that knowledge to hold them. Most interesting of all, they had been loyal to him—connected in a near symbiotic way. Yes, they had been loyal, up to now, all except one. So what had changed the dynamic? Something or someone had changed the dynamic. If she could discover what or who, then she'd have the why.

Brie tuned back in to her surroundings. She was coming to the end of Route 27 where it intersected with Coastal Route 1. She slowed to a stop and turned left onto Route 1. Within a mile or two she was descending toward the Sheepscot River and rolling across the long bridge that spanned the sprawling Sheepscot. She put her window down and sniffed the air, pick-ing up the brackish smell of the tidal surge.

Then she was across the bridge, entering Wiscasset, stop-ping at the intersection with Water Street to let a couple of young boys pass on their bikes. Leaves rattled along the side-walks and rose in miniature cyclones along Main Street as cars passed by. She turned her head to the left and caught a won-derful aroma coming from Annie's Restaurant on the corner. It smelled like homemade soup or chowder, something they were known for, along with their savory pizzas. She'd shared a delicious Greek pizza at Annie's with Jack Le Beau when she'd visited one weekend in late September. He lived right here in Wiscasset with Angus, his giant dog. She wished she had time to stop for a visit, but that wouldn't be happening today. She had to get to her interview with Dr. Whitmore and then beat it back to the ship.

She wound up the hill through Wiscasset without encoun-tering the usual glut of traffic that backed up the hill and down onto the bridge during the summer, and within minutes she rolled out the west side of the village and picked up speed along Route 1. Bath was just a few miles ahead, and not far beyond lay the town of Brunswick, where she was headed.

Chapter 28

Nathanial Bowditch College had sat firmly anchored in the heart of Brunswick, Maine, for over two hundred years. A first-rate institution, Bowditch attracted gifted students and ranked in the top ten of small liberal arts colleges in the US. The campus stretched gracefully over its 250 acres of academic buildings, residence halls, playing fields, and athletic facilities.

Mrs. Robbins had sent a map of the campus to Brie's phone and described the building that housed the history department where Dr. Thaddeaus Whitmore had his office. In her email, Mrs. Robbins had said to look for an old, red brick building with a tall tower at the front that sat on the quadrangle.

Brie parked Dent's SUV in the visitor lot a short ways beyond the main gate to the campus. Remembering she'd been out in the wind all day, she checked the mirror. Her hair, which had started the day in a neat braid, had loosened up, with strands gone rogue all over the place. She looked around and spotted a dark blue Maine State Police ball cap on the back seat. She pulled the cap on, tucking the end of her braid up inside along with any loose strands. She checked the mirror again—much better. Tidy, and official to boot. She climbed out of the car, clipped her badge on the waistband of her khakis, and headed at a brisk walk toward the quadrangle.

The wind was picking up, shaking down the trees, filling the air with a fiery barrage of red and orange leaves. Overhead, a "mackerel sky" was making up—an omen of bad weather in the offing. It was 5:50, just time enough to get to the professor's office before her appointment.

She spotted the quadrangle up ahead and, on the far side, the building with the tower. She hurried across the wide lawn, climbed the granite steps, and entered the building. Silence. At this time of day, most of the students would be in their dorms or heading for the dining hall. She found the stairway and climbed to the third floor and followed Mrs. Robbin's directions to the professor's office.

She came around a corner and saw a man partway down the hall.

"Detective Beaumont?" he asked.

"That's right," Brie said. "You must be Dr. Whitmore."

"At your service." He stopped next to a door on his left and unlocked it. "Please come in." He gestured with his arm and stood to one side to let Brie pass through first. "Please take a seat," the professor said.

Brie sat in one of the chairs in front of a heavy wood desk with ornate carving around the edge. The top of the desk was covered with piles of student papers. The office itself was of good size, lined with bookshelves full to overflowing. Across the room, two leather armchairs sat on either side of a tall window that overlooked the quadrangle.

Thaddeus Whitmore appeared to be in his late fifties, a big man with broad shoulders who could have played football in his youth. Brie thought he had the rumpled professor look down to a T, with his zip neck sweatshirt, brown cords and desert boots that looked like they'd walked all the way from the sixties. His salt-and-pepper hair stuck out Einstein-like, and his brown horn-rimmed glasses showed a scratch on the right lens just off his center of vision.

"Mrs. Robbins left me a text that you are from the Maine State Police." He came around the desk and thumped his briefcase down on the floor. "I suppose this involves some criminal charge against one of my students." He sat down on the other side of the desk and waited to hear the worst.

"Actually, no," Brie said. "I'd like to ask you some questions about a former professor at the college here—a Dr. Alexander Smith. Did you know him?"

"Yes, I knew him," Whitmore said and got very busy straightening up a stack of papers. Brie got the immediate impression that he had not liked Smith.

"Let me fill you in a little on the situation, Dr. Whitmore." Brie proceeded to tell him that a man had been murdered aboard the *Maine Wind* and that Alexander Smith was one of five suspects.

Thaddeus Whitmore looked momentarily disoriented, like what she was saying didn't compute.

"At this point, with the exception of one man whom we deem physically incapable of the crime, the other four are all suspects. And frankly, in interviewing Alexander Smith, I got the sense he was hiding something, which of course made me curious about his tenure here at the college."

"I see," Whitmore said, but offered nothing else, and Brie began to think that getting anything out of him might be like prying open a clam shell.

"In my interview with him, Smith mentioned someone named Edward. When I asked who he was, Smith said he was a colleague. I believe his exact words were, 'no one important.' But for some reason, that didn't ring true."

Dr. Whitmore seemed taken aback by what he'd just heard. He shifted in his chair and straightened up some more papers.

"I believe you are referring to Dr. Edward Holmes, a former professor here in the history department. A brilliant scholar."

The subtext seemed to imply that, in his estimation, Smith was not.

"Dr. Holmes died very suddenly of a heart attack, oh, maybe three and a half years ago," Whitmore said.

"And was it your impression that he and Dr. Smith were friends?" Brie asked.

"They were definitely friends—both taught American history. That was Edward's field of expertise."

"And Dr. Smith's as well, I take it."

"Well, yes, I suppose so."

"So why would Smith say that Edward Holmes was, quote, 'no one important'?"

"That's a very good question, Detective." He looked directly at her when he said it, and behind the horn-rimmed glasses, Brie read some kind of a challenge in his eyes.

She waited for him to say more, but Whitmore had clammed up again.

"When he came aboard the *Maine Wind*, Dr. Smith told us he was retired from teaching—that he was now a writer."

"Did he now?" Whitmore said rhetorically.

"Well, actually, to be accurate, he didn't mention the writing. In fact, he seemed a bit uncomfortable that it had come up. Scott Hogan, our mate on the ship, is quite a maritime history buff. He recognized the name and asked if Smith had written a current and apparently very well received book on John Paul Jones." She took the book out of the bag that sat on her lap and laid it on the desk. "I stopped and bought a copy of it on the way here."

"And why did you buy the book, Detective?" Dr. Whitmore asked, and again Brie sensed something unsaid, like they were playing a game of fill in the blanks—a game she knew well since filling in the blanks was her stock in trade.

"It seemed like a logical thing to do since I was coming here to talk to you about Dr. Smith. Of course, I'm curious about the book, being a lover of the sea and ships, but as a detective, I'm used to learning all I can about the suspects in a case." She paused and studied him for a long moment. "I get the sense there's something you're not saying, Doctor.

Something about these two men—something that troubles you."

Whitmore stood up from his chair and wandered over to the window. "One has to be very careful making any kind of accusations about a colleague, Detective."

She waited for him to say more but suspected he wouldn't without some kind of prompting.

"Doctor Whitmore, a man has been murdered. Alexander Smith is a suspect in that murder. If there's anything you know that can shed light on the character of this man, you need to be forthcoming about it."

"I could be exposing myself to liability, maybe even a lawsuit. And there's the reputation of the college to consider."

"Doctor Whitmore, as a scholar, the pursuit of truth must be paramount for you, I would think. Finding the truth—that's also my stock in trade. In creating a profile of the victim, I have learned that he was very adept—even gifted—at acquiring information about those he brought into his inner circle—damning information, I might add—information that one of them may have been willing to kill to protect. So if you know something about Doctor Smith that could be of help in this investigation, you need to divulge that information. And let me remind you that I can subpoena your testimony. But I don't think that should be necessary, should it now, Doctor?"

Whitmore let out a sigh and turned from the window. "You're very persuasive, Detective. And, I might add, very articulate." He returned to his chair and sat down. From his expression, it may as well have been the hot seat.

"All right, here it is. I don't believe Alexander Smith wrote this book." He reached over and picked it up. "I believe this was Edward Holmes' work. I believe Smith knew about the manuscript—was possibly the only person other than Doctor Holmes who did. I think when Edward died suddenly, Alexander saw an opportunity to publish something of substance, which, by the way, is every scholar's dream. I think he saw that opportunity and he took it."

Brie sat silently assimilating and assessing the accusation that Thaddeus Whitmore had just made.

"You're not implying that Smith had anything to do with Edward Holmes' death, are you?"

Whitmore waved that away. "Heavens, no—the man's no murderer, in my opinion. But I believe he's a thief and a plagiarist."

"So, you don't think he'd be capable of murder?"

Dr. Whitmore studied her. "They say anyone will kill if given the right provocation. Now if what I suspect is true, and it comes out, it will mean financial ruin for Doctor Smith." He searched her eyes, as if the answers all lay there. "What do *you* think, Detective Beaumont? Is that enough provocation to turn a peace-loving academic into a killer? Personally, I still don't think so."

"Based on past experience alone, I'd have to say yes. It's one doozy of a motive, assuming the victim somehow got wind of it."

Dr. Whitmore slumped back in his chair, looking like he'd just been interrogated by the Gestapo.

"It's been a heavy load to carry, Doctor. You must be relieved to share your suspicions about this."

"I have no proof, you understand. But I knew Doctor Holmes' writing well—I knew his style."

"Had he published other books?" Brie asked.

"No, and that's the problem. He had published lots of articles in scholarly journals, but no books. Now, an expert could compare the writing styles and maybe make a case, but it would be a very hard thing to prove, I believe."

"It's hard to believe that no one else would have known about Holmes' work—seen the manuscript, helped him with the research."

"Edward Holmes was a very private man. Brilliant, but not socially adept. I actually think that had he grown up in this day and time, he might have been placed somewhere on the autism spectrum. Except for his friendship with Alex, he was not close to anyone in the department, nor from what I ever saw, anyone in the broader community of the college."

"I see," Brie said. "So, because of that, Smith would have had a unique opportunity to know about and ultimately make off with Dr. Holmes' manuscript. Especially since Holmes' death was so sudden."

"I believe that's the case," Whitmore said.

"What about Dr. Holmes' computer? What happened to that after he died?"

"He used his personal computer," Whitmore said. "When the family—as I recall, it was his brother and sister—came to collect his possessions, they took the computer."

"If they still have it, our computer forensics unit might be able to find some proof of the manuscript on it."

"Even if they deleted his files?" Whitmore asked.

"Nothing is ever fully deleted from a hard drive," Brie said. "If Dr. Holmes wrote the book on that computer, and someone in his family still has it, my guess is computer forensics will find the proof."

"It would be wonderful if Doctor Holmes could be credited for what was his last body of work."

"Doctor Whitmore, who here on the campus might have communicated with Edward Holmes' family when he died?"

"I assume that would have been the dean."

"See if you can locate any record of phone numbers or addresses for Edward Holmes' family. If you do, you can contact me or Lieutenant Dent Fenton at the Maine State Police." Brie wrote down Dent's name and phone number for Dr. Whitmore and also gave him one of her cards from the Maine State Police.

She stood up. "I won't keep you any longer, Doctor. Thank you for your help. You've shed important light on this case." She gestured toward the book. "May I?"

"Oh, by all means." Whitmore handed back Smith's book, and she put it in the bag and tucked it under her left arm.

She shook the professor's hand and turned to leave. But at the door she turned back to him. "And have heart, Doctor; I'm with Shakespeare. I believe 'the truth will out.'"

"Thank you, Detective. I hope that will be the case. Good luck with your investigation."

Brie left the office and made her way down the stairs and out of the building. The sun was low on the horizon, setting up an autumn bonfire in the western sky behind the cloud deck. She made her way across the quadrangle into a northeast wind that had picked up since she'd entered the building. *Should be falling off this time of night*, she thought. *Best get back to the ship. Something's brewing.*

Chapter 29

Brie climbed into Dent's SUV and tossed the bag with the book onto the passenger seat. She sat for a few moments, thinking about what she had just learned from Dr. Whitmore about the alleged theft of Edward Holmes' manuscript. If it were true—and she believed it was—and if Peter Bendorff had found out about it—which she believed he very well could have—it certainly created a pretty damning motive for Alexander Smith to have committed the murder.

She pulled out her small notebook and glanced over the notes she'd just made during the interview. Dr. Whitmore had said that in his estimation, Smith was a thief and a plagiarist, but not a killer. She remembered the words: 'the man's no murderer.' She wondered if that was the truth. As for the theft of the manuscript, time would tell whether or not Edward Holmes' computer could be located and searched for evidence of the manuscript. Without that, Dr. Whitmore was right: it would be very hard to prove that Smith had stolen the work.

Brie flipped back a couple pages in her notebook and came across the number she had jotted down for Jane Jarvis, Lyle Jarvis' mother. It was a loose end she needed to address, so she took out her phone.

She had turned her phone off during the interview with Dr. Whitmore, so she scrolled down her call list to be sure she hadn't missed any important calls. There were a couple earlier calls from Dent, but nothing in the past hour and a half. She also remembered that he'd sent her an email with an attachment that she'd never looked at. Something to do with Leo's

Mafia uncle, as she recalled. Dent had told her she might find it interesting. Probably provided a glimpse into the world Leo had come from. She reminded herself to take a look at it when she got back to the ship.

She punched in the number for Jane Jarvis from her notebook and leaned her arm against the driver's side door as she waited for her to pick up.

After three rings a woman answered with a desperate sounding "Hello," like she was afraid she might miss the call.

"Is this Jane Jarvis?"

"Y-yes . . ." The word stumbled out.

"This is Detective Brie Beaumont from the Maine State Police."

"Whatta you . . . want?" The words trailed off, and suddenly Jane Jarvis sounded very far away, almost as if she'd left planet Earth. Not a geographical, but rather, Brie sensed, an emotional detachment. She could tell that the woman on the other end of the call had been drinking.

"I'd like to ask you some questions if that's all right, Mrs. Jarvis."

"I need Lyle to come home," she bleated out, suddenly very much present. "He's on some goddamn ship somewhere." The words came out slurred. "And now Peter's dead. My brother's dead!" She said it like Brie might not know. But also, maybe, to convince herself of the terrible fact. She sounded incredulous—like she didn't quite accept that it could be the truth. "My brother's dead. Whatta'm I gonna do?" she slurred out.

"I would think, Mrs. Jarvis, anything you can that might help to prove your son is innocent," Brie said in a calm, level tone.

There was silence at the other end, but from the response that finally came back, it was almost as if she had slapped Jane Jarvis hard on the face. The voice was suddenly stone sober. "I'll do anything I can, Detective." Brie could almost see her straightening up in her chair, shaking off the self-pity. "Tell me what I can do."

"For now, you can answer some questions about your son and his relationship to the—" She started to say *victim* but thought better of it. "—to your brother."

"I'll do my best," Jane said, and Brie could hear her voice shake at the mention of her brother.

"When I interviewed Lyle, he seemed to have quite a grudge against his uncle. Seems he felt Peter Bendorff kept his heel down pretty hard on him."

"He said that, and he was always grousing about it, but his life was getting better," Mrs. Jarvis said. "Peter gave him a good job and paid him well. Lyle had a nice apartment in a house near where Pete lived. Lyle's always been clever with computers. He liked his job. Didn't tell me much about it— probably thought I wouldn't understand what he was talking about. I could tell he was good at it, though. I think he was proud of that."

What Jane Jarvis was saying jibed with what Rusty Boardman had told her. So if Jarvis was guilty, maybe the motive lay elsewhere.

"Your brother was planning to fake his suicide and leave the country. Could Lyle have resented him for that, do you think?"

Again, silence from the other end. "I think it would have scared Lyle. It would have scared all of us if we had known."

"And who would all of us be?" Brie asked.

The response that came back had an edge to it, like Brie should understand—like she shouldn't have to ask. "All of us that depended on him," Jane said.

Brie decided to move on. "Mrs. Jarvis, had Lyle ever been treated for anger management?" She was thinking about the scene at lunch—Jarvis throwing Joe Callum overboard.

"Why would he need that?" she asked defensively.

Brie fell silent, deciding how to tackle the denial.

Suddenly Jane was talking again. "Don't get me wrong. He gets angry. Really angry. But he takes it out on things, not people."

Brie's eyebrows went up when she heard that. *I guess Joe Callum is the exception,* she thought. "Can you give me an example?" she asked. "Does he like to break things?"

"More like tear things up. Tear things apart with his hands."

"I see," Brie said, thinking of the crime scene aboard the *Maine Wind*. The wig Bendorff had worn that had been cut up or torn apart.

"Do you think that behavior could escalate, Mrs Jarvis— that he could become angry enough to hurt someone?"

"Lyle has a gentle side," she said. "You should see him with animals. He was always trying to help little injured creatures when he was a boy."

"Mrs. Jarvis, was Lyle ever physically abused? Maybe by your husband before he left, back when Lyle was twelve?"

There was silence from the other end, which gave Brie her answer.

Finally, grudgingly, "I don't see what that has to do with anything."

Brie didn't respond. Lyle Jarvis may have been gentle with the creatures of the world. But it was the humans who had hurt him. And so it was the humans he would lash out against. Brie decided to leave him at the top of her suspect list for now, followed closely by Alexander Smith, who had a whole lot to lose financially if the truth ever came out about his book.

She thanked Jane Jarvis for her time. Mrs. Jarvis pleaded with her again to send Lyle home, and on that note, they ended the call.

Brie made a couple of notes in her notebook and checked her watch. It was just past six thirty. She turned over the ignition on the SUV, rolled down through Brunswick, and picked up the spur of four-lane that ran between Brunswick and Bath and over the Sagadahoc Bridge that spanned the Kennebec River between Bath and Woolwich. As she rolled out onto the bridge, the Bath Iron works, where some of the world's most formidable ships were built, lay below her, off to the right. Known simply as "The Yard," it dominated the western shore of the river.

A strong gust of wind buffeted the car as she reached the middle of the bridge. Brie looked to her right, down the broad reach of the Kennebec. An angry sky was boiling up in the south. Instinctively she depressed the accelerator, eager to reach the junction with Route 27, eager to get back to the ship.

She tried to switch her mind into neutral as the Maine landscape rolled by and the light drained from the day. She'd been intensely focused on the case since before midnight last night, and the first creeping tendrils of a dull headache were beginning to twine up the back of her head. She switched on the radio and found NPR, which was playing classical music. She set the cruise and leaned back into the seat. In about fifteen minutes she entered the outskirts of Wiscasset and rolled on down through the village and out onto the bridge over the Sheepscot River without any of the usual delays.

A few minutes farther along, she came to the junctions of Routes 1 and 27 and turned right. She wondered if the Evidence Response Team was still aboard working the crime scene or whether they had finished and brought Peter Bendorff's body ashore. George had probably served dinner by now. Her stomach rumbled just thinking about beef and roasted vegetables and oven-baked bread from the woodstove.

A little farther along she pulled to the side of the road and brought up Scott's number. She figured she was about fifteen minutes from Boothbay Harbor. Scott might as well start in with the yawl boat. He answered on the second ring.

"Hey, Brie. Where you at?"

"About fifteen minutes out, Scott. Is the forensic team still there?"

"Just packing up to leave. The captain called the Coasties out from the Boothbay Coast Guard Station to transport the body. The yawl boat wasn't quite big enough to accommodate the litter."

"Is Dent Fenton still aboard?" Brie asked.

"Yup. He was wondering if you want him to leave Detective Dupuis aboard overnight."

"Is he nearby, Scott? I'd like to talk to him."

"Hang on, Brie. I see him forward."

Brie switched her phone to speaker mode and pulled back out onto the road. In a few moments Dent came on Scott's phone.

"Brie. Glad you called. We're just clearing out. The Coast Guard is here loading the body, and the evidence team and I are going to hitch a ride with them back to shore. But I'm wondering if you want me to post Marty aboard overnight?"

"I wouldn't turn that down, Dent. I have some work to do on the case when I get back aboard, so it would be great to have an extra cop on hand."

"I'll let him know, Brie. Are we any closer to an arrest?" he asked. "If there are any of these guys you consider dangerous, I can take them off the ship—hold them for up to forty-eight hours."

She had forgotten to tell him about the commotion at lunch, so she filled him in on how Jarvis had thrown Callum overboard.

"Is Callum pressing charges?"

"He hasn't said anything yet. But getting back to your question about taking any of them into custody, I think it might be better to leave all the pieces in place. Let this thing play out. Right now, Jarvis and Alexander Smith are the chief suspects. I want to listen to the interviews again when I get back to the ship."

"Smith, eh? That's a surprise. Isn't he the college professor?"

"Former," Brie said. "I just interviewed the chair of the History Department at Bowditch College, where Smith used to teach." Just then, Brie heard someone ask Dent a question.

"You can fill me in later, Brie. I have to go. I'll leave Marty aboard."

"Let me know if the phone records show anything, Dent. Any connections."

"Will do," he said. "I'll call you later."

They ended the call. Within ten minutes Brie entered the outskirts of Boothbay, and the road started to descend toward the harbor.

It was nearly dark in the village when Brie parked Dent's SUV in the lot above the public dock and started down to the float. She could hear the throaty diesel engine of the yawl boat out across the water, heading her way. She waited by the ladder where Scott had dropped her off, and within five minutes, he made his approach, shifting the yawl's engine into neutral as he floated up to the dock. Brie climbed down the ladder and stepped onto the forwardmost thwart and down into the yawl as Scott made a slow pass. She sat in the bow and gave the yawl a push free of the ladder. Scott circled to port and headed across the harbor toward the outer anchorages where *Maine Wind* lay.

Chapter 30

The sea reflected the dying light of the autumn day. Fog was forming in the harbor as the land cooled quickly, and an offshore breeze scurried down off the warm earth and out over the cool waters of the harbor, where it condensed into fog. As they motored toward the ship, a pretty good chop was making up, and Brie noticed the wind had worked its way into the east. The sky looked unusually bright ahead of the advancing storm front moving in from the south. At least they were tucked in a safe harbor where they could ride it out.

The thought had no more than crossed her mind when Scott called forward. "The captain's weighing anchor as soon as you're back aboard. He wants to get in front of the storm."

Brie turned and looked at Scott in disbelief but didn't try to say anything.

Five minutes later they made their approach to *Maine Wind*. Scott idled the engine and they drifted up to the starboard side, where Brie got hold of the ladder and climbed aboard. Scott circled the yawl back to the stern of the ship.

On deck, Ed Browning and John were laying out the halyards to port and starboard for raising sail. Brie headed aft to talk to John.

When he saw her approaching, he straightened up. "Brie. Glad you're back. How did your interview go?"

"Just fine. I've now added Alex Smith to the suspect list. But more on that later. Scott said we're weighing anchor."

John nodded toward the ominous-looking sky in the south. Thick cumulonimbus clouds the shape and color of anvils crowded the horizon. "There's a gale bearing down on us. If we wait till tomorrow morning, we won't get out. We could be caught here for several days. What's more, there's a hurricane headed for the southeastern seaboard. It's expected to make its way right up the coast."

"But setting off in the dark with a storm bearing down and a killer aboard—do you think that's wise?"

"Look, Brie. I'll handle the ship and the weather. I expect you and Marty to keep a lid on the rest till we make port. Is that clear?"

"Yes sir."

"Come below. There's something I have to show you." John preceded her down the aft companionway and ushered her into his cabin.

Brie immediately saw the chart table and the knife stabbed through the pieces of ripped-up chart.

"Hope we don't need that chart to get home," she said.

"Fortunately, no."

"When did this happen?" Brie asked.

"It was here when I came below to sleep. I should have come and gotten you, but you were busy with the lab techs and Dent up forward. And I was exhausted, Brie. I needed to sleep."

"Did you show this to Dent?"

John looked sheepish. "About an hour ago, Scott came below to tell me the police needed to call the Coast Guard to take the body ashore. The Coasties came out from Boothbay Station, and in all the uproar, I forgot about all this." He gestured toward the chart table.

"I'll get a paper bag from George and bag this as evidence. I'll give it to Dent when we get back to Camden." She started to leave and then stopped. "On the other hand, since it's still here, let's see if we can get some use out of it."

She stepped out of John's cabin, walked across the passageway to Lyle Jarvis cabin and knocked on the door.

When Jarvis opened the door, she said, "Please come with me, Lyle."

She escorted him across the passageway and into the captain's cabin. She gestured toward the knife stuck into the chart table. "Did you do this?"

Jarvis took a step backward, but John stepped between him and the cabin door.

"I want the truth, Mr. Jarvis," Brie said.

His eyes darted around the cabin as they had when she'd interviewed him. Finally they settled on the knife and the torn-up chart. "I was angry at the captain for yelling at me," Jarvis said.

"Is that so?" Brie said. "Did you forget that you threw someone overboard?" She gave him her arctic stare. "Joe Callum could have drowned."

Jarvis refused to look at her.

"You don't have any impulse control whatsoever, do you? Which makes me think that, driven by escalating anger, you killed Peter Bendorff. You never wanted him to run your life, but the thought of him bowing out terrified you, didn't it? Did it make you angry enough to kill him?"

"No. NO! Shit no. I don't know what you're talking about. I was glad he was leaving the country. I finally got to have my life back. I didn't mind working for the company, but like I told you, I hated him running my life. But I didn't kill him. I wouldn't do that."

"Why should I believe you?" Brie asked.

Jarvis sighed and dropped his head, and she thought she actually glimpsed tears in his eyes. "Because I know he cared about me," he said with surprising gentleness. "He was the only man who ever did."

Brie studied him for a long moment, wondering if he was just another good actor in this bizarre little troupe of players. "You can return to your cabin for now," she said.

"We'll be raising sail in a short while," the captain told him. "I expect you on deck to help when you hear the call."

"We're going back out there?" Jarvis looked alarmed. "There's a storm coming."

"That's my problem, not yours," the captain said. "Now, please return to your cabin."

Jarvis left, and Brie and John headed back up on deck. John called Scott and Ed Browning aft. "Let's get busy reefing the main and foresail. As soon as we're done, we'll get the anchor up. We'll raise sail a little farther out toward Squirrel Island and haul the yawl up."

He turned to Brie. "Did you eat yet?"

"No."

"After we're done with the reefing, head below. George has some warm food on the stove for you. You should eat before we get underway."

"We need to find some raingear for Marty."

"I already talked to George, since he and Marty are about the same size. He fixed Marty up with a pair of sea boots and let him borrow his raingear. George'll be turning in soon, so he won't need them overnight."

"Great," Brie said. "I just hope he doesn't get seasick. We're probably in for a bumpy ride."

"By the way, Dent took Marty's car since you weren't back, and Marty was sailing with us."

"I'm sure they'll sort it all out tomorrow when we get back to port," Brie said.

John, Brie, and Scott climbed atop the cabin, spaced themselves out, and worked together tying the reefing lines on the mainsail around the boom. Ed Browning went forward and worked on reefing the foresail. When they were done, Scott sent Brie below to eat and went to help Ed finish the foresail. Before going below, Brie sent Marty aft, telling him to keep a weather eye on Jarvis.

Down in the galley, Old Faithful was still radiating plenty of heat. It felt good. Outside the temperature was dropping, and Brie was a little chilled. She could vaguely remember lunch, but her stomach told her it was a distant memory.

George was in the corner of the galley doing the washing up from dinner, and Joe Callum was there helping dry and stow the dishes. As she came down the ladder, George turned and nodded toward the stove. "Your dinner's waiting, Brie."

"Thanks, George." She lifted the tin foil on the big pan that held the roasted vegetables. "Umm, that smells wonderful." Joe handed her a plate, and she scooped a large serving of the roasted vegetables onto it. The next pan contained roast beef, perfectly cooked to medium rare, and a saucepan alongside held rich, dark mushroom gravy. Brie helped herself to the meat and ladled on some gravy. A tin foil packet on the back of the stove held half a loaf of crusty honey wheat bread with a heavily seeded top. Brie grabbed two pieces, poured herself a mug of steaming coffee from the pot atop the stove, and went over to the table and slid onto the bench.

The food was flat-out comfort ahead of what she knew would be a long night. She had plenty of work to do on the case, delving into the reports Dent Fenton had sent and the interviews she'd conducted, hoping to find something—some clue, some crack into which she could shine the light of a detective's insight and instinct. But she was also part of the crew and knew she might be needed topside if the storm caught up with them and things got wild.

She forked up the savory roasted vegetables that smelled of rosemary and thyme, along with the beef and mushroom gravy. She mopped up any gravy that got away with her crusty bread. Like all of George's meals, it was a little bit of heaven. She was partway through the dinner when she realized this was the last of George's dinners she would be eating. They'd make port by tomorrow, and that would be it—the end of the season. She felt a sudden sadness that she'd missed sharing this last dinner with her crewmates. She took a swallow of the rich dark coffee and focused on enjoying every bite that remained on her plate.

"That was absolutely delicious, George," she said when she finished. "I don't know what I'm going to do without you."

"Oh, you'll be fine, Brie. You have a way of figuring things out."

She wasn't so sure. For the first time in her life, this summer had been filled with healthy, nutritious meals—three squares a day—made from the best whole foods Maine had to offer, and cooked by a master chef. Of course, if she'd said that to George, he would have pooh-poohed it. But it was the truth.

Joe Callum was just finishing lifting the heavy trays of mugs behind the rails when she thought of something she needed to ask him. "Joe, when you're done there, could I talk to you, please?" she said.

"Sure."

He said it immediately, but even so, the word held a trace of hesitation, and Brie noticed uncertainty in his eyes when he glanced over at her. He was still a suspect, and though he didn't top her list, he had the physical capability and, being in the same compartment as Peter Bendorff, the best opportunity to commit the murder. What's more, he'd had a heated argument with the victim the night they'd boarded.

Just then she heard the cranking of the windlass as the guys began bringing up the anchor.

"I'll head up on deck and see if the captain needs an extra hand," George said.

"Call down if he needs me," Brie said.

"Roger that." George headed up the ladder.

Callum came over and sat opposite her. She set her plate aside but kept her mug of coffee. She reached in her back pocket and took out her small notebook and pen.

"Just a couple of questions, Joe."

"Sure." The same word. Same reluctant feel to it.

She studied him for a moment. "As you know from this afternoon, Lyle Jarvis is on a hair trigger."

"I guess *so*," Callum said.

"Is that something you've seen before, working with him at Bendorff Enterprises?"

"Oh, yeah. Everyone knows he's a hothead. He's always making a scene about something."

"And how does that behavior manifest?" she asked.

"Well, he yells a lot. Terribly unprofessional in a business setting, but he gets away with it because of his connection to Peter. I mean, *got* away with it . . ."

Brie waved that away. "I understand. Anything else?"

Callum smiled. "We call him 'The Shredder' at work, 'cause he's always ripping something up."

"Like what? Can you give me an example?"

"It could be anything. A memo he doesn't like the sound of, work of his own he's displeased with for some reason . . . any kind of a note from Peter."

"So it's a behavior that anyone working with him would know about," Brie said.

"Sure. No doubt about that. Why?"

"Just fleshing out a picture of Jarvis—trying to nail down a few things."

Callum looked away, but not before she caught something in his eyes—smugness, maybe arrogance. She made a mental note of it, wondering what really made Joe Callum tick.

She moved on. "So, you lied about your former employer, Joe. And I've since learned quite a bit about what happened during your employment at Hopkins Lilliwell."

He straightened up and stared directly at her. "I think you mean after my employment there."

"I think I said what I mean," Brie said, engaging his stare.

"If you think I'm going to incriminate myself, you're wrong. Nothing was ever proven, or I would have been arrested."

"Here's what I think, Joe. I think you embezzled that money. I think that's why Bendorff hired you. He knew he could get you to color outside the lines. Maybe cook the books? It was his MO—finding people with a past and leveraging them to do his will."

Callum leaned toward her and locked eyes with her. "Even if that were true, it doesn't make me a killer. Jarvis though—Jarvis has the soul of a killer. I believe the evidence will prove him guilty."

Brie kept the eye contact going. "That may be, Mr. Callum. But for whatever reason, I'm not convinced of it yet." She went for the redirect. "You were overheard arguing with Peter Bendorff the night you both came aboard ship. What were you arguing about?"

Callum sat back and let out a sigh. "Since coming to Bendorff Enterprises, Peter had tasked me with a certain amount of oversight of his nephew, Lyle Jarvis. He expected me to continue that oversight after he went on to his new life. I told him I wouldn't do it. He didn't like hearing that, and we argued."

"So if Peter went away, so would the expectation."

"Look, why would I kill Peter? More likely I'd try to talk him out of what he was doing."

"Did you?"

"Sure. Lots of times. But his mind was made up."

Brie made some more notes and then stood up, put her notebook in her pocket, and picked up her plate and mug. "You can return to your cabin, Joe, but we'll need everyone topside in a few minutes to raise sail."

Callum got up and headed for the ladder without saying another word.

She heard the crank on the windlass stop and then the sound of the heavy anchor being maneuvered up onto the starboard gunwale and tied off by the guys. Shortly thereafter the yawl boat fired up, and the ship started to make headway.

Brie washed her dishes and silverware and laid them on the drainer. She reached for a dry towel that hung above the stove and dried her plate and utensils. The troubling truth of this case was that three of the five men aboard had strong enough motives that there was actually a kind of safety in numbers in the situation for each of them. Without any further forensic evidence or some kind of new information, the case could easily grind to a standstill—an intolerable situation for any good detective.

She stowed her dishes and headed for her berth to put on a heavy sweater and grab her watch cap.

Chapter 31

Darkness was coming on fast as *Maine Wind* chugged toward the mouth of Boothbay Harbor. The captain had called for all hands, and the five passengers, crew, and Detective Marty Dupuis stood ready to raise sail. They rounded up near Squirrel Island and hauled the yawl first and then lined up to port and starboard to get the mainsail up. It took slightly less effort with the reef tied in.

The sea still had an oily roll to it, but outside the harbor they knew there'd be a good chop running. Winds were gusting to 25 knots with seas running three to six feet. Once they were underway, the captain signaled for Brie to come aft.

"Tell the passengers to clear the deck and stay below in their cabins. Once they're below, secure the forward and amidships hatches."

"Aye, Captain."

"I'm putting Scott and Ed on bow watch, and I'm taking the helm. You're free to use my cabin if you need to work on the case. I'll call down if we need you on deck, but right now conditions are manageable."

She started to walk away.

"Oh, and tell Marty to come aft. He's got no sea legs. He needs to stay back here with me as things roughen up. If I need a hand, I'll put him to work, and he'll be in position to keep a weather eye on Jarvis down here in the aft compartment."

Brie went forward and asked the men to return to their cabins. Lyle Jarvis and Leo looked relieved to be allowed to go below. She admonished all of them to stay in their berths below decks as the seas would be rough. "If you try to sit or stand up, you'll get seasick. So stay horizontal. If you have to come topside for any reason, put on your PFD. They're in the passageway outside your cabins. No one on deck without one. Is that clear?"

The men nodded and retreated to their cabins. Brie helped Marty get strapped into his PFD and sent him aft to stand by with the captain. She went below to put on her rain jacket and PFD and then headed topside, where she secured the forward and amidships hatches. As they cleared the harbor, John set a heading northeast. The wind was on their starboard beam—a favorable point of sail—and the *Maine Wind*, a seaworthy vessel, heeled to port, hunkered down, and took the seas in stride.

When she came aft, John handed her the key to his cabin. "Since the incident with the chart, it stays locked," he said.

Brie nodded. "Call out if you need me."

"Will do."

She went below and let herself into the captain's cabin. She reached up and flipped on the small overhead light that ran off the ship's battery, took off her PFD and rain jacket, and hung them on a peg on the cabin wall.

She'd left her laptop stowed in the drawer of John's chart table, and she took it out, plugged it into the auxiliary power, sat down, and booted it up. She went immediately to her email, and while they were still picking up a signal from Boothbay, she downloaded the email and attachment Dent had sent her earlier. He'd come across the article while running down the facts on Leo's criminal past. Apparently it contained something about Leo's deceased Mafia uncle that Dent thought she might find interesting. She'd been in no rush to get to it because, after talking to Leo's hand surgeon, it was clear Leo could not have committed the murder.

Brie also found the report Dent had written on his interview with Rebecca Bendorff and downloaded that as well.

There were no new emails, so she settled in to read what she'd downloaded and to listen to the interviews she'd conducted with the suspects.

She decided to start with the interview Dent had done with Bendorff's wife. Dent had given her the gist of it over the phone earlier in the day, but she wanted to read through the report for herself since it was a key interview, and one she had not conducted. She opened the document she'd just downloaded. Marty Dupuis had written the report, and she ran her eye over the information at the top in a cursory way.

Rebecca Lise Bendorff
550 Baxter Boulevard
Portland, Maine
DOB: 11/04/1971
Marital Status: Married 21 years
Employment: Bendorff Enterprises
Former Arrests/Convictions: 0

Brie read down through the report. Much of it she'd already learned from Dent. Rebecca Bendorff appeared to know nothing about her husband's plan to fake his suicide and "completely fell apart" at the news of his murder, which Lieutenant Dent Fenton and Detective Marty Dupuis had delivered that morning.

The report also confirmed that there was no life insurance, and that the lack of it had been a bone of contention in their marriage. Dent had asked if the couple had children, and Rebecca Bendorff had said no. The report described her employment for Bendorff Enterprises. She worked with the residential properties Bendorff Enterprises acquired, making decisions about upgrades and hiring workmen for the projects.

Dent had asked how well she had known the men who were on the ship with her husband. She had said that, except for Lyle Jarvis, she didn't know any of the men on the ship very well, confirming what Alexander Smith had told Brie, that Peter Bendorff kept his family very separate from his employees and personal friends.

Finally, Rebecca Bendorff had accused Lyle Jarvis of the murder. The report stated that she'd always believed Peter's connection with Jarvis would lead to no good, that she believed Peter was trying to make up for not doing more financially for his sister, Jane Jarvis, when Lyle was young.

Brie closed the report. Except for the fact about there being no children in the marriage, it had revealed nothing new. She and Dent Fenton had discussed all the important points earlier. For whatever reason, though, she felt unsettled by the report and glanced over the text again, at the same time trying to conjure up a picture of Rebecca Bendorff in her mind.

She sat for a few moments listening to *Maine Wind's* chorus of sounds—creaks, squeaks, and groans—that was ever-present below decks when they were underway. She'd taken comfort in those sounds ever since coming aboard in May, and she took comfort in them now. To her, the ship had a life, and this was its language. *Maine Wind* had tales to tell, tales of adventure, and her storm-seasoned planks and timbers whispered of the one currently underway. She took her small recorder out of the drawer, turned it on, and sat there letting it capture the ship's haunting sounds. When she left here in a few days, this would be a scintilla of *Maine Wind's* vital essence that she could take with her—an echo of the ship's heart and soul, captured in time.

After a little while, she turned off the recorder and put it back in the drawer. The case weighed on her, heavy as the advancing storm. The lack of resolution here was deeply troubling. She had suspects and motives aplenty. All but one of the suspects had means, and all of them had had opportunity. *So how to find a needle in a haystack?* she wondered.

After a moment the little voice in her head whispered, "Burn down the haystack." Brie sat thinking about what that could possibly mean. What she finally decided was that she needed to sweep away everything she knew—*burn down the haystack*. Start fresh; see what appears.

Chapter 32

B rie went to her documents folder to retrieve the article Dent had sent her. Something about Leo's Mafia brethren, specifically his notorious uncle. *What was his name?* She flipped through her notebook and found it—Francis Luigi.

"Let's see what this is all about." She opened the document. It was a news story from the *Portland Press Herald*, dated August 6, 2013, and right away the headline caught her attention.

Portland May Play Role in Solving Mystery of 1990 Boston Art Heist

Brie knew about this crime. They had studied the case in one of her criminal justice courses in college. In 1990, half a billion dollars in art had been stolen from Boston's Isabella Stewart Gardner Museum. Two thieves dressed as police officers had bluffed their way into the poorly-secured museum and stolen thirteen masterworks of art—all uninsured—by Vermeer, Degas, Manet, and Rembrandt and escaped into the night in a red car. The case, unsolved to this day, and considered one of the world's most baffling crime mysteries, was still under investigation by the FBI.

The incident chronicled in the news story in the *Press Herald* had taken place in the parking lot of a Portland seafood restaurant and was considered the biggest break in the Gardner Museum art heist in years. The incident involved two men, Michael Callente and Robert Cerillo—former Mafia members and suspects in the art robbery—and their wives. In 2013, under questioning by the FBI, Callente's wife said that her husband had handed two paintings over to Robert Cerillo in the parking lot of the Portland seafood restaurant that day. She said her husband had put the paintings in the trunk of their car that morning before they left their home in central Maine to drive to Portland, two hours away.

Farther down, the news story mentioned that Callente and Cerillo had worked for notorious Mafia capo Francis Luigi and that Luigi had been investigated at the time of the heist in March of 1990. Brie sat back. *So there's the connection Dent was talking about—the connection to Leo's uncle, Francis Luigi.*

The FBI's theory was that former mobster Michael Callente, who died not long after the goings-on in the Portland parking lot, had hidden the stolen paintings from the Gardner Museum heist on his property in central Maine. However, searches of the property by the FBI failed to turn up any evidence of the stolen art.

The words "Maine" and "property" got Brie's attention and shot a pulse of adrenaline through her. *What had happened to that property?* she wondered. Peter Bendorff's stock in trade was acquiring businesses and property. What if he had read this very article back in 2013 and decided to go after that property when Callente died? And what if Leo hadn't come here on a whim, just to get out of the big city? What if he was also on the trail of that art? Was it possible that Peter Bendorff's death and this notorious art heist were somehow linked?

She pulled out her phone, hoping she still had reception. She saw bars, brought up Dent Fenton's number, and sent the call.

Dent answered on the second ring. "Brie. Are you underway?"

"Yes, Dent. Where are you?"

"Still at headquarters."

"I just read that news story you sent earlier today about the Maine connection to the Boston art heist in 1990. Fantastic to think that those priceless paintings may have found their way to a little town in central Maine."

"I don't really think it could have any bearing on the Bendorff case. Leo was in prison when the art heist took place. But the uncle's name showed up in his file along with his ties to organized crime, and a note that the FBI had investigated Luigi, the uncle, at the time of the art heist, but found no concrete connections to the crime. I sent it to you as context on Leo Dombello."

"That may be, Dent, but I've got a funny feeling about all of this."

"Really? You think it might have some bearing on the case?"

"I don't know. You got Leo connected to the uncle who used to be the boss of these two Mafia bozos in the Portland parking lot, one of whom—Callente—decided to go back to nature and live in the middle of the Maine woods. My experience, that's not how these guys roll. Then, after Callente dies, there's the wife's testimony that he had the paintings—that he gave two of them to Cerillo that day in Portland in that parking lot outside the seafood restaurant."

"But what's any of that got to do with Peter Bendorff?"

"Bendorff Enterprises specialized in acquiring businesses and property," Brie said. "I want to know who currently owns that property in central Maine that Michael Callente owned."

"Huh, very interesting thought, Brie. Let me get into the public records and see what I find."

Brie heard him clicking away on his keyboard, and topside she could hear the wind ramping up, starting to hum in the rigging. She waited, feeling that tingle of excitement, like a wild thing inside her, at the possibility of a real break in the case.

As she waited for Dent to find the property records, she was thinking about Alex Smith's account of Leo joining the theater group that he and Peter Bendorff had been part of.

What had Smith said? *It seemed like Leo was after something.* At the time Brie had thought Alex Smith was jealous of Peter's interest in Leo, but what if Alex was right? What if Leo *was* after something? Something Peter Bendorff now controlled.

After a couple minutes, Dent came back on the line. "Brie, that was a stroke of brilliance. The Callente property near Madison, Maine, was purchased by none other than Peter Bendorff in September of 2014. Callente's wife signed the papers. The death master file shows Callente died in August, so Bendorff didn't let any grass grow under his feet before approaching the widow."

"And according to my interviews, Leo moved to Maine shortly after that," Brie said. "So we have to assume that Leo had either followed the case of the stolen art or that his uncle put him on the trail of it before he died."

"Think about it, Brie. He comes out of prison. He's broke. The uncle is dying—maybe he had something to do with the art heist, maybe not. But Luigi knows Callente and Cerillo—they worked for him. So he tells Leo he thinks Callente hid the art in Maine. But now Callente dies, and Bendorff snaps up the property. He probably had his eye on it since 2013 when that article came out in the *Press Herald*."

"So Leo comes to Maine and works his way into Peter Bendorff's inner circle. When I interviewed Alexander Smith, he told me how Leo Dombello joined the theater group that he and Peter were part of."

"Well, that explains the disguise Bendorff pulled off."

"Smith said that it seemed like Leo was after something from Peter. I wrote it off as jealously, but obviously the professor was more astute than I thought."

"All those years of figuring out what his students were up to," Dent said. "I think we can assume that was no coincidence —that Leo followed Peter Bendorff and figured out how he could insert himself into Bendorff's life, how he could appear to meet him accidentally."

"And Leo's a natural character, so it made the whole theater connection believable. Problem is, Leo couldn't have commited the murder. His hand surgeon attested to that," Brie said. "So if access to the missing art is the motive in Bendorff's murder, then Leo must have had an accomplice."

"You think it's Lyle Jarvis?" Dent asked.

Brie thought for a minute. "No, I don't. When I interviewed Leo, he seemed to have nothing but disdain for Jarvis. Plus, I have testimony from two people, including Lyle Jarvis' mother, that he was happy with his life and his job, even though he complained about being under Peter Bendorff's heel. And even though the shredding of the wig and breaking of the glasses at the murder scene bear Jarvis' MO, everyone that worked with him knew about that behavior."

"So who's the next most likely suspect?"

"There's Alexander Smith, but somehow, I just don't make the former college professor for a killer. Plagiarism and theft of intellectual property, yes, but murder? I don't buy it."

"So that leaves Callum and Boardman," Dent said.

"Aside from being squeaky clean, Boardman has no motive."

"So that leaves Callum," Dent said.

Brie didn't say anything, but from the beginning she hadn't thought Callum was a fit for the crime. He seemed genuinely attached to Peter Bendorff.

"I want to go back over the interviews, Dent. See if anything jumps out."

"I'm expecting the report on the phone records any time now."

"Great. Call me when you get that. We're still near the coast, so I should have a signal."

"Good detective work, Brie—tracking that connection between Bendorff and the Callente property."

"Thanks, Dent."

"Here we thought Leo was just looking for a new lease on life."

"Maybe it falls under the heading 'you can't teach an old dog new tricks.'"

"Well, not an old Mafia dog, it seems."

They ended the call.

Brie sat back in the chair for a moment, listening to the ship talking to her in its familiar creaks and groans. She had that phrase stuck in her head. *New lease on life.* Why? What did it mean? *New lease . . .* She tapped her fingers on John's chart table as the ship rolled with the seas.

Suddenly a thought struck her like a lightning bolt. She knew why the Rebecca Bendorf interview had left her feeling unsettled. Her subconscious mind had noticed something in that report that her conscious mind had read right over. She leaned forward and opened the report and sat there staring at the name on the top of the report. Rebecca Lise Bendorff. She had looked at it a few minutes ago when she'd read the report, but now the middle name blazed off the page at her. Lise. Not a common name, but one she'd heard the night the men had boarded the ship. It had been quietly spoken into a phone up on deck that night. *Lise.* She remembered coming up from the galley and hearing someone on deck say that name into his phone. Rusty Boardman. She recalled now that he had looked startled at seeing her suddenly appear on deck, and she had thought she'd just interrupted a private call with his girlfriend because of the way he had said her name, with a soft, intimate note. In all the chaos that had followed over the last few days, that occurrence had drifted into the background noise of facts and questions, interviews and discoveries, evidence and impressions that pile up in any open case.

It was a stunning realization—one that changed everything —and she sat processing the information. First of all, if Lise was in fact Rebecca Bendorff, she had lied. In the interview,

Dent had asked her if she knew any of the men aboard the ship with her husband. She had stated that, except for Lyle Jarvis, she didn't know any of them very well. Secondly, it gave Boardman something he hadn't had before—a motive. If he was having an affair with Rebecca Bendorff, that gave him a strong motive in the murder of her husband.

And Brie had a pretty good idea how the two of them had met. Rebecca Bendorff was in charge of renovations on the residential properties her husband acquired. Boardman was in charge of security for all properties and would have been dispatched promptly to that particular property to secure it, and possibly look for a hidden vault that Bendorff was hoping existed on the property. Brie guessed that was when Boardman and Rebecca Bendorff—whom he called "Lise"—had met.

All of this connected to the theory that had taken shape in Brie's mind. She flipped through her notebook for her notes on the Boardman interview. *He was hired . . . two and a half years ago. Well, what a coincidence,* she thought. *The same year the Mafia guy dies up in the Maine woods and Bendorff acquires his property is also the same year Leo Dombello moves to Portland and Bendorff hires Rusty Boardman—ex-military security.* Coincidence? No. In detective work it's what you call a convergence of events. The pieces were in motion, sliding past one another, slipping into place, like a finely wrought Chinese puzzle box.

But other questions and facts were shooting through her brain now—lightning fast, like gamma rays. Why kill Peter Bendorff when Bendorff was planning to disappear? Boardman would have had clear access to the wife at that point.

The obvious answer had to do with the value of the stolen art—half a billion dollars. If the art had been found, then Bendorff must have had a deal going with Leo to fence the art and put that money somewhere—maybe in an offshore account where he could live on it for the rest of his life. How the timing of that was supposed to work out in relation to Peter Bendorff's disappearance was another question, but one thing was clear: Leo must have gotten greedy. So he cut a deal with Boardman.

But why would Boardman go for it? He was a straight arrow. What had bent him? What had turned him into someone who could be bought? And what had turned him into a killer? The answer was a familiar one to any detective: love and money.

Maybe Boardman worried that he couldn't support Lise in the manner to which she was accustomed. And who knew what might happen to Bendorff Enterprises and all the property it controlled? From the interviews Brie had conducted, it sounded like Peter Bendorff walked a thin line between legal and illegal practices.

What they needed now was proof. They needed to establish a connection between Leo and Boardman. Maybe if she got Leo back in here, squeezed him enough, he'd admit to a connection. Maybe she could even leverage him into giving up Boardman if they could offer him a reduced sentence.

Her head was spinning. The whole case had taken an absolutely fantastic turn. If she was right about Boardman being the killer, she had to think about the dangers of confronting him —about the security of the ship and the other passengers.

At that moment her phone rang. It was Dent Fenton. She moved to the far corner of John's cabin. With the noise of the ship and the elements, there was little chance that Boardman could hear her in his cabin across the passageway. But she wasn't taking any chances. She answered the call and spoke as softly as possible.

"Hello, Dent. I have news. Since talking to you, I've uncovered what looks like a romantic connection between Rusty Boardman and Bendorff's wife that gives Boardman a motive."

"Really!" Dent said, and Brie could almost see him sitting up straight in his chair at this news.

She filled him in on the name Lise and what had occurred on deck that first night, and how the nickel had finally dropped when she saw the name on the report.

"This is huge, Brie."

"Did the phone records show any connection between Rusty Boardman and Rebecca Bendorff?" she asked.

"That's why I was calling. The guys just finished cross-referencing all the phone records of the suspects and the Bendorffs. I'm looking at it now, but the report doesn't show any calls between Boardman and either of Rebecca Bendorff's numbers."

"I have to believe, being who he is, that Boardman would have insisted they use burner phones. What about Leo Dombello and Boardman? Anything there?" She flipped through her notebook. "When I interviewed Leo, he said that except for Peter and Alex, he didn't know any of the others personally."

There was silence, and she knew Dent was studying the report.

"You're in luck, Brie. There's one call from Leo's number to Boardman's cell phone last month. And it's the briefest of calls—only twenty seconds long."

"Just long enough for Boardman to tell him never to call that number again," Brie said.

"That'd be my guess. But nonetheless, there it is. And it establishes a connection between them."

"That's great, Dent. I think it's time I get Leo back in here and sit on him. He's been a bad egg all his adult life. Shouldn't be too hard to get him to crack. Do you think the DA would go for a reduced sentence if we can get him to give up Boardman as the killer?"

"I think he might go for that," Dent said. "There's something else that might tie in, too—that might relate to why Bendorff hired Rusty Boardman. I remember reading in Boardman's military record about him being sent into Vietnam in 1989 as part of a Special Forces unit working with the Vietnamese government to locate the remains of MIAs. Even though he'd never been in Vietnam, apparently Boardman, with the help of GPR—Ground Penetrating Radar that had been developed by the military in the seventies—had this uncanny ability, even all those years after the war, to locate the POW pits where the Viet Cong had imprisoned American soldiers. He and his team recovered the remains of dozens of soldiers and finally brought those boys home to rest."

"Interesting," Brie said. "I guess finding that vault on the former Callente property would be child's play for Boardman after what you're describing. Sad, though, that someone who served with such honor ever got involved with Peter Bendorff. When I interviewed him, he said there had been an article in the *Press Herald* about his decorated career when he left the military and moved back to Portland. He said that Peter Bendorff had seen that article and contacted him about the job."

"And now we know why," Dent said.

"It's time to get Leo in here and see what I can squeeze out of him," Brie said. "We already know a lot, which ups the chances that he'll crack."

"That's right, but you need to be extremely careful, Brie. It's a whole other ballgame now that we've made Boardman as the killer."

"I've thought about that, Dent. It's good I've got Marty here for backup."

"Even so, for everyone's safety, it's important that Boardman doesn't know we've tumbled to the whole thing. We'll be on the dock to arrest him when he comes off the ship in Camden tomorrow morning."

"Roger that, Dent. I'll see what I can get out of Leo."

"Keep me posted." He gave her the Maine State Police radio frequency. "In case we lose cell contact, you can reach me via the ship's radio or have the Coast Guard patch through a call if need be."

Brie jotted down the frequency, and they ended the call. She sat tapping her pen on the chart table. If she hoped to turn Leo, she needed to review the interview she'd done with him earlier. She took her digital recorder out of the drawer and backtracked through the interviews till she got to Leo's. She flipped to a fresh page in her notebook and began listening to the interview.

She was amazed at Leo's tone and how well he had played her—the feigned sadness and concern about how Peter had died and whether he had suffered. And his words, "You can't think I had anything to do with Peter's death . . . We were friends. I cared about him." As it turned out, Leo really was a studied actor and a practiced liar. You needed a machete to cut through the innocent curmudgeon, friendly-uncle-teaches-his-nephews-how-to-bake-bread act.

He was a master manipulator who beat Peter Bendorff at his own game, Brie thought. She shook her head as she listened to the rest of the interview, amazed that, despite what she now knew about Leo Dombello, she still had a hard time not being entertained by his act.

Brie turned off the recorder. Time to go topside and talk to Marty and John. She pulled on her rain jacket, buckled her PFD, and stepped out of the cabin. A single hurricane lamp hung from the overhead swung pendulum-like, casting spectral light around the passageway. Topside she could hear the roar of the wind. She locked the captain's door and headed up the ladder.

Chapter 33

A cold, salty wind struck Brie full in the face as she made the deck. Except for the lanterns hung in the rigging as running lights, total darkness engulfed the ship. No moon, no stars. Mounting seas rolled out of the darkness to starboard like tremendous folds of black liquid silk. The storm had yet to catch them, but it had sent its harbingers ahead in the form of wind and seas to prepare them for what was in store.

John had the helm, and in the lantern light Brie saw he was one hundred percent focused on the task at hand. She stepped over to Marty, who stood behind the helm, feet spread wide for balance, his barrel chest even more exaggerated by his orange PFD.

She signaled for him to go further aft, away from the companionway, and then leaned in close and spoke over the roar of the wind. "There's been a break in the case. I believe Boardman is our man. I've just talked to Dent."

Marty nodded. "What can I do?" he said over the wind.

Brie leaned in again. "You feeling seasick at all?"

"No. Thought for sure I would be."

"Then I need you to go forward and get Leo and bring him aft. I need to talk to him. He won't want to come, but there'll be less backtalk if you go for him."

Marty looked toward the bow, and Brie saw a flash of uncertainty in his eyes about navigating the pitching deck in the dark.

"Take the starboard deck and hold on to the lifeline above the gunwale. Those sea boots you borrowed from George have good grip on the deck."

"Which cabin, Brie?"

"Cabin three. And make sure you buckle him into his PFD."

"Roger that."

Marty headed forward, and Brie stepped up to the helm and stood on John's right to be farther from the companionway. He tipped his head toward her, and she spoke into his ear. "There's been a development in the case, John. Something's come to light."

Now he turned his head and studied her eyes in the lantern light, looking for some clue.

"Can't say too much." She nodded toward the companionway and lowered her voice. "The ship has ears, if you catch my drift."

He leaned close to her and said, "I need to know."

Brie nodded. *Of course he does. He's the captain.*

She took hold of the collar of his rain jacket and put her mouth to his ear. "It's Boardman," she said, just loud enough for him to hear.

He turned and looked at her, and she saw the alarm, dark and intense, in his eyes. Of everyone aboard, Rusty Boardman, with his military background, could potentially pose the greatest threat.

"Are we safe?" he asked.

"Yes. I've talked to Dent. He'll have the Mounties on hand when we dock tomorrow. And we have Marty aboard. We just need to maintain the status quo—get through the night."

John studied her face but said nothing.

She leaned in again. "I've sent Marty for Leo. I need to question him some more. He's part of the equation. Do you think we could be overheard in your cabin?"

John was silent for a moment but then leaned in. "I don't think so. Boardman's across the passageway to starboard. With the ship's creaking and the wind, there's plenty of noise down there."

"Don't forget snoring," Brie said, trying to lighten the mood.

John smiled. "That too."

She slipped her arms around his waist and gave him a hug, as much to fortify herself as him. Just then she saw Leo and Marty up forward. Marty ushered Leo over to the starboard rail and walked close behind him, giving him some support against the wind and the pitch of the deck. *Marty is as surefooted as any of the mates aboard,* Brie thought. Then she remembered that he was a fly fisherman, used to keeping his balance in rushing rivers. She needn't have worried about his surefootedness on deck. Marty was as adaptable as any person Brie had ever met, and she admired him for that. *Whatever is called for, he just rolls with it.*

When they got near the helm, Marty took hold of Leo and steered him around behind the captain and over to the ladder. Marty went down first to make sure someone was there if Leo slipped. Leo wasn't young, and Brie was pretty sure he hadn't spent any time in rushing rivers. She followed them down the ladder and was fishing the key out of her pocket when Boardman's cabin door opened and he stepped into the passageway. Leo looked startled by his appearance, and a brief moment of nonverbal communication seemed to pass between them.

Boardman's gaze traveled to Brie and on to Marty. Did he intuit that something was up? Was it her imagination, or was the tension in the passageway as palpable as it seemed? She wished the timing had been different. Or maybe his entrance into the passageway at that moment was no accident. She unlocked the door and ushered Leo into the captain's cabin. Marty stationed himself outside the door, and Boardman crossed to the head and stepped inside.

Brie flipped on the battery-operated light over the chart table, and it cast a dim light around the cabin. There was a second light on the overhead, and she flipped it on. Leo waddled across the cabin and crawled into John's berth. "You can talk to me if you must, but I need to lie down. I don't feel well."

"That's fine, Leo. Are you seasick?"

"I was fine till your copper friend dragged me out of bed."

"Sorry, Leo, but I need to talk to you." She took off her PFD and jacket. She turned on her recorder, got the stool from the corner, and sat opposite him. "I think there are some things you neglected to tell me when we spoke this morning." *This morning? My interview with him seems like a week ago.*

"Okay, so I've got a record. And I've been in prison." He draped a thick arm over his eyes. "You didn't ask me about it, so I didn't tell you. Think of it as our own little version of 'Don't Ask, Don't Tell.' Anyway, I knew you'd find out soon enough."

"I don't start out with the assumption that everyone is a criminal, Leo. That kind of attitude gets too many cops in trouble. I believe in the tenet of 'innocent until proven guilty.'"

"Good for you," Leo said in a flippant way.

"On the other hand, it's my job to find out where guilt lies." *And right now it's lying on John's berth,* she thought.

Leo had no comment, so she pressed on. "Tell me about the art, Leo."

"What art?"

"The art from the Gardner Museum heist in Boston in 1990."

She thought she saw him flinch ever so slightly. "I was in prison in 1990." He removed the arm from over his eyes and peered at her. "You're supposed to be looking for Peter's killer."

"Look, Leo, you can stonewall, but here are the facts. Your uncle, Francis Luigi, if not involved in the art heist, knew the guys who were. One of them, Michael Callente, moved to Maine, bought property, and later died here. Within a month after his death, Peter Bendorff had acquired his property. Coincidence? I don't think so. It was big news in Maine when two of the paintings from the infamous art heist were thought to have changed hands in the parking lot of a Portland restaurant. My guess is, from that point on, Peter Bendorff was closely tracking the property where Callente lived up in central Maine."

"The FBI searched that property twice and found nothing," Leo blurted out.

"Oh, so you do know about the art and the property. Did your uncle tell you about that?"

Leo lay silent.

"Anyway, moving on. So Bendorff buys the property, and right after that you move to Maine and end up in a theater group with Peter Bendorff. Coincidence? I don't think so. You're deep in it, Leo."

Leo lay silent.

"But wait. There's more," Brie said, stifling a smile. "Phone records show a call placed by you last month to Rusty Boardman's cell phone, even though, of the men on the ship, you claimed to know only Peter Bendorff and Alex Smith. You also claimed that the night of the faked suicide, after we allowed everyone to go to bed, that you slept soundly for the rest of the night. But Alexander Smith has testified that when he came down to use the head, around four twenty, he heard you moving around in your cabin."

"So shoot me," Leo said sarcastically.

"Don't tempt me, Leo."

Leo let out a sigh.

"I talked to your hand surgeon, Dr. Andrews."

Leo looked hopeful that this might be his big break.

"Dr. Andrews told me you couldn't have murdered Peter Bendorff with your hands in the shape they're in."

"Ha! I told you so." Leo pointed a stubby finger at her.

"However . . . you certainly could have masterminded the whole thing, and I believe you did. And I believe the reason you were up moving around in your cabin was that you were the lookout for Boardman when he committed the murder."

"No! You've got it all wrong." Suddenly Leo was on his feet, gesticulating wildly with his hands.

Brie was on her feet, too—hand on her gun in her holster.

"I just wanted the art. I never wanted Peter to die. I loved him."

"You don't need to exaggerate, Leo."

"I'm not." He sat on the edge of the berth and buried his face in his hands. "I'm not," he sobbed.

Brie sat down on the stool, stunned. Maybe Leo had not been acting in her first interview with him when he'd asked how Peter died and if he had suffered. If she was to believe what was unfolding before her, Leo Dombello had been in love with Peter Bendorff.

"If that's the truth, Leo, and you're not involved in the murder, then you need to start talking. You need to tell me everything you know about the stolen art and Boardman's connection to it."

Leo threw his hands up. "All right . . . all right."

"First of all, you claim you loved Peter Bendorff. If that's the case, why steal the paintings from him?" she asked.

"I didn't say my feelings were returned. Peter was entertained by me, but that's all. And well, I'm pretty much broke. After I got to know Pete, worked my way into his inner circle, I told him I could set up some offshore accounts for him. And along the way, I casually mentioned that I had fenced art and jewelry. Just to plant the seed."

"So you set up offshore accounts for him. What did you get in return?"

"I laundered mob money through his businesses and got a cut. It wasn't much of a living, but it was something. So you see, I needed that art."

Brie smiled to herself at the logic of criminals.

"I needed the art, but Rusty Boardman held all the cards. He was the security expert, the one who was going to find that vault, and he was this decorated hero. Mr. Honorable. I knew I had no chance at the art once Peter hired him." Leo let out a dramatic sigh.

"Go on," Brie said.

"But then one day I followed Boardman out to the old Callente property. Rebecca Bendorff was there, and it didn't take long for me to size up what was going on between them. That's when I knew how I'd get to Boardman."

"So you threatened to tell Peter about their affair if he didn't throw in with you."

Leo shrugged and held out his hands in an innocent gesture. "Neither one of them was going to be able to fence that art without me. I was the one with the connections. So I went to work on Boardman. Told him if he'd let me know when he found the vault, I'd cut him in. Pete sure wasn't going to do that."

"So what was the plan?" Brie asked.

"It was supposed to be a three-way split. Of course, Pete didn't know that. That was just between me and Boardman."

"Did you find the stolen art?" Brie asked, amazed that there might finally be a resolution to this decades-old crime.

"Yes we did," Leo said, an odd note of pride in his voice. "A vault had been constructed deep into the side of a hill on the far corner of the property. It was a good-sized property. Thirty, forty acres of woods. I'm sure all the work had been done off the books by Callente's mob connections. My uncle got wind of it. Said Callente was smart, that he didn't build the vault right away, that he had stashed the art elsewhere. The FBI searched and searched and finally they backed off. That's when Callente went ahead with the construction.

"The plan was to open the vault before we told Peter about it and if we found anything, take our cut. Boardman had the skills needed to open the vault and crack the safe we found inside. The safe was the size of a small room. Inside it, we found ten of the original thirteen artworks. Two were handed off that day in Portland. And the other one—who knows? Probably sold on the black market."

"So the plan was for you and Boardman to each take some of the art and then tell Peter Bendorff what?"

"We planned to each take three of the paintings and leave four of them for Peter. Then Boardman would tell Pete he'd found the vault, and Pete would be none the wiser. It still meant tens of millions for Pete. I was the lynchpin, you might say. It all depended on me using my black market connections in Europe to fence the art."

"And Rebecca Bendorff, how was she involved in any of this?"

"She wasn't. She was clean. She didn't know anything about the art or Peter's plan to disappear. Boardman said if I told Lise—that's what he called her—if I ever told her anything, he'd kill me. And I believed him. He saw the money from the art as a way to support her in the manner she was used to."

"Did he say that?"

"No, I just knew."

"So why would he kill him, Leo? He's got the money, he's got the girl. Why? What's his motive, when Bendorff was taking himself off the map?"

"Protecting himself, maybe. Or fear of revenge if Pete ever found out he'd been double-crossed. He told me he was nervous about Peter finding out about the art swindle, and

Boardman doesn't scare easy. But he knew Peter could make his life miserable even from a distance. He had the connections to do it. Alive, Peter Bendorff was a loose end."

Leo turned his tired eyes on Brie. "Peter was a shrewd guy, and he liked to have control over people. That's why he sought out employees and friends that he would have some hold over. Now Boardman, he was the exception to that rule. Pete needed his skill set."

"You were an exception too, Leo."

"You're right. All my crimes are pretty much a matter of record." Leo sighed. "Pete was bound to meet his match sooner or later."

"And he met his match in you. Is that right, Leo?"

Leo shrugged. "I was born to the criminal life. Peter . . . well, he was no match for that. In my family, crime is a business. You do what you have to do to get a certain result, but no more. Pete was an easy target, but he didn't deserve to die. This might surprise you, but he was a generous guy. Rusty Boardman went too far." Leo's gaze came unfocused. "You know the ironic part?"

"What?"

"Six months ago, Peter told me to set up an offshore account in his wife's name and put his share from the sale of the art in it. He made me swear I wouldn't tell anybody about the account and that I'd never tell her where the money came from. He said he had all the money he'd ever need and that he wanted her to be taken care of should anything happen to the company." Leo let out a sigh. "So Boardman killed Pete for nothing. He could've had the wife. She would've had the money from the art. They could have lived happily ever after, and him with his nose clean."

"Well, not that clean," Brie said. "He was still involved in one of the biggest art heists in history."

Leo shrugged like it was no big deal.

"So I take it the art is gone?"

Leo pursed his lips and nodded.

"You need to turn state's evidence on Boardman. Tell the police about his part in finding and stealing the art from Bendorff, and about his affair with Bendorff's wife and what you witnessed between them. All that goes to motive. If you do, and you give up your black market connections to the stolen art, we'll work with the Feds to get you a lighter sentence."

Leo threw his arms up in disgust. "What difference does it make? I'm gonna die in prison anyway."

"But which prison will it be, Leo? We could work a deal to get you in a better spot—a safer spot where . . ." She stopped talking and turned her head. Over the noise of the wind, she was picking up a sound—the throaty roar of a boat engine, what sounded like a lobsterboat. And it was close by. The pitch of the sound was getting higher—the boat was approaching. She stood and grabbed her rain jacket off the hook next to the berth. "Stay right here, Leo."

She turned toward the cabin door, and all of a sudden there was a loud fracas in the passageway. She threw the jacket aside, drew her gun, and bolted from the cabin. Marty lay in the passageway, dazed, and Rusty Boardman was just clearing the ladder onto the deck. Brie bounded up the ladder in time to see Boardman climb up on the rail.

"Stop," she shouted and leveled her gun at him just as he dove headlong into the sea.

"What the hell's going on, Brie?" John shouted from the helm.

She rushed to the rail and searched the black water for some sign of Boardman. Then Marty was at her side, and within seconds Scott appeared aft with a search light. He turned it on and trained it on the water just in time to see Boardman pull himself out of the water and over the side of a lobsterboat a hundred yards from the ship.

"Get a light on that boat's call numbers," Brie shouted, but the lobsterboat was already accelerating, speeding away into the darkness.

Brie raised an arm to mark the boat's heading. "What's his bearing, John?"

John looked from the compass to Brie's arm. "Bearing zero —eight—zero." He reached over and picked up the radio receiver and hailed the Coast Guard.

"Mayday—Mayday—Mayday."

Chapter 34

Off on the the eastern horizon, lightning strobed, and the sound of thunder rolled across the ink dark sea. Captain DuLac delivered the distress call again.

"Mayday—Mayday—Mayday. This is *Maine Wind— Maine Wind—Maine Wind*. Whiskey—Alpha—Three—Two—Niner—Seven. Mayday. Marshall Point Light bears zero—four—five magnetic. Distance eight miles. We are en route to Camden, Maine, transporting a murder suspect. Maine State Police aboard. Suspect has escaped overboard and boarded a lobsterboat. I say again, suspect has escaped overboard and boarded lobsterboat. Their heading is due east toward Canadian waters. Need your assistance to intercept fleeing vessel and apprehend suspect. Over."

"*Maine Wind*, this is the US Coast Guard. We have received your coordinates and have a fix on your position. We are tracking a second vessel on AIS traveling at twenty-eight knots, heading east. We are sending an RB-M in pursuit of the fleeing vessel. We will coordinate with Canadian Coast Guard in event we cannot overtake fleeing vessel. Over."

"Request you rendezvous with us and take Officer Beaumont aboard. She can identify the suspect. Over."

"Roger. We will rendezvous and take Officer Beaumont aboard. ETA—twenty-two fifteen. Stay on Channel Twenty-two for further communication. Over."

"Roger, Coast Guard. We will continue to monitor. This is *Maine Wind* Whiskey—Alpha—Three—Two—Niner—Seven. Over and out."

Lightning and thunder made a steady advance on their position now, and the wind had ratcheted up to near gale force.

"Head back to the bow, Scott. I need both you and Ed up there in these conditions. Douse that jib and rig the storm jib."

"Aye, Captain."

Scott headed forward, listing along the starboard deck toward the bow.

"Marty!" Brie called out and signaled him over. "Take Leo back to his cabin and get him secured."

Marty headed down the ladder to collect Leo.

"I need to go below and get on my raingear, John."

"Go now," he said. "The Coast Guard is on the way. ETA twenty-five minutes. I'm going to hold to this heading as long as I can, but if the wind ramps up much more, we'll need to heave to and ride this out."

"Aye, Captain."

Brie went down the ladder to John's cabin to retrieve her rain jacket. She pulled it on, zipped it up, and slipped her PFD over her head and buckled it in place. She headed back up the ladder and along the starboard deck, leaning toward the rail and into the strong wind to keep her balance. She pushed the companionway hatch back, descended the ladder into the galley, and took off her PFD and jacket.

Her sea boots and foul weather bibs were at the back of the galley where the crew hung their wet gear. She grabbed the boots and overalls and listed toward one of the benches behind the table to sit and put them on. She pulled her Maine State Police ID out of her pants pocket and put it into her jacket pocket. Then she wrestled her way into the bib overalls as the ship's bow rose and fell, bucking the rising seas like a harpooned whale. She stood, pulled the suspenders up over her shoulders, and stuffed her feet into her sea boots. The lamps and George's pots and pans swayed wildly on their hooks. She could hear the wind topside whistling like a mad banshee, and now she heard the rain start down, a thousand boney fingers hitting the deck all at once.

She pulled her rain jacket back on, put her inflatable PFD over her head and buckled it. Her gun was buried under her foul weather gear. If necessary she could always get to it, but if it came to a shootout, the Coast Guard carried weapons far more effective than her Glock.

She put on her ball cap, pulled up her hood and tightened it down, and listed across the galley toward the ladder. She climbed the rungs, hands on the brass rails for balance, as *Maine Wind* heeled steeply to port. She slid the companionway hatch back, scrambled up the last few rungs, and secured the hatch.

Up on deck things were getting interesting. Rain pounded down, and she could barely make out the quarterdeck, where the captain stood at the helm. Boarding seas crashed over the bow as the ship dove into the trenches. The captain had ordered Scott and Ed farther aft for safety, and they were up on the galley house shortening the foresail.

Brie grasped the lifeline and headed aft along the starboard deck. Just then, Marty came up the ladder from the amidships compartment, where he had just stowed Leo, and listed toward her. He fell in behind her at the rail, buffering some of the savagery of wind and rain they were driving into. Brie and Marty did the foul weather sailor's walk aft, leaning forward, feet spread wide for balance.

Back at the helm, Brie leaned in to get an update from the captain. "We're going to heave to so the Coast Guard can take you aboard," he shouted over the wind. "We'll stay hove to until the storm weakens, for the comfort of the passengers. After Scott and Ed back the jib, I want you three to ease the main and foresheets."

"Aye, Captain."

Brie headed forward.

"Prepare to heave to," the captain called over the wind.
The crew took their positions.

"Ready about?"

"Ready."

"Hard alee."

John cranked the big ship's wheel around, steering upwind to starboard. When they were dead into the wind, Scott released the jib sheet over to port, and Brie and Ed hauled the storm jib in and belayed it off on the starboard side. The captain eased the ship back off the wind a few points so they were hove to, sailing upwind. The crewmates made their way aft and eased the fore and mainsheets.

Back aft, John hailed the Coast Guard on Channel 22. "Coast Guard, this is *Maine Wind*, Whiskey—Alpha—Three—Two—Niner—Seven. We are hove to, awaiting your arrival. Over."

"We have you in sight, *Maine Wind*. ETA five minutes. We will make our approach to starboard. Have Officer Beaumont ready to board. Over."

"Roger, Coast Guard. *Maine Wind* over and out."

Chapter 35

B rie heard the hum of the RB-M's engines even before its lights penetrated the heavy gloom of rain and darkness. By the time the boat came fully into sight, it was almost upon them. The RB-M throttled down and coasted up on the windward side of *Maine Wind*. Brie was at the starboard rail waiting. She and Scott lowered the boarding ladder, and she shinnied down it and stepped onto the heaving deck of the Coast Guard response boat, where she was greeted by one of the seamen.

"Welcome aboard, Ma'am," he shouted over the wind. "Follow me, please." He ushered her into the door at the back of the pilothouse.

The helmsman, seated in the forward starboard chair, turned and greeted her. "Petty Officer Joseph Adams, Ma'am."

Brie extended her hand. "Detective Brie Beaumont, Maine State Police." She pulled her ID from her pocket and flipped it open. "I'm carrying my off-duty weapon, a Glock nine millimeter."

"Noted," Adams said. "I've been apprised of the situation. We have the fleeing vessel on radar and should overtake them. ETA at their position approximately one hour. Rough seas ahead though, so take a seat and strap in, Detective."

Brie took the seat diagonally behind Petty Officer Adams and buckled her seatbelt as the response boat pulled away from *Maine Wind*. Petty Officer Adams throttled up the engines and they sped east. It was a surreal feeling. The elements raged around them, but the ride was surprisingly smooth and quiet as the RB-M rose up on its twin water jets and accelerated over the turbulent waters—a sensation more akin to flying than traveling by boat.

Being a former Great Lakes sailor, Brie was fully aware of the indispensable function of the Coast Guard on both inland and coastal waterways and took an interest in any new developments in the service. She had read about the Coast Guard's new Response Boat—Medium, but state of the art seemed an understatement for the technology currently surrounding her. Propelled by two Rolls Royce FF Series water jets, the twin diesel engines sent the 45-foot RB-M through the water at speeds up to 42.5 knots with a range of 250 nautical miles when traveling at 30 knots. The water jets eliminated the need for propellers beneath the boat, which protected the engines and made for safer retrieval of victims from the water.

Inside the climate-controlled pilothouse, there was no jolting or bouncing as Brie and the three Coast Guardsmen rode in shock-mitigating seats designed for crew comfort and endurance. The seas ran out of the northeast now, and the RB-M took them in stride as they washed over her decks, occasionally engulfing the pilothouse. At those moments the experience felt akin to being in a submarine as the seas momentarily swallowed the pilothouse, surging past windows placed overhead and all around the top of the house.

From where she sat, Brie could see the radar screen on the starboard console in front of the helmsman's chair. They were slowly gaining on the fleeing lobsterboat. She glanced at her watch—just shy of eleven p.m. She closed her eyes momentarily, lulled by the comfort of the seat and the jet-propelled ride. The day had been long and exhausting. She just needed a moment's rest.

*   *   *

Brie jolted awake when she heard the response boat's loudhailer. "This is the United States Coast Guard. Heave to and prepare to be boarded."

The RB-M's search lights were trained on the fleeing vessel, which gave no response but appeared to speed up.

Petty Officer Adams keyed the mic. "I say again, heave to, heave to. This is the US Coast Guard," the loudhailer broadcast.

The renegade lobsterboat accelerated, driving through storm and night-blackened seas—charging up the crests of mounting waves and surfing down their backs. Brie was wide awake now, staring through the response boat's rain-besieged windshield, riveted on the scene unfolding all around them. The RB-M's search lights revealed tumultuous seas, building, mounting as the storm intensified. She thought about *Maine Wind*, hove to, riding it out, and hoped they were safe.

An array of equipment was mounted atop the pilothouse: lights, radar scanner, and mast that held communication antennas. The wind whistled and keened through all that equipment, and seas broke over them as they maintained their pursuit of the fleeing vessel.

The officer at the helm switched on the loudhailer. "This is the Coast Guard. Reduce speed and heave to or risk capsizing in these seas. I say again, reduce speed and heave to."

No response from the lobsterboat.

"Arrogant SOBs," the helmsman said, just loud enough for Brie to pick up.

"They're really traveling," Brie said, loud enough for Petty Officer Adams to hear.

He turned his head slightly. "Some of these lobsterboats with their souped-up engines can do fifty to sixty miles per hour. They're tempting fate on a night like this, though."

The chase continued over the next twenty minutes, with the Coast Guard repeatedly pulling alongside the fleeing lobsterboat, ordering them to heave to. But to no avail.

Petty Officer Adams had just radioed the Coast Guard at Station Bar Harbor and St. Johns, New Brunswick for assistance in intercepting the fleeing vessel when the navigator seated to his left shouted, "Captain, look there, look there!"

Brie squinted through the windshield of the response boat and couldn't believe what she was seeing. The mother of all monstrous seas rose up before them, ancient, vast, deadly, and determined. A solid black wall of water that seemed to have no top to it—a juggernaut, a ship-eater, if ever there had been one.

Petty Officer Adams pushed the throttle full open and veered northeast, steering the boat directly up the face of the monster sea. He hailed the lobsterboat once more. "Fleeing vessel—beware rogue wave. Beware rogue wave. Heave to. Heave to." And then the Coast Guard response boat went vertical. Brie was pressed back in her seat by the extreme angle of the wave and the speed the response boat had achieved. It was the elevator ride from hell, and within seconds they burst through the top of the behemoth wave and careened down its gargantuan back.

"Holy Mother of God," the young seaman next to her exclaimed. "There went one of my nine lives."

Brie wasn't sure if he was swearing or praying, but his words certainly captured the feeling in the pilothouse.

Petty Officer Adams came about and headed southwest in the direction they had just come from.

"Nothing showing on the radar," the navigator said. "No sign of the boat. It's like the sea just swallowed them up."

Petty Officer Adams sent a distress call, requesting a helicopter and additional search boats to scour the waters for any trace of the lost vessel, and they continued searching for the next forty-five minutes, until the relief boats arrived. Petty Officer Adams received a call with orders to return to Station Boothbay. The RB-Ms were needed for fast response to unfolding emergencies at sea. Adams set a heading southwest and sent a call to *Maine Wind* on Channel 22.

"*Maine Wind—Maine Wind—Maine Wind.* This is the Coast Guard. Please radio your coordinates. Over."

John came back immediately and gave their position.

"We are returning Detective Beaumont to your position. Over."

"We read you, Coast Guard. Will be on lookout. Over and out."

The very sound of John's voice comforted Brie. All she wanted was to see *Maine Wind* safely in her berth in Camden and know this ordeal was finally at an end.

The trip back to *Maine Wind* took a little under an hour. After the worst of the storm had passed, John had once again set course for home port. When the Coast Guard response boat was a few minutes out, *Maine Wind* hove to temporarily to receive Brie back aboard. John sent her below to sleep and would listen to no objections from her that she should stand watch.

"Scott and Ed haven't had to run down a killer the last twenty-four hours. Go. Sleep. That's an order."

He smiled when he said it, but Brie knew when she was outgunned. "Aye, Captain." She headed below, stowed her raingear at the back of the galley, and headed for her berth. She crawled under her covers, and it was lights out the minute her head hit the pillow.

Chapter 36

Brie woke to the sound of George clanking around in the galley. She heard the squeal of the feeding door on Old Faithful and knew he must be getting the oven up to temperature to bake some wonderful, savory concoction for breakfast. She rolled out of her berth. She was still in her clothes from the night before. She grabbed her towel and toiletries and headed for the shower in the amidships compartment.

She was back down at her berth within fifteen minutes. She climbed into a clean pair of cargo khakis and a snug-fitting, hooded, black fleece top, and worked her wet hair into a French braid. It was cold up on deck, having been officially fall now for several weeks, so she pulled on her watch cap, donned her heavy jacket, and headed out into the galley.

"The first pot of coffee is done, Brie. Like a cup?"

"I'd love a cup, George."

"Scott told me about what happened last night with Boardman." He poured her a mugful and handed it to her. "The whole thing is almost unbelievable."

"I know," Brie said. "The final frenzied act in this crazy drama. I've seen a lot in my time as a cop, but last night—that might be the capper." She wrapped her hands covetously around the mug and took a sip. "Ahhh. That's the stuff, George. Don't ever stop making this wonderful brew."

"Did you see the captain on deck?"

"No, Scott's at the helm. We're just approaching Vinalhaven off to starboard. I'll get the deck swabbed topside and then come down and help in the galley. I take it we're eating on the fly."

"Yup, Scott said the captain's dead set on getting back to port by nine or ten a. m. at the latest."

Brie finished her mug of coffee and headed up on deck. She went to the bosun's box and got out her mop and bucket, which she lowered over the side via the line attached to fill with seawater for swabbing the deck. The familiar routine of morning deck chores felt good after all the craziness of the past couple days.

Ed appeared on deck now and went for his bucket and mop and started down the port side of the deck. Brie finished her side and sluiced everything down with a few buckets of seawater, then went to check in with Scott.

"Morning, Brie. Did you sleep well?"

"Like the dead. Not to coin any moribund metaphors."

"Sure don't need any of those. The captain filled me in on the bizarre outcome with Rusty Boardman and the sinking of that lobsterboat."

"I suppose the word will come down eventually about who was involved—whose boat that was. I'm afraid I'll be long gone by then."

"You leave for Minnesota tomorrow?"

"Yup." Brie was silent for a moment.

"We'll all miss you, Brie. It goes without saying."

"Thanks, Scott." Brie suddenly felt her emotions well up —probably the stress of the past twenty-four hours. She turned her head away so Scott wouldn't see. "I should go below and help George with the breakfast."

"Go," Scott said. "We've got things under control up here. You come take the helm after breakfast, though. It'll be your last chance."

Brie turned and gave him a two-fingered salute as she headed forward.

Down in the galley she helped George prep the batter for blueberry pancakes, and they cut up and combined all the fruit that was left from the voyage into a large bowl to go with the breakfast. Then they worked side by side at the stove, frying bacon and sausages and making several dozen pancakes. Ed came below when he'd finished the chores and helped get the dishes and everything up on deck for the breakfast service.

Dawn had broken ghost gray, but since then the sun had burned through the fog, and a fresh breeze had blown in a fine morning at sea. By 0800 the four remaining shipmates had come topside, and George rang the ship's bell for breakfast. The breakfast was delicious, but it was a sober crowd—made even more so when the captain, in answer to questions about Rusty Boardman's whereabouts, explained that Boardman had tried to flee the ship last night in a vessel that was later lost at sea. John nixed any further questions by saying that the Coast Guard was still searching for survivors. There were lots of other questions about the case, which Brie refused to comment on because the case was still officially open.

Brie finished her breakfast and spelled Scott at the helm, and later, with John beside her, she brought *Maine Wind* into its home waters, where they headed upwind and lowered and furled the sails for the last time. All hands got on the lines and lowered the yawl, and Scott climbed down the ladder, fired up the yawl, and pushed the ship the rest of the way into the harbor to her berth. Brie stayed at the wheel with John by her side until it was time to man the docking lines.

The Maine State Police had been radioed about their arrival and were there to take Leo into custody for his part in the sale of stolen art from the Gardner Museum heist. Later, after the other passengers had departed, they emptied Leo's cabin and took his possessions back to John's boat yard for storage, until the police decided what should be done with them.

Joe Callum decided not to press charges against Lyle Jarvis for throwing him overboard. And in a rare moment of concession, Jarvis actually offered Callum a sincere apology. As to Alexander Smith and the questions about his book, it remained to be seen what would transpire, and whether Dr. Holmes' computer could be located and searched for evidence of the manuscript.

Brie and Scott went about the ship collecting all the towels and bed linens. They took them into town to the Laundromat and then bagged and boxed them for storage over the winter. George emptied and cleaned the galley from top to bottom, and all of a sudden it was time to say goodbye. Scott and George packed their seabags and left the ship, but not before long hugs were exchanged and a few tears were shed by Brie.

In the afternoon, Brie met Dent Fenton and Marty Dupuis at the Maine State Police Troop D headquarters in Augusta. Brie spent several hours filling out reports on the case and turning over her notes and recordings of the interviews with the passengers. She called Joe Wolf, the ME, to fill him in on the disposition of the case. The Evidence Response Team had just begun processing what they had collected from the crime scene aboard ship, so it was way too early to know if any evidence would turn up connecting Rusty Boardman to the murder. But his motives had been established, and his jumping ship was apparently the act of a desperate and guilty man.

Finally, it was time for more goodbyes. Brie turned over her badge and ID to Dent, gave him and Marty big hugs, and promised she would stay in touch. Dent told her he expected to hand that badge back to her in a few months, after she had sorted things out back in Minnesota. "You know your sea captain can't live without you," he said, and Brie thought she detected just a shade of something in his voice—regret, maybe, that he hadn't found her first. It was five o'clock when she left the troop headquarters and headed back toward the ship in John's truck.

Chapter 37

Before dinner, Brie and John wandered around the village of Camden so Brie could buy gifts for her mom and her friend Ariel. She and her mom were scheduled to go up North for a few days by Lake Superior as soon as she got home. She hadn't spent any prolonged time with her mother for several years, and this would be their chance to really kick back and catch up on each other's lives.

In a shop that sold lovely stoneware, Brie bought her mom a set of coffee mugs painted with Maine blueberries and a coffee table book about houses of Maine that were designed to fit the land. In a small gift shop farther up the street, Brie found a miniature working sextant that she bought for Ariel. It was a piece of whimsy but also an authentic representation of the connection between sea and sky. She thought Ariel would love it. After all, her friend spent a lot of time with her head in the clouds, figuratively speaking.

Then she and John meandered back down the street to Waterfront to have dinner. The wind had died down and the evening was lovely, so they asked to be seated out on the covered deck and were given a table right next to the harbor. They'd shared a bottle of Pinot Noir and a wonderful dinner of steamed lobster and fresh seared halibut with all the trimmings. Brie had told John it had to be lobster because it would be her last chance for a while. They lingered over dessert—cheesecake for Brie and key lime pie for John—and rich black coffee. After dinner, they strolled along through the village a little more and back to the small park where the Megunticook River thundered down a waterfall and emptied into the harbor.

"I still don't know why Boardman would have jumped ship like that in the middle of a storm. What was he thinking?" John asked.

"He was probably thinking he was about to be caught. He saw me bring Leo into your cabin last night. Maybe he thought Leo would try to cut a deal—reveal Boardman's involvement with the stolen art. Boardman was so far off the map by that point, I guess he thought his only option was to try to run. The police don't know yet who the other guy on the lobsterboat was, but obviously he had to be a friend or relative who thought he could get Boardman into hiding, maybe in the Canadian Maritimes."

"Crazy."

"Yup."

"And what about Leo? What will happen to him?"

"The Feds will prosecute, since he was involved in the transport of stolen goods across state lines, and the Gardner Museum heist was already in their jurisdiction."

"You gotta admit it was hard not to like Leo, though."

"You're right. He's a character, but sadly, one who was born to a life of crime."

John slid an arm around Brie, and they stood under the lights in the park, listening to the waterfall.

"You know one of the stranger coincidences in this whole thing?"

"What?" John asked.

"Remember when we were at Sentinel Island in July?"

"Sure."

"Well, the artist that went missing from there—Amanda Whitcomb? Remember the story that old Harriet Patterson, the island matriarch, told about Amanda's involvement with that man and his black market art ring when she was living in France as a young artist?"

"I do remember."

"She said that man had come to America, to the island, just a few years ago, looking for Amanda. An odd coincidence, don't you think, considering the Maine connection to the stolen art?"

"Do you think he really came here looking for Amanda?"

"It would have been nice to think he came back for her, but—call me a cynic—I didn't believe it then, and now I really don't. I'll bet you anything if he wasn't connected to the stolen art, he was looking to be."

"You'll have to fill Dent in," John said.

"It's a lead the FBI could follow," Brie said. "It wouldn't be hard for them to learn who he was. Somebody in the Whitcomb family would have to know."

Brie and John walked back toward *Maine Wind* so Brie could get packed for her flight the next day.

*　　*　　*

Later that night they stood on *Maine Wind's* deck under a canopy of stars. Diners and revelers had gone home, and they had the harbor to themselves.

"Look there, in the northwest. There's Vega, Deneb, and Altair," Brie said.

"We stood on this same deck back in May, looking at those same stars. Remember?"

"How could I forget, John? It was the night we first kissed."

"I was fascinated by this woman, this detective, who knew her way around the stars like that. I didn't want to lose you."

"Well, you didn't, and I'm awfully glad of it."

He gathered her into his arms. "So here we are with the stars again. And this our last night aboard."

Brie felt a moment of panic. "Not forever."

John kissed her forehead. "Not if I can help it."

Brie put her head against his shoulder, and they stood there not talking, just feeling the warmth of each other.

"Brie, look at me."

She did.

"I love you. Just wanted to say it again."

"I love you too, John."

"We've been through a lot these past five months. I'm glad we finally got that out."

"Me too."

"Now, if you'll come below, I'd like to show you just how much."

Brie smiled up at him. "Lead on, my captain."

Chapter 38

Brie sat on the tarmac at the Portland Jetport, waiting for the plane to take off. John had driven her to the airport late this morning. They had left Camden early so they'd have time to stop in Wiscasset and say goodbye to Jack Le Beau, the retired detective whom Brie had worked with on this case and the one on Apparition Island.

Brie had brought Angus a giant rawhide bone as a gift, and she gave Jack a hand-knitted wool sweater she'd bought for him in Stonington when they had anchored there in late September. The four of them—that included Angus, of course—sat out on Jack's porch and ate doughnuts and drank coffee. "A last meal particularly suited to a couple of cops," John had joked.

Then on the way down to Portland, Brie had called Dent and told him about the possible connection with the guy from France who had once been involved in the black market art world. She gave Dent Harriet Patterson's name on Sentinel Island and the Whitcomb family name so he could pass the information along to the FBI. She also suggested to Dent that Leo Dombello might know who the Frenchman was.

The plane began to taxi toward the runway. Brie leaned back in her seat and closed her eyes, thinking about John, thinking about the glorious, sleepless night they had spent showing each other the depth of their love.

And suddenly the plane was racing down the runway, lifting off, climbing out over the ocean. Banking, banking, preparing to head west.

Brie looked out her window. Far below her, the sea rolled away, ancient and deep as time. She closed her eyes. And there was John at the helm, heading upwind, heading for their next adventure. The jet engines droned, but she was elsewhere. She felt the deck pitch beneath her feet. Felt the cool sea air on her face. Smelled the salt. Heard the roar of the wind in the canvas. Heard *Maine Wind's* rigging creak. And John's voice, and the familiar chorus.

"Ready about?"

"Ready."

"Helm's alee."

Author's Note

The details surrounding the art heist at the Isabella Stewart Gardner Museum in Boston in March of 1990 are factual, and while the names Michael Callente and Robert Cerillo have been fictionalized, elements of the story involving the missing art and the state of Maine are also true. One of the suspects in the robbery did purchase land in central Maine and lived there until his death. His wife later testified that two of the ten stolen paintings changed hands in the parking lot of a Portland seafood restaurant in 2003. And while Leo Dombello's uncle, Francis Luigi, is a fictional character, the two suspects in the Gardner Museum art heist at one time worked for former Boston mobster Robert Luisi. To this day no trace has ever been found of the stolen art, valued at half a billion dollars.

DEATH
in the
Blood Moon

Coming in the fall of 2018

My next book, featuring Detective Brie Beaumont, will be set in Minnesota, on the north shore of Lake Superior, and in Maine. I hope all my New England readers will enjoy visiting Brie's home state. Here is a short quote from the book.

"This was an ancient place, where wild, tumultuous rivers rushed down deep gorges of billion-year-old basalt—lava laid down, miles thick, by volcanoes, eons ago, when the continent tried to rift apart; where the spirits of the voyageurs and the indigenous peoples—the Ojibwe and the Cree—still brood over the great lake known as Kitchigame."

From *Death in the Blood Moon*
by Jenifer LeClair

Glossary of Sailing Terms

Abaft: In or behind the stern of the ship.

Aft: Toward the back of the boat.

Abeam: At right angles to the boat.

AIS: Long range automatic identification system. Used by the Coast Guard to track vessels at sea.

Alee: Helm's alee or hard alee is the command for tacking or coming about.

Amidships: In the middle of the boat.

Athwartships: In a direction at right angles to the fore-and-aft line of the vessel.

ATON: Aid to navigation.

Back the jib: To rig to windward so the wind hits the front of the sail rather than the back. Used when heaving to.

Ballantine: To coil a halyard into three overlapping piles. The finished pile of line looks like a 3-leaf clover. Ballantining keeps the line from fouling as the sail is doused or lowered.

Batten down the hatches: Secure a ship's hatch-tarpaulins, especially when rough weather is expected.

Beam reach: Also "reach." To sail across the wind, or with the wind abeam.

Bearing: The angle from the boat to an object.

Beating: Sailing close-hauled, or as close to the wind as is efficient.

Belaying pin: A wood pin used onboard ship to secure a line fastened around it.

Berth: A fixed bed or bunk on a ship, train, or other means of transport. Also, a ship's allotted place at a wharf or dock.

Bollard: A thick, low post, usually of iron or steel, mounted on a wharf or the like, to which mooring lines from vessels are attached.

Boom: The spar that extends and supports the foot of the sail.

Bow: The most forward part of the boat.

Bowsprit: Permanent spar attached to the bow, to which jib-stays and forestays are fastened.

Close-hauled: Sailing as close to the wind as is efficient; also beating or on the wind.

Come about: Also "tack." To bring the boat across the wind to a new heading.

Companionway: A set of steps leading from a ship's deck down to a cabin or lower deck.

Davits: Outboard rigging for raising and lowering the ship's yawl boat or dory.

Dodger: A canvas cover over a cockpit or a companionway.

Dory: A small multipurpose craft usually propelled by pulling (using oars) or sailing.

Downwind: Away from the direction from which the wind blows.

Foremast: On a schooner, the mast closer to the bow.

Foresail: The sail that is rigged on the foremast.

Furl: To roll or fold up and secure neatly, as a sail against a spar or a flag against its staff

Gaff: The spar that supports the top edge of a four-sided sail.

Gaff-rigged: A boat with four-sided sails rigged to gaffs.

Galley: A boat's kitchen.

Gam: A social visit at sea between ships or ship's crew.

Grabrail: A handrail running along the edge of the deckhouse or cabin top.

Gunwale (pronounced *gunnel*): A boat's rail at the edge of the deck.

Hatch: An opening in a deck, covered by a hatch cover.

Halyard: A line that hoists a sail and keeps it up.

Head: A boat's bathroom.

Heading: The course, or direction the boat is pointing.

Headsail: Pronounced "hed-sal." Any of various jibs or staysails set forward of the foremast of a vessel.

Heave to: To turn into the wind and set sails to stop or gain control in heavy weather.

Heaving line: A line thrown outboard to another vessel or to a person in the water.

Heel: The tilt or laying over of a boat caused by wind.

Helm: The tiller or steering wheel.

Hurricane hole: An area for safe anchorage, with good protection from the wind on as many sides as possible.

Jib: A sail carried on the headstay or forestay.

Jibe: To change tacks by heading off, or turning away from the wind, until the sails swing across the boat.

Knot: One nautical mile per hour.

Lace-lines: Also reefing lines. Used to secure a sail to the bowsprit or boom.

Lazarette: A small hold, usually in the stern, for stores and gear.

Lee deck: The side of the ship away from the wind.

Lee of the island: The side of the island sheltered from the wind.

Leeward: Away from the direction of the wind. Pronounced *lu-ard.*

Longboat: The longest boat carried by a sailing ship.

Luff: When a sailing vessel is steered far enough toward the direction of the wind, or the sheet controlling a sail is eased so far past optimal trim that airflow over the surfaces of the sail is disrupted and the sail begins to "flap" or "luff."

Make off or Make fast: To secure a line to a belaying pin or cleat.

Mainmast: Mast farthest aft on a schooner. Carries the mainsail.

Mainsail: The sail attached to the largest mast on the boat.

Mainsheet: The line that controls the mainsail.

Making up: Building; getting bigger, as in "the seas were making up."

Mal de mer: Seasickness.

Mayday: An international radio distress signal used by ships and aircraft.

Middle watch: 0000 – 0400, or 12:00 – 4:00 a.m.

Outboard: On, toward, or near the outside, especially of a ship.

Painter: The bow line on a dinghy.

Pan-Pan: Three calls of pan-pan in radiotelephone communications is used to signify that there is an urgency on board a boat, ship, aircraft, or other vehicle but that, for the time being at least, there is no immediate danger to anyone's life or to the vessel itself. This is referred to as a state of urgency.

Peak halyard: Raises the end of the gaff farthest from the mast.

PFDs: Personal flotation devices.

Pitch: Movement of the vessel on the athwartships axis, causing the bow and stern to rise and fall alternately.

Port: The left side of the ship when facing forward.

Port tack: Sailing to windward with the wind coming over the port side of the boat.

Quarter: The side of the boat near the stern.

Ratlines: System of tarred rungs used to climb to the top of the mast.

RB-M: Response Boat Medium. A 45-foot US Coast Guard response vessel.

Reef: A part of a sail that is rolled and tied down to reduce the area exposed to the wind. Verb: to shorten (sail) by tying in one or more reefs.

Rode: The anchor line.

Running: Sailing with the wind astern.

Running rigging: The term for the rigging of a sailing vessel that is used for raising, lowering, and controlling the sails, as opposed to the standing rigging, which supports the mast and other spars.

Saloon: The main cabin on a ship.

Scandalize the forepeak: On a gaff-rigged vessel, lowering the peak of the sail to slow the vessel.

Schooner: A boat with two or more masts: the foremast or fore-wardmost mast is shorter that the mainmast.

Scuppers: Holes in the rail or gunwale that allow water drain-age.

Sea-kindly: A vessel's ability to move comfortably, or without undue strain, in rough seas.

Sea-worthy: A vessel able to survive heavy weather.

Sennit: Braided small stuff or cordage of many varieties. Used for everything from lanyards to chafing gear.

Sole: A cabin or cockpit floor.

Spindrift: The spray of salt water blown along the surface of the sea in heavy winds.

Starboard: The right side of the ship when facing forward.

Starboard tack: Sailing to windward with the wind coming over the starboard side of the boat.

Staysail: A small headsail set between the jib and the foremast.

Stem: The forward edge of the bow.

Stern: The aftmost part of the hull.

Storm jib: a small heavy jib for use in a high wind.

Thwarts: The seats in a dory or dinghy.

Upwind: Toward the wind.

Windlass: Winch used to raise a ship's anchor

Windward: Upwind.

Yaw: A side-to-side movement of the bow of the ship, usually in heavy seas.

Yawl boat: A small, powerful motorized boat used to push a mo-torless vessel.

CPSIA information can be obtained
at www.ICGtesting.com
Printed in the USA
LVOW12s1149090217
523553LV00003B/4/P